YESTERDAY'S SUN

Please return/renew this item
by the last date shown.
Books may also be renewed by
phone and Internet
Telford and Wrekin Libraries

YESTERDAY'S SUN

Amanda Brooke

WINDSOR
PARAGON

First published 2012
by Harper
This Large Print edition published 2012
by AudioGO Ltd
by arrangement with
HarperCollins*Publishers*

Hardcover   ISBN: 978 1 445 82584 7
Softcover   ISBN: 978 1 445 82585 4

Telford & Wrekin

Libraries

British Library Cataloguing in Publication Data available

Printed and bound in Great Britain by
MPG Books Group Limited

To Jessica and Nathan
For making me what I am
A mother

PROLOGUE

One hand of the clock swept across the other, marking that brief and unstoppable moment where one day ends and another begins. Holly lay in bed rubbing the swell of her stomach and soothing her unborn child against the cold tremor of fear that had swept across her body, as unstoppable as the hands of the clock.

It took Holly a considerable amount of effort to roll from her back onto her side. She had to manoeuvre her bump carefully while at the same time suppressing countless grunts and groans for fear of waking Tom, who was facing away from her, gently snoring. Holly nuzzled closer to him until her nose felt the familiar tickle of his untamed locks. She breathed in deeply, savouring his warm, sweet smell.

'I love you,' she whispered. The sound of her voice was barely audible, but then Holly had become an expert at keeping quiet. She had spent so many restless nights lying next to him, fighting the urge to break her silence and to tell him that the day she would leave him was drawing ever nearer.

'Today's the day,' she told him. 'You're going to become a father and what an amazing daddy you're going to be. But it's not going to be easy. You'll think you won't be able to cope, but you will. You'll be angry with me for leaving you both, but eventually you'll understand. One day, you'll look at our daughter and you'll know what I know. You'll know that she was worth the sacrifice.'

Tom shifted restlessly in his sleep and Holly held her breath. She didn't want to wake him, not yet. But she had to give voice to her apology, even if she didn't want him to hear it. It was one of the last things on her 'to do' list. That and give birth, of course.

Holly had spent the last few months preparing for the arrival of her daughter and, just as importantly, preparing for her departure from their lives. Tom loved Holly for her obsession with plans, something that bordered on neurosis, but even he would be shocked to discover how well she had prepared for this day. But how else could she die peacefully?

'I love you,' Holly repeated. A single tear rolled down her cheek and she felt the burden of knowledge pulling her down far more heavily than the baby she was carrying. 'I'm so sorry that I didn't tell you, couldn't tell you. However terrifying this is for me, it would have been unbearable for you. I've had to take some tough decisions and I've learnt the hard way that the best decisions are never the obvious ones. And I've learnt something else too. I've learnt that love endures, sometimes in the most amazing ways. I promise you, I'll be there at your side in your darkest hours.'

A sob escaped and this time it was loud enough to stir Tom. He turned sleepily towards her. 'Are you OK?' he mumbled sleepily, and then startled himself awake. 'Is it time?'

'Time? Not quite yet,' Holly assured him with a rueful smile despite herself. Time had been her enemy from the moment they had moved into the gatehouse, the house they now called home. That had been only eighteen months ago and her

2

thoughts returned to that pivotal moment when time began to run out for her.

Holly closed the front door and leaned heavily against it, breathing out a huge sigh of relief. The removal men had been miracle workers, transforming the empty shell they had arrived at that morning into something that Holly could now call home. The house had once been an imposing gatehouse, sitting at the entrance to the majestic Hardmonton Hall, but the Hall was now a burned out ruin and the gatehouse had been all but forgotten, set just outside the tiny village of Fincross. Despite its grey stone walls and peeling paint, Holly had fallen in love with the house. It had stood the test of time far better than the Hall itself and seemed the ideal place to build a home and settle down, perhaps for ever.

Still leaning against the door, Holly took a furtive look at her reflection in the full-length mirror which had been left propped up against the wall, waiting to be hung. The house, correction, her home may have improved its looks during the day, but she was definitely looking worse for wear. Her long blonde hair was usually her crowning glory to compensate for her otherwise average looks, but it was now pulled back in a bedraggled ponytail. The little make-up she had put on at the start of the day was no more than a memory, having retreated into the tiny wrinkles at the corners of her blue, almond-shaped eyes.

She hoped she looked more tired than old. After all, she was only twenty-nine and she felt as if her life was just beginning. Married for only two years, this was the first place she and Tom had actually owned and the first chance they had had to put down proper roots.

Ignoring her reflection, Holly took in her new surroundings. The hall ran down the centre of the house, with a door on the left leading to a small reception room that would become Tom's study. The door to the right led to a larger reception room, which would be their living room, and the half-open door gave teasing glimpses of familiar pieces of furniture in their new surroundings. The city-living furniture was a harsh contrast to the chintz-inspired wallpaper and hardwood floors, but Holly had rather eccentric tastes and liked the conflict in styles.

'I've checked the list and I think it's complete,' Tom said, appearing in the doorway at the furthest end of the hall, which led from the kitchen.

Tom looked even more dishevelled than Holly in his well-worn jeans and T-shirt. The look did nothing to flatter his tall, wiry stature or show off the toned body which Holly knew lay beneath. The difference between the two of them was that this worn-out look was normal for Tom. He was far too interested in the world around him to pay any attention to himself. That was probably why he made such a good journalist. He was warm and approachable, never smarmy, never intimidating, and people opened up easily to him.

Holly had resisted the urge to smarten him up, not least because it was the contrast to her own style that appealed to her. Holly was an artist and, when she wasn't knee-deep in plaster of Paris and paint, she liked to dress up in carefully contrasting combinations of vintage and contemporary clothes, a style which was also reflected in her artwork. The other reason Holly accepted Tom's unkempt style was purely selfish. He spent a lot of time working away and she didn't want him impressing the ladies too much.

'What list?' Holly asked suspiciously. 'There's still tons of work to do. It's going to take weeks before we're properly unpacked and that's before we even start thinking about redecorating.'

'Not the moving-house list,' Tom corrected her, 'THE LIST.' He was stepping slowly towards her with his left hand out in front of him, inspecting an imaginary piece of paper on his upturned palm. He stopped two feet in front of her.

'You do realize that you're looking at an empty hand?'

Tom ignored her. 'Find boyfriend. Tick! Find gallery to exhibit your artwork. Tick! Get married. Tick! Establish select clientele to buy said works of art. Tick! Earn enough to give up your job. Tick!' Each time he said, 'Tick!' Tom was using the index finger on his other hand as an imaginary pen to mark off each accomplishment.

'And finally?' asked Holly, already knowing the answer.

Tom moved a step closer. 'Move to the country and live happily ever after.'

'Tick,' whispered Holly just before Tom kissed her.

After an indecent amount of time, Tom took a breath. 'And I do believe, Mrs Corrigan, that you've completed your list a whole six months ahead of schedule.'

'I do believe you're right, Mr Corrigan,' Holly answered smugly.

7

Perhaps smug was the wrong word. Eternally grateful might be better. Holly had worked hard at her five-year life plan but, in truth, her success at finding the perfect husband and blossoming career had been more luck than management. In fact, she owed it all to a drunken accountant.

When Holly was twenty-five, having left art school with an armful of accolades but no real idea of how she was going to make a living out of her talent, she had found herself juggling countless part-time jobs to make ends meet. The jobs had been accumulated as she worked her way through college and, when she left, she'd carried on with them until they began to consume so much of her day that art became a luxury she couldn't afford, let alone find the time or energy to work on.

Her epiphany arrived one night in the shape of a middle-aged city worker who staggered drunkenly into the backstreet bar she was working in. Her hero, after several attempts, claimed a seat at the bar and immediately took Holly hostage with a lengthy monologue about his wonderful life and recent promotion in a leading accountancy firm. It wasn't until the drunk told her about how his promotion was all part of his five-year plan that Holly, the neurotic list maker, started to pay attention. Suddenly realizing how aimless her own life was, she had asked herself why, if this good-for-nothing drunk could succeed, couldn't she? She went home that night and couldn't sleep until she had set out on paper the goals she wanted to achieve in the next five years.

Within a year, Holly had a new direction. She had traded in her collection of part-time jobs for one full-time job in a television studio, working behind the scenes on production and finally putting her talents to good use. It had also meant that she had enough spare time to develop her artwork and earn occasional commissions through contacts with a local art gallery.

Next on her list was her love life. That wasn't supposed to happen until year three, but Tom arrived ahead of schedule. He had been visiting the TV studio for a job interview, and left a few hours later not only with a new job but with a new girlfriend too.

Holly had spotted him wandering around the props section, obviously lost. He had emerged from the interview on a high, having being offered a job as a special correspondent on environmental issues, but what started out as a snooping expedition around the studio quickly turned into an endless journey through a maze.

Tom Corrigan wasn't exactly what Holly had in mind for husband material. On the face of it, they couldn't have been more different. There was the obvious contrast in their looks. Her pale, mousey complexion was even more pronounced in comparison to Tom's tall, dark, handsome looks. There were other fundamental differences too. She was organized, he was not. She prepared for and expected failure; Tom saw every setback as an opportunity. She admitted when she needed help; Tom, the man who had just been given the opportunity to travel the country, wasn't about to admit any time soon that he couldn't even find his way out of the studio. After bumping into Holly on that fateful tour of the studio, he neglected to mention that he was lost and offered to hang around and help her until she was finished for the day, at which point he would escort her off the premises and take her to dinner.

'I can see the cogs turning,' Tom warned her, drawing her out of her reverie. 'Starting the next five-year plan already?'

'I'm quite happy working my way through my current lists, thank you,' replied Holly. 'The unpacking, the redecorating, my new studio, not to mention the new commission for Mrs Bronson.'

'Quite happy?' Tom asked her with mock surprise.

Holly smiled. 'Very happy. Quite possibly very, very happy.'

'Quite possibly?' he said, raising a mischievous eyebrow.

'Give it up already,' Holly scolded. 'Are we going to stand here all day in the hall arguing about the scale of my happiness, or are we going to make use of some of the other rooms?'

'What a good idea. How about I get the champagne and meet you in the bedroom in precisely two minutes?'

'Sounds like a plan to me,' answered Holly, but Tom was already heading back to the kitchen.

*   *   *

The next morning, Tom and Holly were as reluctant to leave their bed as they had been eager to jump into it the night before. Tom was on leave from work for two weeks, so there was no alarm clock demanding their attention, no fixed routine to comply with, nothing to do but finish their unpacking and explore their new surroundings. They just had to get out of bed first.

The bed faced the large picture window, which looked out onto a rambling garden bordered by a rambling orchard and, beyond that, the rambling English countryside. It was a bright spring morning and the sun was doing its best to rouse the new incumbents of the gatehouse out of their deep sleep. The insistent sunshine played patterns across the white linen curtains, fluttered down the pale blue walls, skipped across the polished wooden floor and crept stealthily across Holly's sleeping face, tickling her into wakefulness.

Her first thoughts quickly formed into a list of all the things that needed to be done, urgent actions vying for attention. Holly silenced those thoughts, mentally folding over the pages of her newly formed list. They could wait. She wanted to savour at least one day with her husband in their new home with no one else's needs to satisfy except their own. Time at home with Tom was going to be at a premium in the coming months.

No sooner had they closed the deal on the gatehouse, a house which they had chosen specifically because it was within commuting distance of London, than Tom was offered a new job. It was an offer he couldn't refuse, not least because the studio was going through a painful reorganization and he was one of the lucky ones. At least he was keeping his job, although he would now be expected to do more work front of camera, covering politics as well as environmental issues, and he could also expect to be sent further afield. The further afield clause in his contract arrived sooner than expected and his first assignment was a six-week stint in Belgium, making his commute a little longer than either of them had anticipated.

11

'Are you awake?' Tom asked.

'Hmmm,' answered Holly, turning towards him so that they were nose to nose.

'Whoa, morning breath!' teased Tom.

'You can talk, you smell like a man.'

'Thank you.'

'I hadn't finished,' Holly corrected him. 'You smell like a man who's spent the night licking the carpet of one of those really old pubs where your shoes stick to the floor. In fact, I can see you've still got half the carpet coated on your tongue.'

'So you don't want a kiss then?'

'Are you sure you can cope with my morning breath?' challenged Holly. She deliberately breathed out each word.

'I'm willing to take the chance if you don't mind risking a mouthful of old pub carpet.' Tom poked his tongue out and licked the tip of Holly's nose.

'I've had worse things in my mouth.'

'Now there's a challenge,' grinned Tom.

'Not only do you have a tongue that smells like the gutter, you've got a mind that's already there.'

Tom glided his body over towards Holly, sliding his hand across her torso and then slipping his legs between hers. It was a well-rehearsed and familiar manoeuvre that placed him over her and left Holly breathless.

'I can talk dirty, if you want me to,' Tom offered.

Holly wrapped her arms around his neck before letting her fingers trail down his spine. Hidden beneath the shadow of Tom's body, Holly could only sense the dappling of morning light as it played across his back.

'How dirty?'

'Well . . .' Tom said. He drew out the word with a

12

teasing hiss, then he smiled, or was it a smirk? 'I'm not talking five-year plans here.'

'I should hope not,' replied Holly. She was watching the curves of his mouth intently, the dampness of his lips, the glimpse of his tongue. She pushed her body towards him, encouraging him on.

'Oh, no,' Tom said, ignoring her blatant desire. 'I'm not even talking seven years.' He kissed her nose. 'Not even ten.'

Holly tangled her fingers in the luxurious waves of his hair. She reached up to kiss him but he moved his head away. He hadn't finished teasing her yet.

'I might be talking twenty years here. Hell, no, I'm perverted enough to even count on forty.'

'You have a sick mind, Tom Corrigan,' agreed Holly. Her body was tingling with anticipation and she writhed beneath him. She could tease too.

'I want a plan that takes us right up to our dotage, in this house, surrounded by our family, our children, our children's children and maybe even our children's children's children.'

For a fraction of a second, Holly's body froze. Then she blinked hard in an attempt to push away the fear that had fluttered across her eyes. She forced a smile, hoping that Tom hadn't noticed her reaction, hoping that she could resurrect the moment, but the air in her ballooning passion had well and truly popped.

'What?' Tom asked with a quizzical look that pierced Holly's heart. 'Does the thought of children terrify you so much?'

'No,' lied Holly.

'Yes, it does,' insisted Tom. He leaned his body over to her right side, resting his arms. The moment

13

for passion had most definitely been lost.

'I want children,' insisted Holly. 'It's just the being a mother part that I struggle with.'

'You want to give me children. That's different from wanting them yourself,' corrected Tom, his tone a mixture of concern and frustration. 'And you can and will be a good mum. It's not hereditary, you know.'

Tom was, of course, referring to her childhood. Holly was the product of a broken home, broken long before the bitter divorce that followed. Her mother had left home when Holly was only eight years old, but rather than feel abandoned, she had actually felt relief. Her mother had had a perverse attitude to motherhood and replaced love with cruelty, nurturing with scorn. After the divorce, Holly saw little of her and by the time she was a teenager her mother had drunk herself into an early grave. Her father by contrast was distant and completely uninterested in his daughter, but in some ways that made him every bit as cruel. He left Holly to bring herself up, so when she moved into student digs at the age of eighteen she never returned home again, not even for his funeral.

'I know it's not hereditary, but you learn by example. You really don't know how lucky you are with your family. Yours is so, it's so . . .' Holly just couldn't find the words. Tom knew all about her childhood, but he could never really know what it was like to grow up without the security of a loving family. 'It's so linear,' she said at last.

'Linear?' laughed Tom. 'What does that mean?'

'You have a mum and a dad who love and support you, and they had parents who loved and supported them. Your grandparents probably had wonderful parents too, and so it goes on and on, handed down, generation after generation.'

Tom's parents were wonderful in Holly's eyes and she was sometimes overwhelmed by the way they had accepted her into their family and loved her like one of their own. Being part of a classic nuclear family had been a steep and very emotional learning curve for Holly. When Tom's grandmother Edith had died recently, Holly had witnessed first-hand how the family had drawn strength from each other, how their love for Edith had somehow bridged the void that her death had left in their lives.

'We're not that perfect,' Tom replied. 'We have the odd black sheep in the family.'

'Oh, but you are perfect. Compared to my family, you are.' Holly gently touched the side of Tom's face. 'What if I'm the weak link that's going to break the chain in your family? What if I can't learn to be the kind of mother that your family has been built on through the generations?'

'Don't ever think you're weak. Yes, your parents were weak and that had an effect on you, but it had the opposite effect. You're the strongest person I know. Your parents were awful at parenting but that just means you're going to make sure you're the best mum you possibly could be. You have to believe that.'

Tom's body had become tense and she could feel a growing anger inside him. Anger that she knew was directed at her parents and at himself for not being able to heal her and banish the demons of her past.

'I know I have to believe in myself,' conceded Holly, although she didn't think she ever would.

15

But Tom wasn't going to rest until she had her next plan all worked out. Not that he needed a plan to work to. Tom was a free spirit who preferred to make things up as he went along, but he was thirty-two now and he was desperate to be a father or to at least know that he would be one day.

Tears had started to well in Holly's eyes and the sunlight that surrounded Tom's head was a blurred halo. The only thing Holly could see clearly was his soft green eyes.

'Hey, you're crying,' Tom said, sounding shocked.

Holly blinked, willing the tears to disappear. 'I'm not,' she lied defiantly.

'Ah, I forgot, you never cry.'

'I do. Not that I am now, but I do.'

'When?'

Holly paused, struggling to find a recent example that would prove Tom wrong. 'There was that film, the one where the dog died.'

Tom frowned as he tried to remember. Then he stifled a laugh. 'That must have been over two years ago, I don't think we were even married then.'

'But I cried, point proven.'

'OK, point proven,' conceded Tom. 'But I don't want to push you into anything you don't want for yourself. I had hoped that when Lisa had her baby and then Penny, you'd just want to follow suit, but I can see it's not going to be that simple. If you're not ready to start talking babies yet, then I understand.'

Lisa and Penny were the closest thing Holly had to friends in London and they'd had their babies within a year of each other. She knew Tom had been disappointed when Holly hadn't miraculously become broody at the sight of a newborn. Little

16

did he know that her enthusiasm to move to the country had in part been fuelled by a desire to put as much distance between herself and the endless baby chatter.

'Once I've got the house in order, then we can start on the next five-year plan. A joint one this time, and making a baby will most definitely be on the list,' she told him.

'A baby? Singular?' Tom said. His body had begun to relax again and he was back in teasing mode. 'Have you looked at this body? It's a well-tuned baby-making machine if ever there was one. You won't be able to so much as look at me without getting pregnant.'

'Hold on, tiger,' smiled Holly, relaxing too. 'I think that baby-making machine of yours could do with a little more practice.'

'Your wish is my command,' replied Tom.

It was lunchtime before they managed to explore the rest of their new home.

*   *   *

The days disappeared in a blur and Tom's departure was drawing painfully near, painfully fast. They had unpacked everything that needed to be unpacked, cleaned everything that needed cleaning and replaced as many of the things that needed replacing as they could afford. What little savings they had left had already been set aside to pay for the renovation of a small outbuilding at the side of the house that was going to be used as Holly's studio.

Tom's parents had visited, bearing gifts and even helping out with the physical demands of turning

17

the gatehouse into a home. Typical of Diane and Jack, they had stayed long enough to help but hadn't outstayed their welcome. They knew without being told that Holly and Tom had a lot of quality time to try to cram into two weeks.

Diane had made sure the kitchen was organized and fully stocked with a range of cooking essentials before she left. She was keen to support Holly in one of her new projects. Holly wanted to learn to cook. Her dad had been keen to show Holly the basics, if only to keep himself well fed, but the basics had involved how to open tins of beans, how to pierce the cellophane before putting ready meals in the microwave, how to make instant noodles, that kind of thing. Now Holly and Tom were living so far away from the conveniences of fast-food takeaways and restaurants on every corner, she was keen to improve her skills. The move into the country was more than simply a change of address; Holly wanted it to be a change of lifestyle.

'It's a beautiful house, Holly. Jack and I are so happy for you both,' Diane told her as they unpacked a mind-boggling assortment of kitchen utensils. 'And Mum would be too. It makes the pain of losing her a little easier to bear, knowing that her legacy is to help you and Tom start a new life of your own.'

'I'm just sorry Grandma Edith isn't here to see her money being well spent. It means a lot to me and Tom that you're happy with how we've used the inheritance.'

'It's all about investing in the future. This is where it all starts for you and Tom. This is where your family will be made.'

Diane gave Holly a hug and didn't see the cloud

18

of doubt pass over her face. Holly only wished she had the same kind of confidence in herself that the entire Corrigan family seemed to have.

Three days before Tom was due to leave, Holly's to-do list was complete and the house was officially in order. The builders had already started work on the outbuilding and, although Holly was happy to sit back and let them get on with it, Tom obviously felt some kind of threat to his masculinity so he took up his own physical challenge by clearing the overgrown garden.

Leaving the men to their labours, Holly stayed indoors to start work on the preliminary sketches for her new commission. Mrs Bronson was a young wife with a very rich and very much older husband. To celebrate the birth of their first child together, as opposed to the numerous children her husband had fathered from a variety of previous marriages and dalliances, Mrs Bronson wanted to mark the occasion with a sculpture. It would need to be a substantial piece and would become a permanent and prominent feature in the entrance hall to their mansion.

Naturally, the theme of the sculpture was mother and child. Given the theme, Holly had been reluctant to take on the commission, which would take at least six months to complete, but the money was too good to turn down.

She had set out her sketch pads in the study that morning, full of good intentions but with a distinct lack of inspiration. Money alone wasn't incentive enough to get her creative juices flowing. She just didn't have that same depth of feeling she usually had to draw upon. She knew nothing about the miraculous bond between mother and child that

19

everyone else seemed to drone on about.

Holly couldn't recall a single memory of her childhood where she had felt that kind of bond. She had spent most of her formative years feeling either alone or afraid. Her mother had been in her teens when she had discovered she was pregnant. A hasty marriage and an unwanted child had come as a nasty shock to her and she hadn't been prepared or willing to give up her freedom.

With a young child to care for, her mother's social life had been severely restricted, so she often brought the party lifestyle she craved into the house. Holly had vivid memories of a house full of hangers-on, either recovering from the last party or waiting for the next. Her mum was always centre of attention, dancing barefoot through the house whether there was music playing or not. She always looked her happiest when she was dancing and everyone was drawn to her, even Holly, like a moth to the flame, eager to share her mother's excitement. She could remember one time when her mum had picked her up and twirled her around the room to squeals of delight from her daughter, but Holly was never sure whether that had actually happened. She suspected it was merely a false memory of a longed-for dream. The memories Holly could rely on were those where her mum would stop dancing and point an accusing finger at her daughter before proclaiming to everyone that this was the creature who had ruined her life. The look on her mother's face was one of pure loathing, and that was the image that Holly recalled when she thought of motherhood.

Until Tom, Holly hadn't even managed to witness responsible parenting second-hand. In her early years, she had been isolated from other children, their parents having already labelled Holly as a problem child because of her family life. As a teenager, she had been naturally drawn to the other orphaned fledglings that had been pushed out of the nest too soon.

Her art had been her saviour in more ways than one. It had been a form of escapism, a part of her life she could control and succeed in and, in hindsight, it had also been an effective form of therapy. She had put a lot of anger into her earlier work and it was only after meeting Tom that she found she could express positive emotion in her art too. The love between a man and a woman she now understood; the love between a mother and a child she didn't. She was drawing a blank, literally.

She had spent two hours going through the motions of sketching images, but still hadn't come up with any ideas that were sufficiently original or thought-provoking. She'd sketched out some obvious images of a mother holding her child, a mother nursing her child, a mother kissing her child. Desperate for a new perspective, she'd even sketched out an image of the moment of birth. Possibly not the kind of statue Mrs Bronson would want greeting her guests in the entrance to her home.

Holly had a meeting scheduled with Mrs Bronson in less than a week's time and she was starting to debate whether or not to cancel the commission altogether. If she went ahead and produced a sub-standard piece of work then that would damage her reputation, which was still in its embryonic stages. On the other hand, reneging on a deal would be equally damaging to her career.

Putting down her sketch pad, Holly headed into the kitchen. The room was large, with enough space for a dining table at its centre. It might have been the outbuilding which had drawn Holly to the property, but it was the kitchen that had sold the place to both her and Tom. The wooden units were painted white, the walls were green and the terracotta floor tiles extended out through the back door and across to a small terrace, which led onto the immense if slightly untamed garden and the countryside beyond.

Holly peered out of the kitchen window, searching for Tom. She couldn't see him through the tangle of shrubs and trees, but she knew where he was from the sounds of snapping branches and occasional expletives. Ignoring the urge to go and investigate, she started chopping up vegetables— locally grown produce, of course—and set to work making a large pan of soup to try out on Tom and the builders.

'And what do you think you're up to?'

Holly jumped, narrowly avoiding chopping a finger rather than a carrot. A pair of arms closed around her waist. Tom had spied her from the garden and crept into the house.

'Don't you know better than to frighten a woman when she's armed and dangerous?' warned Holly, brandishing her kitchen knife.

'You're always dangerous. You can cut me to the wick, knife or not.' He leaned down and kissed the back of her neck.

'Don't go getting sidetracked. I want that garden looking spick and span before you disappear off into the sunset.'

'Look, woman!' gasped Tom in amazement,

pointing towards the garden. 'Can't you see the transformation already?'

Holly peered towards the garden, putting a hand up to shade her eyes for effect. 'No, not at all,' she laughed.

'I've practically made a small mountain from all the bracken and deadwood I've cleared. I've even trimmed your bush.'

'A man renowned for his literary prowess and he still lowers the tone with childish innuendo,' remarked Holly. 'And the garden looks like a heap to me.'

'Well, it'll look better when all the garden waste's been cleared,' Tom replied sulkily. 'I just need someone to use their womanly charms on the builders to see if they'll help me get rid of it.'

'Well, I'm busy, in case you hadn't noticed. Go use your own womanly charms on them, I'm sure they'll be impressed.'

Holly let Tom beg a little longer before giving in. She was secretly happy to have an excuse to check on the building work. The outbuilding was set back and to the side of the house and looked like it had been used as a workshop at some point in the past. It was a one-storey brick building about the size of a double garage. Thanks to Billy the foreman, they had made a good start in the last week and had already filled two skips gutting the place. Thankfully the roof hadn't needed to be completely replaced, but Velux roof windows were being installed to add more light. Interior walls had been knocked through and new windows knocked out of the outer walls. Each time Holly checked on their progress, the studio seemed to be getting lighter and lighter.

The studio was a hive of activity and Holly found Billy piling rubble into a wheelbarrow. The foreman was probably nearing retirement but showed no signs of acting his age as he picked up huge blocks of cement with ease. He had round features that did their best to hide the wrinkles on his weathered face and he still had a good head of hair which was quite possibly grey, although Holly could only guess at this because he always seemed to wear a permanent layer of dust that made his hair almost white.

'How's it going, Billy?' Holly shouted over the din of power tools.

'The electrician is coming over tomorrow, so I'd say we'll be plastering the walls by early next week and putting the final touches to the job.'

'You're a miracle worker, you really are.'

Billy beamed a smile at her. 'Glad to be of service. You can always count on me,' he told her. 'Not like that husband of yours. I've said it before and I'll say it again, he shouldn't be leaving you on your own to fend for yourself.'

'Yes, Billy, you have said it before, many times. And like I keep telling you, I can manage perfectly well on my own,' admonished Holly. She was now used to Billy's old-fashioned views and, rather than take offence, she quite liked being treated as the fairer sex, especially when it meant she could wrap him around her finger.

'If there's anything you need, you only have to ask,' he assured her with a kindly twinkle in his eye.

'Well, there is something,' she began. 'But it's that husband of mine who needs the help.'

'We've been watching him hack away at that jungle of yours,' Billy said. 'Kept us amused all

24

morning, it has.'

'Any chance a couple of your lads could help clear away the debris? There's a pan of soup on the go and a ton of crusty bread for your trouble,' pleaded Holly, fluttering her eyelashes for effect.

'Your wish is my command,' agreed Billy. 'But while you're here, you might want to take a look at this. We found it during the clear-out.'

Billy picked up a wooden box from among a heap of building materials stacked up in a corner.

The box was the size of a small shoebox and, although it was difficult to tell underneath the layers of dust, it seemed to be made of oak with brass hinges and a simple clasp. There were engravings around its sides, but again the dust was obscuring the detail.

'Have you opened it?' Holly asked with growing excitement. The box didn't exactly look like it was going to contain a hoard of jewels, but it was ornate enough to suggest it held something of value.

Billy turned the clasp and lifted the lid. Holly's excitement dissipated in a puff of ancient dust as she peered at the assortment of mechanical-looking objects within. Split into two sections, the box held some kind of glass ball on one side and a selection of brass cogs and brackets on the other. 'What is it?' she asked.

'Haven't got a clue,' Billy answered. 'Consider it a gift, from me to you.' Again, he winked at her.

'Thanks, Billy, you really know how to spoil a girl.'

Holly took the box with her back into the house and put it to one side so she could concentrate on getting lunch prepared.

The soup was a success, judging by the speed

in which it was devoured by the workers, and with their lunch break over the builders set to work helping Tom clear the garden. Holly wasn't in a hurry to return to her sketches so she decided to occupy herself with the mysterious wooden box. Having laid some old newspaper on the kitchen table, she set about gently cleaning the box and its contents with soapy water and an old toothbrush. Technically speaking, the toothbrush hadn't been old that morning when Tom had been using it, but it was now.

The box itself gave nothing away as to its purpose, other than some pretty carvings of the sun, moon, stars and what looked like clock faces. The glass ball was the easiest item to clean. It was about two inches in diameter and as Holly wiped away the dust, she could see that it was made of something other than clear glass. The orb had a perfectly smooth surface but, at its core, there was a small, silvery prism that reflected light out from its centre. It glinted softly in the warm sunlight. Setting the orb to one side, Holly concentrated her efforts on the cogs. Beneath the dust and grime the brass shone and that was when she noticed an inscription running around the edge of one of the larger cogs. The inscription was well worn and unreadable in places, but she could just about make out a few words. *Reflection*, was one, *Key*, another and she guessed another said *Time*.

'Found something else to do to avoid the dreaded Mrs Bronson?' Tom asked her. He was covered in scratches from his hard labours, but as Holly peeked out of the window at the garden she had to admit it was starting to take shape.

'Billy found it in the outbuilding. I've cleaned

26

it up, but I've still not got a clue what it is.' Holly showed him the inscription on the cog.

'"In time, reflection is the key to travelling",' Tom read.

Holly's jaw dropped open. 'How on earth did you read that? Some of the words have completely worn away.'

Tom beamed with superiority. 'I keep telling you, I have hidden depths.'

'Is it a well-known saying? I've not heard it before, what does it mean?' she demanded.

'Haven't the foggiest.' Tom shrugged.

'Tom?' Holly asked, eyeing him with suspicion now.

'You know that stone plinth stuck in the middle of the garden with no apparent use? Well, I found a matching top hidden in the overgrowth. It has the same inscription written on it.'

'Show me,' Holly insisted, leaving the array of freshly polished brass cogs to sparkle on the kitchen table.

The stone slab was face-down in the dirt, half buried by years of leaf-fall. It was a deep grey colour with sparkles of quartz glistening through it. Despite working with a wide range of materials in her sculptures, Holly didn't recognize the type of stone at all. The slab was perfectly round and, as Tom had described, it had an inscription, currently upside down, around its outer edge. There was also a large hole in the centre which looked like it would match the top of the plinth perfectly.

'Considering it's been buried beneath all of this mulch, I can't believe how clean it is,' Tom told her, shaking his head in disbelief.

Holly traced her fingers across its cold, smooth

27

surface. Her fingers tingled as if a faint charge of electricity had flowed up from the stone and she pulled her hand away.

'Does it feel weird to you?' Holly asked, unsure if she had imagined it.

Tom gave her a puzzled look and then stroked the surface of the slab. 'Feels like stone to me,' he assured her. 'What were you expecting it to feel like?'

Holly tentatively touched the stone again and this time there was no tingling sensation. She shook her head, dismissing the thought. 'Nothing, it's just me. Can we move it?'

'And do what? You seriously think we can lift it onto the plinth?'

'Yes, of course.' Holly could visualize the stone circle balanced perfectly on top of the plinth and taking centre stage in the garden. It belonged in its rightful place and Holly wasn't going to rest until it was moved.

'Are you sure you don't want to ask the builders?'

'Are you a man or a mouse?' Holly stood with her hands on her hips, challenging him.

'I'm a man, of course. But it doesn't help that my only partner in crime is a feeble woman.'

'Just get on with it,' warned Holly.

Holly put her hands on the stone again, almost hoping its latent power would help them with the task that lay ahead. Tom joined her and they dug their hands deep into the dirt to find a hold. As they lifted the slab, Tom's face went a beautiful shade of puce and he grunted and groaned. Holly matched him groan for groan and could feel the veins in her neck throbbing with the effort. After

28

what seemed like an eternity of laborious shuffling, they dropped the stone to the ground to take a rest.

'Not bad,' panted Tom.

'Sure,' gasped Holly. 'We've moved it all of six inches.' She looked over at the plinth, which was still about twenty feet away. 'At this rate, we'll get there in three days and two hernias.'

There was a tut-tut of disapproval behind her. Holly turned to see Billy shaking his head.

'Mr C, I'm disappointed in you. You should know better than to treat your lady like a common labourer,' he said, before turning around to his workmates who had followed him into the garden. 'No offence, lads.'

Holly was about to tell Billy that heavy lifting was an occupational hazard as far as she was concerned, but then she thought better of it. 'My knight in shining armour,' she said.

Tom groaned as he tried to straighten his back. 'Mine too,' he said, winking at Billy.

Billy and his crew of builders lifted up the stone slab as if it were made of balsa wood and two minutes later they were lifting it over the plinth.

'Hold on a minute,' Holly shouted. She had realized that the inscription was still upside down.

With a little more effort, the slab was turned over and placed on top of the plinth. It was a perfect fit. Everyone gathered around the newly formed table and stared at it.

'It's a clock,' one of Billy's lads said.

'And it's telling me it's time to get back to work,' replied Billy pointedly.

The builders disappeared as quickly as they had arrived, leaving Holly and Tom alone with their puzzle. Billy's lad had been right about it looking

29

like a clock. The top had a large dial carved with Roman numerals in much the same way as a traditional clock. There was still a gaping hole about two inches deep in the centre of the dial where the top of the plinth didn't reach the surface. It was only now that Holly noticed that there were grooves and notches in the upper surface of the plinth and this must be where the dial's mechanism would fit, the mechanism which was no doubt made up from the box of gizmos Billy had discovered. As well as the inscription running around the outer edge, there was an assortment of symbols, similar to those on the box, etched beautifully into the stone surface.

'It's a sundial,' Holly said.

'It's going to make a great feature in the garden.'

'All I need to do now is work out how to fit all the cogs into it and get it to work,' Holly replied, eager to return to the kitchen to retrieve the wooden box and its contents.

'Well, I've done all the hard work, so I'll leave the rest to you. I've still got plenty of clearing to do. Unless you want to help me?' offered Tom.

'Didn't you hear what Billy said? I'm not a common labourer,' grinned Holly.

Holly spent the rest of the afternoon fitting the pieces of the puzzle together. When she had finished, all the cogs were in place in the centre of the dial. Uppermost were four claws, pointing towards the skies, reaching out and waiting desperately to grasp the glass orb. Holly dropped the orb into the claws and it rattled into place, although the claws were opened too wide to hold it snugly. The reflection from the sun as it glinted off the prism deep inside the orb was painfully bright.

30

Holly called Tom over and they both stepped back to admire their new garden centrepiece.

'I thought a sundial was supposed to use shadows, not reflections from the sun,' Tom said as he squinted at the orb. He tried to push it down further into the mechanism to see if the claws would close further around it, but the dial creaked stubbornly and refused to move. 'Looks like you didn't put it together properly.'

Holly thumped him.

'What was that for?'

'You're not supposed to force the claws like that.'

'How do you know?' asked Tom.

'I just do,' replied Holly, a frown appearing on her brow. She didn't know anything about sundials, but this one made her feel uncomfortable. She removed the orb and put it back in the box.

'I'll put this somewhere safe. I don't suppose it's a good idea reflecting sunlight across the garden when there's so much deadwood still around.'

'If that's a hint, then I'll get back to work. Time is running out.'

Tom's words sent a shiver down Holly's spine. She had a sudden sense of foreboding that she couldn't quite explain.

2

The house felt empty. Tom had left for Belgium in the early hours of the morning. Holly had clung onto him until his taxi arrived and Tom had had to prise her fingers away from her vice grip on the lapels of his jacket as she gave him one final kiss, a kiss that would have to last her for six whole weeks.

'It won't be for long. I'll be back before you know it and, besides, it's less than two hours away by plane. If you need me, I could be back in no time at all.'

'I should come with you. Whose stupid idea was it anyway for me to stay at home?'

'Yours,' answered Tom, as kindly as he could.

He was right, it had been her idea. She had to accept that she was at a critical point in her career. Moving out of the city when her work was starting to receive critical acclaim had been a huge risk. Moving out of the country would be vocational suicide.

She had retreated to her bed, where she allowed herself to wallow in self-pity as she sensed the distance growing between them by the minute. She knew she was being self-indulgent; it wasn't as if she hadn't been on her own before. She could quite easily fend for herself, but that wasn't the point. Her dream had been to move into the village with Tom, not to be on her own. As she lay in bed, the cheerful birdsong that accompanied the dawning of the new day only served to mock Holly. At least the weather was a little more sympathetic as the storm clouds gathered overhead. Holly pulled the bedcovers over her head and did her best to go back to sleep. It was Sunday so at least there would be no builders to look after today.

The birds had recovered from their early morning hysteria and settled into just the occasional midday tweets by the time Holly pulled on her sweats, tied back her hair and dragged herself into the kitchen to make a strong cup of coffee. She spotted Tom's half-empty mug of coffee abandoned on the kitchen table and bit her lip to stifle a sob that appeared from nowhere.

'You pathetic idiot,' she told herself. 'Mrs Bronson's sculpture isn't going to create itself.'

She took a deep breath and pulled her shoulders back, willing herself to find the motivation to start moving. As she exhaled, her body sagged like a deflated balloon. She tried again and, before her resolve was allowed to falter a second time, she picked up Tom's mug, gently washed it and put it away, out of sight.

Armed with her coffee, Holly shuffled into the study, where her heart sank a little further. Although this had temporarily become Holly's domain while the studio was being finished off, it was always intended to be Tom's room. Tom, however, wasn't around to make it his own.

The study was at the front of the house and had an open fire, a large bay window and pastel-coloured, flowery wallpaper, all the essentials for a warm and welcoming country cottage feel. In her current mood, however, Holly could see only a cold and uninviting, heartbreakingly empty room. The clean, modern lines of the city-living furniture Holly and Tom had brought with them no longer seemed like a quirky contrast but rather a violent clash of two alien worlds. She was starting to think she was never going to adjust to country life.

The distraction of the decor was too much, so after a half-hearted attempt to make a start at her work she picked herself up and shuffled into the more spacious living room. It had windows to both the front and the back of the house, but even with so much more natural light to work in, she still

33

couldn't settle.

Eventually Holly returned to the kitchen, which was the one room she had no intention of changing. The only furniture they had added was a large wooden kitchen table that had belonged to Grandma Edith. The table had history, a good history.

At last, Holly's thoughts turned to her commission. The showdown with Mrs Bronson was now only three days away. She had a couple of concepts she thought would suit her client's taste, but she still hadn't been able to find something that she personally could put her heart into. She needed to believe in the piece if she was going to bring the chosen design to life. Taking the job had been purely financial and she wasn't proud of that fact. The end result wasn't going to be just about the money, though: her conscience wouldn't let it. She wasn't prepared to produce something that she wouldn't want to put her name to.

Holly picked up the two sketches which were on the short list so far. One was of a mother and child, their arms curved around each other in an unbroken circle. The concept wasn't exactly original, but she intended to make the piece by merging etched black stone with white, which was a trademark she was becoming renowned for. The second sketch showed a swirling image of a mother twirling a child through the air. It had more energy than the first and of the two it was the one Holly preferred. There was still something missing, though. She suspected it lacked the emotional connection between the two figures, something which she knew too little of and it showed in the sketches.

Startled from her inner thoughts by a knock at the door, Holly crept down the hallway and did a quick check in the mirror, which was now properly hung in place on the wall next to the door. She seriously considered running back into the kitchen to hide rather than frighten off her unknown caller with her sullen features and unkempt hair. If she had still been in London it would have been an easy option to take, but here in the village, she felt obliged to welcome her visitor. Reluctantly, Holly opened the door.

'Hello, you must be Holly. I hope I didn't disturb you.' A grey-haired woman with deep brown eyes was sheltering under a huge blue-and-white polka dot umbrella. The rain was thumping savagely against it but, despite her frail appearance, the old lady kept the umbrella firm in her grasp.

'Not at all,' lied Holly, unconsciously rubbing her cheeks to bring some colour to her complexion. She opened her mouth to continue but then had a lengthy internal debate with herself, wondering whether or not to invite this woman into her home.

Was she an old, lonely lady looking for company, a nosy busybody on the hunt for gossip to spread across the village, or a well-disguised saleswoman selling something? Of course, she might simply be what she appeared. A friendly face, welcoming Holly to the community. Whatever the answer, Holly could write off the rest of the afternoon if she let the old lady cross the threshold, but failure to do the right thing now could see her ostracized from the village. She'd been warned by her fellow townies that if you upset the wrong person then a village feud could last generations. Those particular townies had never set foot outside the city and

35

Holly knew it was just scaremongering, but then Holly didn't want to take any chances.

'Perhaps it's the wrong time to call,' the woman suggested sympathetically. 'I'm Jocelyn and I live just down the road in the village. It was only a quick call to introduce myself, but please, tell me to go away if you want. Really, I've got the skin of a rhino, I won't be offended.'

'No, please, where are my manners? Come in.'

Holly relieved Jocelyn of her umbrella and her overcoat and led her into the kitchen. She quickly cleared away her artwork and made space for Jocelyn to sit down. Jocelyn was looking around the room and a gentle smile curved her lips.

'Would you like a hot drink to warm you up?' offered Holly.

'No, honestly, I won't put you to any trouble.'

'It's no trouble, I was about to get another cup for myself.'

With the polite debate laid to rest, Holly put the kettle on and rummaged through the cupboards for proper teacups and some biscuits to offer her guest.

'I heard you're a successful artist and now I can see why. These drawings are amazing,' Jocelyn said, tapping one of the sketches Holly had put to one side.

'Thank you. It keeps me out of trouble.' Holly had only met a handful of people from the village so far. For the last two weeks, she and Tom had been too wrapped up in their own company to pursue introductions with their neighbours beyond the occasional polite 'hello'. It shouldn't have surprised her, however, that the village grapevine had already sized them up.

'Billy has been telling me all about your new

studio. He's quite proud of it.'

'Oh, I see,' Holly didn't see really and was trying to make the right connections. Jocelyn must know Billy quite well, but she looked at least eighty years old, while Billy was perhaps early sixties. 'You're not Billy's wife, are you?' Holly blushed at her own bluntness.

'Good grief, no,' laughed Jocelyn. 'He's a good friend and I love him to bits, but I can only take Billy in small doses.'

Holly laughed. 'I think I know what you mean. He does seem rather set in his ways. He certainly gave Tom a hard time for going off and leaving me.' Presuming that Jocelyn wouldn't know Tom was working away, Holly explained herself more. 'Tom left for Belgium this morning and he'll be away for six long weeks.'

'Yes, I know, it's why I called around, really,' Jocelyn admitted with an awkward smile. 'Billy thought you might need a shoulder to cry on and it was either me or him.'

Holly wondered if there was anything in their lives that would remain private. It was certainly going to take her a while to get used to village life. Perhaps there was a village committee that would need to ratify her next five-year plan, she thought to herself.

'Well, thank you for being so thoughtful,' replied Holly, and she actually meant it. Tom's parents had promised to check on her regularly, but they were two villages away. The few friends she had were all in London and she was just starting to realize that the emptiness she had felt when Tom left was as much to do with feeling isolated as it had been to do with the absence of bodies in the house.

'It's not a problem,' Jocelyn said, taking a sip of her tea and allowing a small hesitation before saying what she said next. 'The truth of the matter is I fancied a sneaky peak inside the house. It's been a long time since I was here last.'

'Really?' asked Holly. 'Did you know someone who lived here before?'

'I was someone who lived here.'

'Really?' gasped Holly. 'When? What was it like? Why did you move?' The questions kept tumbling out of Holly's mouth.

'Oh, it must be at least twenty-five years now,' explained Jocelyn. 'Last time I was in this kitchen it was fitted out in top-of-the-range Formica and the colour scheme was orange and brown.'

'Seventies at its best,' observed Holly.

'You guessed it, although it was the early eighties when I left. My husband wasn't exactly one for decorating.'

'So why did you leave? Who had the house after you?' Holly was eager to know the full history of the house she now called home.

'That's a long story,' sighed Jocelyn. 'I left because I left my husband. He lived in the house a few more years and then it was sold on.'

'I'm sorry. I didn't mean to pry.' More questions were queuing up in Holly's mind, but she had the good grace to curb them.

'That's all right. This house holds some really good memories for me and some,' Jocelyn continued, scrunching her face as she prepared herself for the confession: 'Well, some not so good. I just hope you find happiness here. In fact, I'm sure you will.'

Jocelyn was more keen on telling Holly all

38

about the village than she was about her life in the gatehouse. She offered to introduce her to village life whenever she was ready, whenever she felt like she needed the company. She told her all about the quiz nights at one of the local pubs, the karaoke night at the other, not to mention all the fundraisers and bingo nights at the village hall.

'And then of course there's my teashop, which is opposite the church. Now I will only insist on one thing and that is that you stop by this week so I can treat you to afternoon tea.'

Holly could offer no better response than continuous nodding. Jocelyn was turning out to be the perfect medicine for a lonely heart. 'I will,' she promised.

'Don't go getting all polite on me. I'm sure you think I'm nothing but a hopeless busybody,' Jocelyn confessed. 'But I know from experience how easy it is to become isolated in a small village. You seem to be an independent and determined young lady, but sometimes that can work against you. It worked against me.'

'What do you mean?' asked Holly, hoping Jocelyn would reveal a little more about her history.

'You remind me a little of myself. Maybe it's the connection with the house. I hope that's all it is. I was born and raised in the village, but I had dreams of carving out a career for myself just like you, making my own way in the world.'

'So what happened?'

'I didn't have any talents to rely on, not like you. I put off marriage as long as I could but, eventually, I conformed to tradition. I didn't come from a time or a place where it was the done thing for women to have a career of their own, or a life of their own, for that matter.'

'So you became a housewife? In this house?'

'Yes. In the beginning it was actually good. My son was born and my husband had a good job. He ran his own carpentry business.'

'And the outbuilding was his workshop,' guessed Holly. 'So what went wrong? Sorry, is that too personal?'

'It's a long story. A long, long story and I won't bore you with it now. I've taken up enough of your time,' replied Jocelyn, draining the last of her tea.

Holly was a little disappointed. Her interest in this woman's past life had been piqued. She wanted to know the details and she didn't mind if it took the rest of the day.

Jocelyn stood up, clearing up the plates and cups before putting them on the tray. 'No, please, I can't let you do that. You're my guest,' reproached Holly.

'Indulge an old lady,' Jocelyn said with a half-hidden grin. 'I like to clean up after myself. Besides, I wanted to have a better look out the window and into the garden.'

'You can have a full tour of the house if you like,' laughed Holly.

'Now that would be cheeky and I really do have to be getting along.'

'It's still raining,' warned Holly. 'Are you sure you want to go yet?'

'A little rain won't do me any harm. Besides, it's good for the garden.' Jocelyn turned and peered out of the window. Her body imperceptibly sagged.

'Tom made a start on it, but I don't think it's been touched for quite some time,' explained Holly, feeling the need to apologize for the ramshackle state of the garden.

'I see you've resurrected the moondial.' Jocelyn was looking intently at the stone table.

'Moondial? Do you mean the sundial?'

Before Holly had a chance to quiz Jocelyn further, the phone rang. It was Tom. He had arrived safely at his new digs in Belgium.

'I'll leave you to it,' mouthed Jocelyn.

Holly was torn between being a gracious host and speaking to Tom. For the brief time Jocelyn had been there, Holly had forgotten how lonely she had been, but those feelings crashed against her chest once more. Holly put a hand on Jocelyn's shoulder. 'Thank you,' she whispered.

With a series of determined hand signals, Holly was ordered to stay in the kitchen and Jocelyn saw herself out of the house. 'I've just made a new friend,' Holly told Tom. 'She's almost made today bearable.'

*   *   *

Holly treated herself to a large glass of wine and a deep bubble bath before bedtime, a combination which she hoped would guarantee a peaceful night's sleep. Although it wasn't unusual for Tom to spend nights away, their current separation was going to be the longest of their marriage. To ease their shared loneliness, Tom had promised to set time aside each and every morning and evening to speak to Holly on the phone, so with glass in hand, surrounded by soft pillows, Holly let Tom whisper sweet nothings to her as she lay in bed.

When they could put it off no longer, Holly reluctantly said goodnight and put down the phone.

She turned off the lights but didn't manage to switch off her mind so easily. Holly's best-laid plans of a peaceful night became snagged in a tangle of thoughts. The separation from Tom, the new house, the village, the commission she couldn't find inspiration for, all of these kept her tossing and turning long past midnight. To her surprise, it wasn't thoughts of Tom and more particularly Tom's absence that preoccupied her mind most of all. It was Jocelyn.

Holly had taken an immediate liking to Jocelyn. When the old lady had arrived on her doorstep uninvited, it had been the last thing Holly had wanted. But as it turned out, she had been sorry to see her go. There was still so much she wanted to know about the gatehouse's previous occupants, and Jocelyn intrigued her. She had the distinct feeling they were going to be good friends. The thought comforted her and in some ways appeased her curiosity.

Try as she might to clear her mind, the effort simply made her concentrate even more on the thoughts she was trying to ignore. The hours slipped by as she tossed and turned until she eventually admitted defeat and stretched her arms wide then opened her eyes. The digital glow of the clock revealed it was 2:07 a.m. Moonlight was seeping through the window blind, filling the room with nature's very own lunar mood lighting. Holly's heart skipped a beat as Jocelyn's words echoed in her mind. 'I see you've resurrected the moondial,' she'd said, just as Holly had been distracted by Tom's phone call. Was that what had been playing on her mind? If it was, there was only one way to chase away the demons that had kept sleep firmly out of reach.

Holly tumbled out of bed and opened the blinds. A perfectly formed full moon had risen above a bubbling sea of clouds. The storm that had plagued the day was now a distant memory, receding into the night. Holly drew her eyes away from the moon and looked down towards the garden, which was painted in a hundred shades of grey. It wasn't the white speckled blossom winking at her from the orchard or the occasional daffodil bobbing its ghostly white head against the night that drew her attention but the moondial. It was positioned perfectly in the centre of the garden to catch the full effect of the moonlight. It practically shone.

Though she couldn't explain why, Holly felt drawn to the dial as it glinted invitingly at her. Once the idea of taking a closer look had formed in her mind, she couldn't ignore it. She almost laughed at her own foolishness as she slipped into a T-shirt and jog pants and headed downstairs. She slipped on a pair of trainers and then, before going out through the kitchen door, Holly had another, equally bemusing idea. She retrieved the wooden box that contained the final piece of the moondial puzzle and took it with her out into the garden.

Spring hadn't quite chased away the winter chills and Holly shivered against the cold April night. The ground was damp and the grass was so long and overgrown that her jog pants soon became soaked up to her knees.

Holly felt a knot of anxiety building inside her as she approached the dial. The garden that had seemed neglected and forlorn by day took on a more menacing feel by night as the wind stirred up the dead bracken strewn across the outer edges of the garden so that it rustled with the echoes of extinguished life.

She could almost believe that she was being controlled by an invisible puppeteer as she placed the box on top of the dial and opened it. She lifted the orb up to catch the moonlight and it glimmered with excitement as shards of light reached out like beacons from the prism embedded in its core.

Carefully placing the orb in the centre of the dial, where it clattered against the brass claws, Holly was mesmerized as she watched it absorbing the fragments of moonlight until the orb glowed into life, becoming a miniature moon caught within the claws of the dial. Her heart jumped as the mechanism seemed to come to life too and with an ancient clunk, the dial snatched the orb greedily in its claws. In a split second, thin strands of light spread out from the glowing orb, beams of light that started to turn like the frenzied hands of a clock spinning out of control. At that same moment, Holly put out her hand to hold onto the dial for support and an electric current shot up her arm.

Instinctively, Holly pulled her hand away as a shower of moonbeams sparked around her. Reeling from the shock, her legs went from under her and as she fell, her head glanced off the side of the dial. Holly landed on the ground with a thump and stars joined in the merry dance that flittered across her closed eyelids. She could hear the steady ticking of a clock fading into the distance, the sound replaced by the furious beating of her heart.

Winded and badly shaken, she tried to calm herself by taking deep breaths. She leant over, putting her hands on the ground to steady and

44

compose herself. The grass beneath her fingers felt soft and lush as if she was kneeling on a well manicured lawn, not the tangled overgrowth she was expecting.

Holly had an irrational fear that she wasn't in her garden any more, but she was still half blinded and could only use her hands to find her bearings and explore her surroundings. She wondered if the force of the moondial's light show had knocked her further than she had realized, but then she touched the hard surface of the plinth beneath the moondial. It was hard, cold, but reassuringly familiar. Using the top of the dial for support, Holly pulled herself unsteadily to her feet.

Although white worms of light were still crawling across her vision, she could make out vague outlines of other familiar landmarks. The orchard, the studio, the house. Then Holly glanced at the moondial and her heart froze. The orb and the brass mechanism had disappeared, as had the wooden box which had been left on top of it. Holly spun around, scanning the ground in case they had fallen nearby, but all she saw was a perfectly cut lawn. Her heart would have hammered harder if it wasn't already beating to maximum effect. What just happened? she asked herself.

Shaking uncontrollably, Holly suddenly realized that it wasn't only the shock that was making her shiver. The temperature had dropped by a good few degrees and her T-shirt felt pathetically thin. She tried to bring calm to her shaking body by concentrating on her breathing, which came out in icy vapour clouds that swirled in the air in front of her eyes. The calm was short-lived as she turned to face the house, seeking the comfort of her home.

When she had walked across the garden earlier, her path had only been revealed by the soft glow of the moon. There had been no artificial lights leaching from the house because she hadn't switched any lights on. Now the kitchen window was ablaze with light.

Holly could only imagine that the knock on the head had affected her senses and perhaps her memory was playing tricks on her. She took a deep breath and gave herself a moment to take a more thorough look around her. It didn't help.

Something was wrong with this picture: correction, so many things were wrong with this picture, but she didn't seem able to process her thoughts properly. As she neared the house, her mind could no longer deny the one thing that her sanity had refused to acknowledge. There was a conservatory slap bang in front of the house, running the full width of the living room up to the back door. The conservatory was in darkness, but soft light glowed from the living room beyond.

With faltering steps and a sense of lost reality, Holly crept towards the door that led through to the kitchen. Rather than walk straight back into what was supposed to be her home, she peeked through the window like a thief. To her relief, it was empty, but as she took in the detail, her growing confusion was ramped up to spine-chilling terror, skipping right past the niceties of growing anxiety. The kitchen was still her kitchen, same cupboards, same cooker, same fridge, even the same table, but it was most definitely not the kitchen she had just left. Holly started to wonder how bad the bump on her head must have been to explain away the vast assortment of baby equipment stacked up on every available surface.

Holly could only make herself move by convincing herself that what she was experiencing was some form of hallucination. She just wanted to get into the house and take refuge in her bed, blocking out the alternative universe her mind seemed to have created around her for her own private terror. She stepped towards the back door and tried to open it, but the door handle wouldn't budge. Although the handle felt cold and solid, her hand didn't seem to be applying pressure on it at all and Holly wondered if it was an after-effect of the shock she had received from the moondial. She wrapped her fingers tightly around the handle and, with the kind of effort it would take to open castle gates, Holly finally opened the door and stepped deeper inside her nightmare.

The room smelled different, a mixture of home cooking and warm milk as opposed to the smell of instant noodles and stale wine that she would have expected. Holly didn't feel strong enough or confident enough to go too far into the kitchen, so she rested against a nearby cupboard. She waited and listened, hoping at least one of her senses was still working rationally. She wanted to hear nothing but the familiar silence of an empty house, but it wasn't long before her hearing joined in the game that was pushing her sanity to the limits. She heard distant voices coming from one of the other rooms but moving closer. Whoever was in the house had just entered the hall. Holly's eyes shot between the back door, which was her only means of escape, and the door that led into the hall and which could open at any moment.

Holly stood her ground. This was her house

and she had every right to be here. So why did she feel like a stranger in her own home? There were two voices she could make out, one male, one female. They were soft and muffled and Holly couldn't quite hear what they were saying above the thumping of her own heart. She did hear the now familiar squeak as the front door opened.

With a brief moment to relax from the threat of imminent confrontation, Holly tried to do a reality check. What was happening to her? Could this really be a hallucination? Had the bump on her head made her delusional? Had she been knocked out longer than she thought? Had she spent days unconscious in the garden while squatters had taken up roost in her house? As implausible as it sounded, Holly almost preferred to believe that option rather than consider the state of her mental health.

She walked across the kitchen and was about to take a chance and peek into the hallway when the door opened wide in front of her. Holly gasped and took stumbling steps backwards as a figure loomed in front of her.

'Tom!' Holly cried. 'Thank God you're here.'

She reached both arms towards him but then she froze. The man in front of her looked like her Tom, but there was so much about him that wasn't familiar that it startled her. His hair was cropped short, much shorter than at any other time Holly had known him, but it wasn't this that startled her most. He didn't just look dishevelled, which would have been normal for him, he looked gaunt. But even this wasn't what froze Holly's heart to the core. It was his eyes. His beautiful green eyes looked towards Holly and then right through her.

His eyes looked vacant, dead even.

Tom turned away from Holly without even registering her presence. He picked up a pair of ladies' leather gloves which were lying on the kitchen table on top of a notebook. 'Got them,' he called out before turning and leaving the kitchen.

As the door closed and Holly was left on her own once more, she felt a wave of dizziness wash over her. Finally, she remembered to breathe. With every ounce of composure she had left, Holly staggered towards the door Tom had disappeared through and with more effort than she knew it deserved, she managed to open it by just a fraction. Tom was standing at the front door with his back to her. Diane was there too, standing on the threshold with her hand on Tom's arm, talking to him. Partially reflected in the hall mirror, there was a third figure and, although she couldn't be sure, Holly guessed it was her father-in-law, Jack.

Holly held herself back from a burning desire to rush into Tom's arms and demand that he make everything right. Then she remembered the way he had looked right through her and fear kept her rooted to the spot.

'You know where we are if you need anything,' Diane was telling Tom.

'I know, Mum. We'll be fine.'

'I know we've all agreed now is the right time to let you fend for yourself, but if you need me . . .'

'I know,' insisted Tom. 'I know where you are.'

'Will you leave the boy alone, Di,' Jack said. An arm appeared around Diane's waist as he tried to pull his wife away.

'She's such a fragile, little thing. Now if you're ever unsure about what to do, I've written

49

everything down in the notepad on the table. And I'm always at the end of the phone. If you need anything, ring me.'

'I will, but you know everything's organized. It's not like Holly didn't have everything planned right down to the last nappy for Libby's arrival. You'd think she knew she was never coming home from hospital.' Tom's voice cracked with emotion and there was a pause as he gulped back a sob. 'I know I can't replace her, Mum, but I promise you, I'll look after our baby. She came at such a high price.'

'Poor Holly. It's just so wrong. She would have made such a good mum. Why did she have to . . .' Diane couldn't finish her sentence, she simply let the tears roll down her cheeks.

'You can say the word, Mum. It's not like I could forget,' Tom told her. 'She died. Holly died.'

Holly gripped the door handle. Whether it was fear or determination, her sense of touch seemed to be recovering slightly and the handle felt firm in her grasp, unlike her sanity. Holly could barely gasp in shock because the wind had been knocked out of her body and she felt utterly weak. She wanted to run but couldn't draw her eyes away from the horror that was being played out in front of her like a car crash in slow motion.

'No more of this,' Jack was insisting. 'We said we would go home today. We agreed it was for the best.'

'But it's been less than a month. Tom's world's been turned upside down,' argued Diane.

'Dad's right,' Tom said, straightening his back in firm resolve. 'If we don't do this now, then it's just going to get harder and harder.'

'And if you keep on blubbing, you're not going to

50

be able to see your way down the path to the car,' warned Jack.

'At least let me help you with your case,' insisted Tom, taking a step over the threshold.

'What about Libby?' Diane sobbed.

'She's safe enough in the living room and I'll put the snip on the door.'

No sooner had the figures retreated from view than a sound came from the living room. It was a sound so alien to the house that Holly released the door handle as if, like the moondial, it too had been charged with electricity.

She wanted to turn and run but something about the sound of the baby crying caught her around the chest. Never before had Holly felt a reaction like it to a baby's cries. Instead of moving away, she stepped into the hallway and entered the living room.

The baby was in a bassinet in the corner of the room. Her eyes were open wide and alert. They were bright green, a mirror image of Tom's. When the baby saw Holly, she didn't just stop crying, her whole body relaxed and she stilled herself. She was the most beautiful thing Holly had ever seen. She had wisps of blonde hair and a handful of tiny curls licked her forehead. Her cheeks were perfectly round and her pink lips the cutest Cupid's bow. Holly couldn't resist and she gently stroked the side of her angelic face. The baby responded by moving towards her hand, her little mouth searching for nourishment.

'So what's a tiny wonder like you doing in a nightmare like this?' whispered Holly.

The baby wriggled and gurgled and Holly instinctively reached out to her. She paused only

51

briefly as the urge to hold the baby consumed her. She had never in her life had any desire to hold a baby and she couldn't recall a time when she actually had held one. She slipped her hands beneath the baby's body, her fingers sweeping over the soft, warm folds of the blanket she was wrapped in and Holly went to pick her up. Her fumbling fingers met no resistance and Holly could feel no weight against her hands as she tried to lift the baby out of the bassinet. Holly frowned in frustration as the need to hold the baby overwhelmed her. But no matter how hard she tried, the baby remained firmly in the bassinet and sensing Holly's frustration she began to cry, much louder than before.

'I'm coming,' called Tom's disembodied voice and Holly heard him rush down the hallway and into the kitchen.

Holly stepped away from the bassinet and looked around the room with rising panic. The stack of sympathy cards lined up across the mantelpiece didn't escape her notice but she was more intent on finding a hiding place. She scurried over to the large patio windows which led into the conservatory and slipped into the shadows just as Tom appeared with a baby's feeding bottle in his hand.

He picked the baby up and sat down on the nearest of the two sofas to feed her. He was practically facing Holly and although she knew she wasn't completely hidden, there was still no sign that Tom sensed that she was there.

'Alone at last,' Tom sighed as the baby guzzled her milk urgently.

The room fell silent other than the sound of the baby's gulps and Holly's ragged breathing. She thought her breathing must be so loud

52

that Tom would surely hear her, but still he didn't acknowledge her. She could feel herself withdrawing into the relative comfort of a shock-induced numbness. Her brain had all but stopped trying to make sense of what was happening to her. She chose instead to concentrate on the regular gulps of satisfaction she could hear coming from Libby and it soothed her.

'I know you're there, Holly,' Tom said.

Goosebumps coursed up Holly's arms and down her spine. As if in a trance, Holly stepped out of the shadows and into the living room.

'I'm here Tom,' she said.

Tom was looking towards the patio window, just to the left of Holly, but he had that distant look in his eyes again. Wherever he was looking, it was some place far from the confines of the room. 'I hope you can see me, sweetheart. I hope you can hear me, because I don't think I could go on if I thought you'd completely left me.' Tom's voice was a crackled whisper and he closed his eyes tightly, suppressing the tears that had sprung to his eyes.

Holly rushed forward and knelt in front of him, grabbing his arms and willing him to open his eyes and see her. 'I'm here, Tom! Please, please look at me!' she sobbed.

Tom opened his eyes and Holly shuddered as once again his gaze passed right through her, cutting her like a knife. Holly recoiled from Tom for the very first time in their lives together.

'It hurts, Holly, it hurts so much. Every time I wake up, I remember I'm never going to see you again and my stomach lurches. I can't believe it. I won't believe it. You were fine. You were fit and you were healthy; pregnant, yes, but healthy. You

53

were there one minute and then you just weren't. Every bone in my body aches for you and it hurts so much.'

Tom paused, shaking his head as if to clear his thoughts. 'Mum keeps saying I should let go, let myself cry, but I can't. I'm so scared, Holly, because I swear if I did cry, I don't think I'd be able to stop.' Tom kept gulping for air, drowning himself in unshed tears.

Libby started to wriggle in his arms so Tom pulled the half-finished bottle from her mouth. His face softened slightly as he looked at his daughter and he smiled at her before lifting her onto his shoulder and patting her back. The painted smile disappeared and a look of pain returned to his eyes. 'I'm not ready for you to leave me, Hol. I'm not ready to accept that you're never going to walk back into the room. All your things are exactly as you left them, everything is there, ready for you to come home. Come home, Holly, please just come home.'

A sob escaped and Tom bit his lip to hold himself together. 'I don't want to feel like this any more, it hurts too much. If it wasn't for Libby, I don't think I could go on without you,' he said. Libby gave a huge burp in reply, and Tom forced a smile. He cradled her again in his arms and started feeding her once more.

'Thanks for the vote of confidence, Libby,' he whispered, and the love for his daughter warmed Holly's heart and thawed the numbness that had engulfed her. 'I love you so much and your mummy loves you and she's watching over you.'

Holly couldn't resist stroking the top of Libby's head and as she leaned forward she could feel

54

Tom's warm breath on her face. Her whole body tingled and she knew that this was more real than any dream she had ever had.

'Promise me you'll never leave me,' Tom whispered.

'I promise,' Holly answered, willing Tom to hear her, but he made no response.

Holly rested her head on Tom's lap in submission and closed her eyes. 'This isn't real, Tom, this isn't happening. It's going to be all right.'

Silence filled the room and time ticked by. Holly stayed where she was until the baby finished her bottle and then she reluctantly withdrew as Tom made a move to stand up. She stood up too, facing him as he perched Libby on his shoulder and then picked up the bassinet.

'Bedtime for us, I think,' Tom said with false bravado.

As he turned and headed for the door, Holly put her hand on his shoulder, not wanting him to leave. 'Stay with me,' she pleaded as the sense of panic returned.

Tom paused. 'Stay with me,' he whispered, but then he left the room.

Holly felt close to breaking point and she was paralysed by fear. Her breathing was getting faster and deeper and she started to feel woozy. She was on the verge of hyperventilating. She heard Tom's footsteps going up the stairs and then the creaking of floorboards overhead. For the second time that night, the sound of the baby crying sent her whole body into spasm.

The combination of the need for fresh air and the overwhelming desire to run away was enough to give Holly the strength to leave the house. She stumbled through to the kitchen, fumbled with the door handle before eventually letting herself out of the house and across the garden. It was still cold, much too cold for late April, and the wind whipped around her.

Holly's eyes darted from one side of the garden to the other, wondering what demons lurked in the shadows to strip away the last shreds of her sanity. In answer to her challenge, Holly's attention was drawn towards the orchard. The trees that should have been on the verge of blossom were now forlornly hanging onto withered leaves, fragments of a summer long gone. Holly stumbled on until she reached the moondial.

'I'm not dead, I'm not dead!' she cried out. She sank to her knees and curled herself up into a ball. 'I'm here, Tom. Why can't you see me?' she pleaded.

Holly wasn't sure how long she remained curled up in a ball beneath the moondial. Exhausted and cold, terrified and confused, she didn't know what to do next. It was only when the kitchen light was switched off and the garden was etched in grey once more that Holly lifted her head and looked towards the house.

A few seconds later, a light appeared from her bedroom window. It was the soft glow of a bedside lamp. The bedroom blind was open. Holly tried to remember if she had left the blind open or closed. She sighed deeply. What did it matter? Everything had changed and Holly felt trapped in a world she no longer belonged in. But Tom was in there. If she didn't belong with him, then where did she belong?

Holly rose to her feet and, beneath the watchful gaze of the full moon, felt an urge to go back into the house and run to Tom. She was about to take a step forward when the unmistakeable silhouette of her husband appeared at the bedroom window. He was rocking from side to side and although Holly was raging against the impossibility of it all, she knew he had the baby in his arms. The slow rocking motion of his body suddenly froze. Holly couldn't see his eyes but she knew without a shadow of a doubt that he was looking at her.

It felt as if the world was closing in around her when she fell under Tom's gaze. There was a crushing weight pushing against her chest as the rhythmic sound of a ticking clock grew closer and then stopped with a thud. Whether it was the wind that whipped around her or just sheer exhaustion, Holly stumbled and reached out to the moondial to steady herself. The moment she touched the dial, a host of dancing moonbeams scampered around her. The garden became a blur and the air became heavier and a few degrees warmer.

Holly needed both hands on the dial to keep herself steady. She closed her eyes in an effort to stem the waves of dizziness that ebbed and flowed through her. One of her hands touched something on the dial. Holly blinked to chase away the shadows of light left by the moonbeams. It took a while before she could safely pick up what she had touched. She held it in her hands and a sense of relief washed away the terror. It was the wooden box. The dial mechanism and the orb had all reappeared too. The orb trembled benignly in the loosened grasp of the brass claws. Everything was as it should be.

The wind had eased and as Holly looked towards the orchard, the telltale white buds of spring sparkled against the night. Below her feet, the long grass was just as overgrown as it ever had been. Holly's head snapped towards the house. Her bedroom window was in darkness, as was the whole house, minus one conservatory. The bedroom blind was rolled up but no figure looked down upon her.

Holly snatched the orb from the dial and threw it urgently into the box as if holding it would burn her fingers. Taking the box with her, she ran through the grass, not stopping until she was back in the kitchen where she quickly turned the light on. A quick check confirmed that there was no baby equipment, no notepad on the table.

The tentacles of Holly's living nightmare were slowly releasing their grip on her heart and her mind. Stepping more tentatively into the hallway, Holly checked both reception rooms before heading upstairs. Her bedroom was empty, her bed a writhing mess of bed linen just as she'd left it. The digital display on the clock read 3:21 a.m.

Holly stripped out of her clothes, her jog pants still sodden from the wet grass. She crawled into the comfort of her bed and wrapped herself in her duvet. Unable to even begin to make sense of the last hour, Holly closed her eyes and closed down her mind. The sleep that had previously evaded her came swiftly and mercifully.

3

The ominous glow of the full moon had surrendered to the harsh spring sunlight by the time Holly was shocked into consciousness by someone banging on the front door. Jumping from her bed, she ignored the discarded clothes on the floor and grabbed her dressing gown. Her body ached all over as she made her way downstairs.

'Sorry, Billy, I must have slept in,' she apologized as she rubbed the last remnants of sleep from her eyes.

'Now, now, Mrs Corrigan,' tutted Billy. 'You can't go answering the door in your slinky nightie when there are builders around, you'll have my lads dropping hammers on their toes.'

'It's an old dressing gown, Billy, and I think I'm more likely to frighten them off than anything else,' retorted Holly. She knew she must look a state but was silently grateful for Billy's gallantry as she tried to scrape back her hair into some kind of order.

Billy's mischievous smile dropped and his playful tone was replaced by one of concern. 'Hey, what happened to your face?' he asked.

Holly leaned back and took a look at herself in the hallway mirror. The right side of her cheek was bruised and grazed. 'It's nothing,' Holly said in a robotic tone as the memory of her moonlit walkabout replayed in her mind for the first time since waking.

'If that man of yours has been knocking you about then we'll be having serious words when he gets back,' Billy growled.

'Don't be daft,' Holly said with a smile that didn't quite reach her eyes. 'I'm just a weak and feeble woman who can't be trusted on her own. I tripped in the garden, that's all.'

'Well, it sounds like it was a good idea of mine to send Jocelyn around. I knew you'd need looking after.'

Holly was in no mood for Billy's usual banter, but if she didn't appear her usual self, who knew who else he would be sending around to check on her.

'I'm perfectly capable of taking care of myself, but yes, it was a very good idea. She's a lovely lady,' replied Holly with a smile that was more genuine this time.

'You need to get out more, visit people.'

'Now if I promise I will, could you stop nagging and get on with your work?'

Billy saluted. 'I aim to please. We should have the internal work finished by the end of the week, so if you want to start thinking about those bells and whistles you wanted to add, now would be a good time. After that, if there's anything else you need, you only have to ask.'

'Is that a proposition, Billy?' gasped Holly with a half smile.

Billy actually blushed. 'Erm, well, I was actually thinking, well, what I meant was, erm, the garden could do with a proper makeover. We don't want any more accidents, do we?' he stammered.

Holly shivered as she recalled the sensation of kneeling on the soft lawn. 'Thanks, Billy, but I'm not sure I want to let Tom off the hook with that particular job just yet.'

She brought her chat with Billy to a swift end, promising to make him and his lads a nice cup of tea. With Billy dispatched to the studio, Holly took another look at her reflection in the mirror. She wanted desperately to believe that the events of the previous night had just been a weird and not-so-wonderful nightmare, but the physical evidence was difficult to dismiss.

As she went through the motions of getting showered and dressed, her mind remained focused on finding a rational explanation for what had happened the night before. There was absolutely no doubt that she had left the house during the night. The open kitchen door and the wet jog pants proved without a doubt that she had gone into the garden. The wooden box left abandoned on the kitchen table confirmed that she had been playing with the moondial. But at what point did reality end and her imagination take over?

Everything had a rational explanation up until the point when she had banged her head. Mild concussion might explain her bizarre vision of the future; in fact, it was the only explanation Holly was willing to consider.

Refusing to waste any more time thinking about the hallucination, she readied herself for a full day's work. She went downstairs and made the promised pot of tea for the builders and then a strong cup of coffee for herself. She set out the tools of her trade on the kitchen table, determined to spend the day focused on Mrs Bronson's commission. Being organized and disciplined sometimes conflicted with her creativity, but today she needed something to concentrate her mind on. No distractions.

Tom phoned. There were some distractions that were an exception to the rule and Holly needed the comfort from simply hearing his voice.

'Good morning, my light, my life,' Tom chirped.

'Good morning, my compass, my anchor,' replied Holly, and she was surprised at how relieved she was to have Tom hear and acknowledge her. She thought of the man she had seen the night before, bereft and lost, but quickly pushed the image from her mind.

'Haven't disturbed you, have I?' Tom asked.

'No, not at all. You wouldn't believe how much I've missed you.'

'Not got the substitute installed yet, then?' Tom asked playfully.

Holly smiled, enjoying the normality of the conversation. The tension she had been carrying with her all morning slipped from her body. 'It was a bit fraught earlier,' she told Tom, 'but I've managed to kick the rugby team out of my bed.'

'Only one rugby team? Your stamina must be slipping.'

'So how about you? Sourced out a string of hussies to keep you busy?'

'Oh, there was extensive auditioning last night but no one compares to you.'

'I miss you,' Holly whispered, unable to keep up the pretence any longer.

'I miss you too.'

'I don't think I can bear to be away from you for so long. To hell with Mrs Bronson, I should come and join you.'

There was the longest silence. Holly sensed Tom's agreement but neither of them wanted to break their resolve to see it through.

'No, ignore me,' Holly added quickly before Tom could answer. 'I've had a bad night, that's all and it's only been one day. I'll be fine, honest. It'll take a few days for me to settle and after all, I've got this damned commission to do. Throwing in the towel just isn't an option. I've only got today and tomorrow left to get the designs right. I'll throw myself into my work and I'll be fine. Ignore me. I'll be fine. Honest.'

'Holly.'

'Yes?'

'You're rambling.'

Holly sighed. 'Sorry.'

'So didn't you have a good night?'

'Now that's an understatement.' Holly paused, not sure about how much she could tell Tom without worrying him. 'Now don't go freaking out, but I had a bit of an accident and no, I don't mean I wet the bed.' She hoped the levity in her voice sounded genuine.

'What kind of accident? Are you OK?' Tom's voice was laced with anxiety.

Holly did a quick editing exercise in her mind. Tom was level-headed about most things, but he'd be sending her off for a brain scan if she mentioned hallucinations. 'I was in the garden and slipped. It's just a graze on the cheek, nothing major.'

'You banged your head? Did you knock yourself out? Did you lose consciousness?'

'I watch the medical dramas too, you know. No, I didn't lose consciousness. No concussion, doctor, honest,' Holly said with an air of confidence she didn't feel. 'Although I may have dented the moondial with my head.'

'What do you mean the moondial? Don't you mean the sundial? Are you sure that knock to the head didn't affect your senses?'

'I'm fine,' repeated Holly, a little too curtly. Tom was closer to the truth than he realized. 'It was Jocelyn who called it a moondial and she should know, she lived here first.'

Holly had already told Tom all about her unexpected visitor and mentioning Jocelyn again was a good way to change the subject. Holly hadn't

63

exactly lied to Tom about her fall but she hadn't told him the whole truth either. 'She wasn't very impressed with the rest of the garden though and I was actually embarrassed. So when are you going to spend time at home long enough to get it sorted?' she asked.

It was Tom's turn to be cagey, which eased Holly's conscience. He told her there was still lots of upheaval at the studio and reminded her that everyone there was fighting to keep their job. Demanding where he went and what he did simply wasn't an option.

They chatted a while, until eventually work couldn't be put off any longer for either of them. Holly put the phone down and reluctantly picked up her sketch pad. Her plan was to continue to work up more sketches based on the two designs she had already settled on.

When she opened her sketchbook to the first of her drawings, the one of a mother holding a baby, her eyes were immediately drawn to the image of the baby. Her sketch had only subtle suggestions of form but even so, when she traced the baby's face with her finger it brought to mind the baby of her hallucination. Libby. With a warm rush of emotion, she recalled the moment that she had looked into Libby's eyes and felt an instant connection. Was this what maternal instinct felt like, she wondered, or was she just desperately trying to justify Tom's belief in her?

Holly's gaze turned to the figure of the mother. With new eyes, the pose was all wrong. The figure she had sketched was holding the baby tentatively, almost as if it were a box of spiders ready to crawl up her arm. Holly scored a line through the drawing before she knew what she was doing. Then she turned to the second sketch, which she had thought was the most promising in terms of concept. She still liked the spiralling form of the mother spinning the baby around, but again the pose seemed all wrong and the mother might just as well be twirling her handbag. She scored a line through this drawing too.

With a flutter of panic, Holly knew the pressure was on and she was going to have to work solidly for the next two days to get her proposal ready in time.

*　　　*　　　*

The trip to London was a dramatic gear change from the country life Holly was slowly becoming accustomed to. She left the serenity of the village to catch the early morning train from a nearby town and then battled in vain for a seat, losing it to one of the more seasoned commuters.

The meeting with Mrs Bronson was to take place at the gallery where Holly exhibited and sold her sculptures. It was a small gallery but ideal for her work, partially because of its prime position and select clientele, and partially because she worked well with the proprietor, Sam Peterson. Sam had been extremely supportive of her fledgling career when she had first arrived in London and had played a large part in Holly's success as an artist.

Holly had met Sam through one of the many part-time jobs she had taken after leaving art college. She had worked for a pet-care agency, walking dogs, babysitting rabbits and, in Sam's case, feeding his cats while he was away on one of his many tropical holidays with his partner James. Sam had taken a keen interest in her artwork and had not only encouraged her to keep up with her art after she left college but had eventually offered to exhibit her work in his gallery.

It was a short journey to the gallery on the tube and then on through the bustling crowds, but Holly was starting to feel energized by the hustle and bustle. She was wearing a smart fifties-style tunic dress with matching jacket. The outfit was a shade of pale blue that set off her long blonde hair, which was swept back off her face with a matching headband. It had been a while since Holly had worn something other than jeans and T-shirt, and dressing up made her feel part of the crowd again.

She needed all the energy she could muster, because she was practically running on empty. She had worked nonstop on her designs, sketching into the wee small hours of the night with nothing to keep her company except the waning moon, which peeped through the kitchen window like a brooding monster, narrowing its eye in concentration over Holly's shoulder.

Whilst she had managed to keep most of the details of her hallucination out of her thoughts, she couldn't quite erase the picture of Libby from her mind's eye. She used this to her advantage and breathed new life into the sketches she was creating. At long last, Holly felt a connection with the art piece she was trying to create. The downside to this was that she had also developed a connection with Libby. She may have only been a figment of her imagination, but Libby was the first baby that Holly hadn't been terrified of, the first baby she had wanted to reach out and hold. Libby had sneaked into her heart and there was a part of Holly that almost wished that she was real.

*   *   *

The tinkling of the brass bell over the door announced Holly's arrival at the gallery. The expanse of space that greeted her was bright and modern. White walls reflected the natural light streaming from the glass-fronted gallery, while strategically placed spotlights picked up the selection of brightly coloured and contrasting art pieces to entice the buyers.

The receptionist waved to her and picked up the phone, no doubt announcing her arrival to Sam. As Holly waited, she took the opportunity to do a quick stocktake of the work she had on display and to check out the competition. Holly sold a range of small sculptures through the gallery; some were figures, others more conceptual, but all had Holly's distinctive style of mixing contrasting textures and colour. Holly's work seemed to be becoming more commercial and it was the income from this type of work that paid for her and Tom's luxuries. Holly felt a twinge of disappointment as she noted that only a few pieces of her work were being displayed in this front-of-house section of the gallery.

'Looking for something?' came a soft voice from behind her. Holly turned around to be greeted by the portly features of a middle-aged man with an obvious obsession for tweed.

'Hello, Sam,' beamed Holly, giving her old friend a kiss on each cheek. 'I was just looking for some art pieces by the up-and-coming artist Holly Corrigan, but for the life of me I can't see the kind of collection I was hoping for. Keeping them in a darkened room somewhere, are you?'

'Oh, Holly, Holly, Holly. What suspicious creatures you countryfolk are,' he admonished. 'So you think as soon as you traded in your stilettos for wellies, I'd be putting your artwork out to grass too, do you?'

'Well . . .' grimaced Holly, feeling guilty that she would even suggest that Sam wasn't taking care of her best interests.

'There's one of your pieces over there,' Sam sniffed, pointing to the window front. Holly wasn't sure if his stance reminded her of a school teacher or an air steward.

'Another to the right there and two to the left, there and there.'

Definitely air steward, thought Holly suppressing a grin. 'And the rest?'

'S-O-L-D, sold!'

'All of them?' gasped Holly.

'All of them,' confirmed Sam. 'The recession is officially over. You heard it here first.'

Holly grabbed his arms and they did a little celebratory jig in the middle of the gallery.

'Well done, Sam!'

'Well done, Holly!' corrected Sam. He stopped still and peered at Holly's face. 'Is that a black eye I see beneath the camouflage of make-up? Has that man of yours been beating you up?'

'Why does everyone keep saying that!' demanded Holly. 'Of course he didn't. I fell in the garden, that's all.'

'Hmm,' replied Sam. 'Well, you can tell me all about your new country life later. First we need to deal with your favourite client,' he whispered.

'Oh, God, is she here already?' Holly broke out into a cold sweat at the thought of what she was about to face. 'Is Bronson Junior with her?'

'Thankfully not,' replied Sam, who shared Holly's relief.

Holly was of course referring to Mrs Bronson's offspring or, as Holly tended to view the baby, her latest fashion accessory. Holly might not be an expert in maternal matters, but each time she saw Mrs Bronson with her son it brought to mind a precocious child playing with a new kitten. She wouldn't have been surprised if her client had turned up with the poor child peaking out of one of her oversized handbags.

'Onwards and upwards,' Sam told her, directing her up the stairs to his private office.

*   *   *

The meeting with Mrs Bronson went better than expected. Holly had two fully worked up designs to show her client, but there was only one that she felt able to put her heart into and fortunately for her it was the one Mrs Bronson opted for. It was a spiralling form, depicting not just a mother cradling a baby in her arms, but a whole series of figures below them, symbolizing past generations swirling up through the black stone base towards the two white figures. She would still need to complete a scaled-down version first of all for Mrs Bronson to sign off, but for Holly the hardest part was now over with. She had managed to create the concept and she was as happy with it as she could be under the circumstances and given the struggles she had put herself through.

The bell above the door of the gallery settled into silence and both Holly and Sam breathed a sigh of relief as Mrs Bronson disappeared into the distance.

'Well, that went well,' Holly said cautiously.

'Don't sound so surprised, the design is beautiful. Well done, you. I know it can't have been easy.' Sam knew Holly better than most and he knew all about her troubled childhood. 'I did wonder if it was the right thing for you to take on, but you pulled it off. I don't think I could have bluffed my way through it. Remind me never to play poker with you.'

'What do you mean, bluff?' Holly demanded, although she knew exactly what he meant.

'Holly, I love you dearly, but, well, you're not exactly mother-making material, are you? To pull off an art piece of this scale it takes some insight into all that mother-and-child nonsense and I'm afraid you're just as bad as me: clueless on the subject.'

'New home, new life. Who says I'm not mother-making material?' Holly argued. She could feel the colour rising in her face. A week ago she would have agreed wholeheartedly with Sam, they'd had similar conversations before. But now, with Libby's face appearing like a watermark over everything she saw, Holly didn't want to hear it.

Sam laughed and hugged her to him. 'Maybe you're right, and I hope you are. Just promise me one thing . . .'

'What's that?' Holly asked suspiciously as she unravelled herself from his embrace.

'For goodness' sake, don't bring it with you when you come visit. What's made in the country, stays in

70

the country.'

'I promise!' laughed Holly. 'Now enough of this, let's get down to business. How am I going to replenish your stock?'

Although she loved the idea that her work was becoming sought after, she wasn't prepared to simply churn out sculptures on a conveyor belt to meet demand. Taking on Mrs Bronson's commission had been bad enough. Sam was persuasive however so she went through some ideas with him and promised to get to work on them if time allowed, once her studio was up and running in the next week or so. In truth, a heavy workload was going to be a welcome distraction during Tom's absence.

* * *

Sam did his best to persuade Holly to stay longer but she was on a mission. She had one more job to do before she left for home. Holly said her goodbyes and then weaved her way back across London, heading for the British Library, where she hoped to get some inspiration for the type of stone she would use in Mrs Bronson's sculpture. At least, that was the reason she kept giving herself.

The library was vast and Holly would have felt lost if she hadn't already spent countless hours if not days searching through its obsessively stacked and indexed treasures. She wasted no time in tracking down the reference books she needed to decide upon the stone and even less time on deciding which type of stone to use. Holly closed the last book she had been leafing through and stacked it up with the rest on the reading desk she

71

was occupying. She tapped her fingers distractedly on the stack of books. She hadn't fooled herself. She had already known she would choose black marble for the base of her sculpture, it was the obvious choice, and the upper section would be formed from clay.

A man at the next table cleared his throat and stared meaningfully at Holly. Holly's hand froze mid tap. She hadn't realized she had been tapping so loudly. 'Sorry,' she mouthed.

Holly returned her books and asked a library assistant for help looking up any records of Hardmonton Hall. It wasn't the Hall that interested her as much as it was the origins of the moondial. Her desire to find out more about the dial had nothing to do with her hallucination, she told herself, she was simply doing research on what was a very interesting, if not mysterious, centrepiece in her garden. It took Holly quite a while, with the occasional direction from one very patient and helpful assistant, to gather all of two books on the subject. Sitting back at her reading desk, Holly opened the first book. It was a collected history of English architecture, specializing in Tudor manor houses, and Hardmonton Hall was listed in its index. Holly flicked through until she came to the relevant section. There were only a handful of pages devoted to the Hall, most of which were illustrations and plans of the buildings and grounds. It was in a plan of the ornate gardens that flowed from the back of the Hall that Holly eventually found evidence of the moondial. It was, or had been, located in what appeared to be a large stone circle. The circle was divided into four segments with an inner circle where the moondial would have been sited. From this centrepiece, four wide stone paths led outwards, separated by flower beds of some sort.

The second book was a wild card and Holly held out little hope that it would uncover any more of the dial's history. It was a book on great archaeological expeditions in the nineteenth century and although there was no reference to the Hall itself, there was a reference to one of the previous Lord Hardmontons. Leafing through the book, Holly found the chapter she was looking for. She frowned as she skimmed through page after page of text. Charles Hardmonton had been a renowned explorer involved in expeditions all over the world and, as interesting as this local history was to Holly, she could feel a growing frustration building inside her.

Her impatience grew as she tracked Lord Hardmonton's adventures from one side of the globe to the other and she prepared herself for disappointment as she turned each page. In a fit of pique, she skipped through to the last paragraph. Lord Hardmonton's career as an explorer had come to an abrupt end when he fell out of favour with his sponsors during his last recorded expedition to central Mexico in search of the Temple of Coyolxauhqui, the Aztec moon goddess.

Holly's eyes narrowed in concentration as she read the name again. Could this be the connection to the moondial? Retracing her steps, Holly leafed backwards through the book, checking through the text again to see if there were any other references, but her efforts went unrewarded.

Never one to accept defeat easily, Holly knew she had reached a dead end. She closed the book with such force that the contents of the entire table rattled and then she stood up quickly and her chair scraped against the tiled floor.

'Shush!' hissed the man at the next reading table. It was the same man who had coughed at her earlier. Holly glowered at him.

'Shush yourself,' hissed Holly as she stomped past his desk. 'I'd have been better off at home searching on Google, at least the company would have been better.'

Holly stopped in her tracks as her words echoed across the room and then she did an about turn. Ignoring the snooty glare from her fellow reader, she returned to her desk and reopened the book, found the reference to the name of the Aztec goddess and scribbled it down. Googling for information wasn't such a bad idea.

It was only in the bright May sunshine that Holly started to relax again and her thoughts returned to the day's successes. She had plenty of work to keep her out of trouble and she was keen to return to the village. As Holly entered the train station, she spotted a gift-shop window crammed with teddy bears and she was reminded of Sam's cutting remarks about her lack of maternal feelings. Sam had inadvertently given her the push she needed and, without a moment's hesitation, she strode into the shop and bought her unborn daughter the brightest, pinkest teddy bear she could find.

*　　　*　　　*

Holly hadn't eaten since breakfast and her stomach was rumbling by the time she returned to Fincross late that afternoon. It made the decision to take a

74

detour and pay a visit to Jocelyn's teashop an easy one. She would be fulfilling her promise to the old lady and, besides, she wanted to celebrate her day's achievements and she couldn't do that on her own.

The teashop was picture-postcard perfect with gingham curtains, lace tablecloths and the smell of freshly baked pastries and brewing tea and coffee to entice customers. It was busier than Holly had expected, but she managed to grab a table just as a young couple were leaving.

'What a lovely surprise!' gushed Jocelyn, scurrying from behind the counter to give Holly a bear hug. 'Are you hungry? What can I get you?'

'I'm starving,' Holly confessed. 'What do you recommend?'

'Oh, you'll have to have a cream tea. I've just taken a fresh batch of scones out of the oven so they're lovely and warm. Or, if you're really hungry, you could try an open sandwich, there's plenty to choose from. Or you could have both? You look like you could do with some pampering,' she said, looking purposely at Holly's bruised cheek.

Holly self-consciously put her hand to her face. 'Minor accident,' she explained dismissively before convincing Jocelyn that a cream tea would be more than enough. When it arrived it was clear that she had been treated to extra helpings. Jocelyn took the seat opposite her.

'I'll just rest my legs for five minutes. Lisa can cope on her own for a while.'

'It's a lovely teashop. You've done well here.'

'It wasn't all down to me. My sister Beatrice ran the shop originally. When I left Harry, she was good enough to give me a job, not to mention the flat upstairs. Eventually we became partners and when she died six years ago, God rest her soul, her daughter Lisa took over her share. I love this place, it gave me my life back and I want to carry on working here till my dying day.'

'Is your son involved in the family business?'

'Paul? Oh no,' laughed Jocelyn, the thought obviously tickling her. 'He's in the army. I don't think he'd quite suit a pinny.'

'You must be very proud of him.'

'Oh, I am, I am. He's done so well for himself and things could have been so different.' Jocelyn's eyes seemed to dim, as if a shadow from the past had been cast over her.

'Different in what way?'

Jocelyn waved a hand dismissively as if wafting the shadow away. 'Oh, nothing. He didn't have it easy, that's all. His father was a fervent disciplinarian. Taking Paul away from his influence was the best thing I could have done for him.'

'I'm sorry you didn't have a better life in our house.'

'Well, don't you worry about me, it was a long time ago. Your lives will be happier there, I'm sure of it.'

'Do you think so?' Holly asked, still unsettled by her vision of the future.

'I know so,' confirmed Jocelyn, with a smile that made Holly feel safe and her future secure. 'So how's Billy getting on with your studio?'

'You need to ask? I thought he'd be keeping the whole village informed of his progress.'

'He can be a terrible gossip,' agreed Jocelyn, 'but he knows better than to do it around me. I'd give him a clip around the ear if I caught him. Don't get me wrong, it's not so much the gossip I object to, he just never gets it right, mainly because he's always too busy talking to actually listen.'

Jocelyn and Holly shared a few more jokes at Billy's expense before Jocelyn had to return to work for the teatime rush. Holly attempted to pay for her tea but Jocelyn stubbornly refused, and she was not a woman to be argued with.

'Thank you, Jocelyn, you've been a real tonic. You'll have to let me return the favour and come over to mine one day.'

'Well, don't feel you have to. I don't want to take up your time now that you've got your sculpture to make,' offered Jocelyn, even though her eyes were pleading with Holly not to withdraw the offer.

'I insist.'

Jocelyn smiled gleefully. 'I get every other weekend off and I've not got anything planned, so how about a week on Sunday for brunch?'

'It's a date,' agreed Holly. 'At last I've got something to look forward to other than Tom coming home.'

*   *   *

It didn't take long for Holly's curiosity to get the better of her. The very next morning her sketchbook and pencils had been carefully laid out on the kitchen table but Holly was nowhere to be seen. She had taken her steaming mug of coffee into Tom's study and was waiting impatiently for his computer to whir into life. She wasn't exactly a technophobe, but she didn't particularly see the attraction of the virtual world that the Internet offered. She preferred to interact with a world she could experience with all her senses, but still, needs must, and she hoped the World Wide Web would succeed where the library had failed.

She carefully typed the name of the moon goddess into the search engine and was immediately presented with pages of hyperlinks, some of which provided immediate dead ends, others only tiny snippets of information. It was only when she added Charles Hardmonton's name to the search that she hit pay dirt. She found a research site which not only gave more detail about Lord Hardmonton's last expedition, but it also disclosed information about his fall from grace, information that would have been seen as libellous in its day and wouldn't be found in any textbook.

Lord Hardmonton's last recorded expedition had indeed been in search of the temple of Coyolxauhqui in Central Mexico. He had been a principled explorer and these principles had led to a major dispute with his fellow adventurers and more importantly his sponsors back in England. When they found the temple to the moon goddess, Lord Hardmonton had wanted to preserve it in situ, but he was under pressure from his sponsors to strip the temple of its contents and dispatch them to England. Under the threat of legal action for breach of contract, Lord Hardmonton had reluctantly taken part in what amounted to the ransacking of the site.

Holly couldn't help admiring this nineteenth-century explorer, but his adventures still provided no link to the moondial. She sighed as she scrolled down the page. Further dispute had arisen when Lord Hardmonton arrived back in England. There had been an extensive inventory taken of their hoard, but at some point one of the relics had disappeared in transit. Despite his noble reputation, the finger of suspicion pointed towards Charles Hardmonton. The missing item was never recovered and he was never able to raise the necessary support to finance any further expeditions. He became a recluse and lived out the rest of his life in Hardmonton Hall.

Having drawn a blank, Holly sipped her coffee and stared at the screen. The link between a missing relic from the temple and the moondial was a tenuous one, but Holly wasn't ready to give up just yet. She tried another combination of words, this time adding 'inventory' to the search. To Holly's amazement, one of the first links led to an actual photocopy of the original inventory. The missing item had been highlighted and recorded as the Moon Stone and there were footnotes describing the treasure in greater detail. It was a large ceremonial stone, made from an unspecified grey quartz. The stone was the centrepiece of the temple and was rumoured to be the fabled Moon Stone, used to worship the moon goddess, Coyolxauhqui. The reference also suggested that, rather than being used for sacrifices, this stone was used to invoke visions.

In her haste to reach over and switch off the computer Holly slopped her coffee over the keyboard. She didn't want to read any more. She looked at the mess she'd made with her spilt coffee, which was now dripping off the keyboard and trickling towards some of Tom's papers. With a good excuse to bring her research to an end, Holly jumped up and raced to the kitchen for a cloth. She grabbed a dishcloth from the kitchen sink, but before she turned back towards the study, she glanced out of the window and her body froze. She was staring at the moondial.

She had so far refused to allow her mind to confront directly the idea that the dial had played any role whatsoever in the vision she had seen other than simply being the very hard surface she had hit her head on. Now, she hadn't only found a link to the moondial's past life, she had, if her mind allowed it, found a link to the vision of the future she had foreseen.

The spilt coffee was left to dry of its own accord as Holly did her best to convince herself that she was simply jumping to conclusions; irrational conclusions, at that. Her vision of the future was nothing other than a hallucination, she just had to keep telling herself that.

*   *   *

May seemed to be flying by as Holly settled into a peaceful but industrious routine. Billy had completed her studio in record time so she spent her mornings in there working on the scaled version of Mrs Bronson's sculpture. Her afternoons were set aside for chores and evenings divided equally between sketching new art pieces to satisfy Sam's demands and telephone calls with Tom, not to mention the occasional foray into the village.

Brunch with Jocelyn was a great success and Holly discovered more and more about the history of the village, although the subject of Jocelyn's time in the house was expertly sidestepped. The rest of the village seemed equally unwilling to discuss Jocelyn's past, so Holly's curiosity remained unsatisfied despite her best efforts.

Holly, too, did some sidestepping and kept any conversation with Jocelyn well away from the moondial. Since learning about the Moon Stone, she had become even more resolute in her belief that her vision had just been a hallucination. Her conviction grew as surely as the bruise on her cheek faded.

Stripping away every last remnant of the nightmare that had haunted her, Holly erased the image of Tom's lifeless eyes that looked right through her, deleted the vision of the gatehouse with a conservatory pinned to its back and wiped away the chaos of a house which gave home to a newborn but no new mother. The only image that Holly held sacred was that of the baby and, as she pictured Libby's angelic face, her fingers tingled as she recalled the softness of her cheek.

It was no surprise that the thought of motherhood consumed Holly's thoughts, not least because she was now working intently on Mrs Bronson's sculpture. At night, as she closed her eyes, she thought of Libby and relived that moment when their two hearts connected. Slowly she was beginning to share Tom's enthusiasm for parenthood and she sensed the desire to be a mother growing inside her, a fragile ember that needed nurturing and, when the vision of the baby wasn't enough to keep the spark alive, she used the anger against her mother to fuel her desire to change.

'I've been thinking about the future,' Holly told Tom one night as she snuggled beneath the covers in bed. She had the pink teddy propped on her knee in front of her and she felt a flutter of excitement as she imagined the bear's pink ears being tugged by tiny baby fingers.

'So what are you having for breakfast, then?' Tom teased.

'I was thinking a little bit further ahead than that. How about the next five years?' Holly held her breath, waiting for Tom's excitement to erupt.

'Oh,' he said.

'Well, I was expecting a bit more enthusiasm than that,' Holly replied, feeling a little bit deflated. 'I'm about to tell you I'm ready to start planning for a baby and that's the response I get?'

There was a pause and an irrational fear gripped at Holly's chest.

'You've found someone else,' she gasped.

'Don't be daft. Of course I haven't!' Tom told her, shock rising in his voice. 'Don't ever think that. Look, I'm sorry, I know it's a big step for you and I love that you want to be a mum, I love that you're ready to start a family, I love that you want to have a house full of kids, I love you!'

'Back up a minute,' interrupted Holly. 'Let's just plan one baby at a time, shall we?'

'I know, I know. It's a five-year plan, blah, blah, blah.'

'So what's the problem? Why aren't you going wild with excitement?' Holly asked, pouting her lip like a petulant child even though Tom couldn't see her.

'The studio has called me in for an interview as soon as I'm back in London.'

'Why?' Holly didn't like the tone of his voice. She knew he was still worried about his job, but he was already doing everything they asked of him; surely there was nothing more he could give?

'The reorganization hasn't been able to stop

82

the rot. There's going to be a merger and more changes.'

'But they can't do that, they've already messed you around. Your job's as flexible as it could be, they can't change it any more! Can they?' Holly felt tears stinging her eyes. She had been looking forward to this moment, telling Tom that she was ready to be a mother. It hadn't gone according to plan and the euphoric moment Holly had imagined fizzled and died.

She had planned on keeping her decision to herself until Tom returned home in two weeks, but then she had looked up at the full moon that night and the urge to go back into the garden and put the glass orb once more into the claws of the moondial had unnerved her. She needed to lay claim to the future the moondial was trying to take from her.

'The merger will mean major changes, cutting deeper than anyone expected,' Tom said.

'You're losing your job?' Holly asked, panic rising in her voice. Her income from her artwork wasn't enough to support the two of them, let alone a baby.

'I really don't know. I'm sorry, Hol, I think it's great that you want to start planning for a family, better than great, absolutely monumental. I know how much it must have taken you to get to this point and I feel awful about it.'

'Hey, don't feel awful. It's not your fault and, who knows, it might be good news from the studio.' Holly was usually the more pessimistic of the two, but somehow she sensed there was a need for a little role reversal. Tom was sounding decidedly anxious. 'Maybe they are in dire straits but they've just realized that it's going to take someone as incredible as you to get things back on track. I can understand that.'

'I get the feeling that it'll go one of two ways. Either I'll have no job at all, or they'll use the threat as leverage to get me to do some kind of nightmare job. But, hey, we don't know yet, and even if it is bad, I don't have to accept it. I could always take a chance and go freelance if the worst happens.'

'Suppose,' Holly said glumly. Optimism didn't become her and she was struggling to fight against the sense of impending doom. 'Not exactly the secure future we imagined, then?'

'Hol, we won't know anything for sure for a couple of weeks yet. Let's worry about it when it happens.'

'You're right,' she said in a monotone voice that did little to hide her disappointment. 'Perhaps during your interview you can ask the studio to fill out our five-year plan for us.'

Holly knew it wasn't Tom's fault, yet she couldn't help but feel as though he'd just thrown icy cold water over her fragile plans for motherhood. She suddenly felt so alone with Tom at the end of the phone and the distance between them stretching out further than ever before. Her only company was the pink teddy bear sitting on her knee staring back at her. She played with the label sticking out of the side of its head and it was only then that she noticed the warning written on it. The toy was not for children under two years of age. Perhaps this was a sign that she really wasn't fit to be a mother after all. She couldn't even buy a simple teddy for her baby.

'We'll know in a couple of weeks,' repeated Tom.

Holly bit down hard on her lip. She didn't dare

reply in case her words came out as a sob.

'We'll have babies one day, I promise,' Tom added.

'Will you stay on the phone with me until I go to sleep?' Holly asked.

'I'll stay with you forever.'

4

'Now you look like someone who needs cheering up,' Jocelyn told Holly. She had just arrived for their now usual Sunday brunch and could tell straight away that there was something on Holly's mind.

'I'm fine,' Holly reassured Jocelyn with a weak smile. They were sitting at the kitchen table and Holly lifted a teacup to her mouth to hide her trembling and slightly bruised lips. Since Tom's call, Holly had been nervously biting them to hold back the tears she refused to shed.

'You're not the least bit fine. These eyes may be old but they're not blind,' admonished Jocelyn. She picked up her shopping bag and took out a small cake box. 'Still, there's nothing that can't be put right with a cupcake. Now what do you fancy, lemon or walnut?'

'Tom might be losing his job,' gulped Holly.

'Oh, Holly, I'm sorry.' Jocelyn put down the box and stood up, although the grimace on her face made it clear the manoeuvre was a huge struggle for the old lady. 'Damn these aching joints,' she muttered as she shuffled around the table to give Holly a hug.

'Are you all right?' Holly asked. It was now her turn to look concerned. She was so used to seeing Jocelyn as a strong warhorse that she found it easy to forget that she was an octogenarian.

'Nothing a new pair of hips wouldn't fix,' smiled Jocelyn. 'I remember the days I used to walk back and forth from here to the village two or three times a day. Now just walking from one end of the room wears me out.'

'You should have said. I've got the car outside. I could have picked you up.'

'I wasn't born old and I refuse to give in to it. The day I stop getting from A to B under my own steam is the day I reach my final destination.'

'Well, you sit right back down and I'll get some plates for those cakes.'

Jocelyn sank back into her chair with a relieved sigh. 'So when will you find out about Tom?'

'He's back a week on Thursday and then he's being hauled in to see the studio. He doesn't know what they're planning, but he's not expecting it to be good news. Even if he does keep his job they'll be piling more work on him.' It was Holly's turn to sink back into her chair with a deep sigh, only this sigh had the telltale signs of disappointment.

'He sounds like a resourceful kind of fellow and from what I've seen of him on TV he's gorgeous. I should imagine he could walk into any job he wanted. I'd give him a job,' Jocelyn admitted with a wink.

'Yes, I can imagine!' laughed Holly. 'And however comfortable he looks in front of the camera, he actually hates it. He'd rather do the legwork and let someone else take the credit on screen. But it's not just the job security that worries

86

me,' confessed Holly.

'Want to talk about it?' Jocelyn asked.

'We were about to start planning for a family. You have no idea how difficult it's been for me to even contemplate becoming a mother and now, when I think I'm ready, everything is going wrong. I'm starting to wonder if it was meant to be.' For someone Holly had known for less than two months, she was surprised at how easily she could talk to Jocelyn. There had been very few people in Holly's life that she would have felt able to have this conversation with, and Jocelyn seemed to be filling a gap that had existed since childhood.

'There's still plenty of time. You'll be a mum one day and you'll be a good mum, I can feel it in my bones and, believe me, they speak to me a lot.'

'Did you not think of having more children?' asked Holly innocently. She was still struggling to find out more about Jocelyn's former life.

Jocelyn looked thoughtfully at Holly. 'I married late, had a baby late. I was forty-one when I had Paul, but even if I had been younger, I don't think another baby would have been a good idea. I wasn't blessed with a husband like Tom. Harry was a bully and things just got worse when I had Paul. I think he was actually jealous of the affection I showed Paul, so his behaviour became even worse after the baby was born.'

'I don't suppose you saw motherhood as a blessing in your life then?' Holly asked.

'Oh, the complete opposite,' replied Jocelyn, shaking her head. 'Paul was the best thing that ever happened to me. Harry was an expert in mental torture. He isolated me from my friends and family and slowly but surely wore me down. If it hadn't been for Paul, it could have been so much worse.'

'What do you mean?'

Jocelyn was looking over Holly's shoulder towards the window and the garden beyond. There was a look of fear on her face as if her husband's ghost would appear at the window. 'Paul saved my life. By that, I mean it was because of Paul that I finally left Harry. I couldn't build up the courage to leave for my own protection, but I could for my son, although it took some hard lessons before I realized that.' Jocelyn's voice had withered to a whisper and the age-worn wrinkles around her eyes seemed to cut deeper into her face. Her whole body shuddered, despite the warmth of the morning sun streaming through the window.

'Are you all right?' Holly asked.

'I'm fine. I think someone just walked over my grave.' Again, there was that furtive glance towards the window. 'I'm sorry, Holly, it's so hard to go back to that part of my life.'

'No, it's me who should apologize. I don't think I quite realized how awful a time you had here. I'm so sorry,' said Holly.

'Don't be sorry, be hopeful. Don't give up on your dreams yet, Holly.'

For a split second, Holly didn't think about her dreams but her nightmares. 'Perhaps I should be careful what I wish for,' she said to Jocelyn. 'Now, enough serious talk; these cakes aren't going to eat themselves.'

*　　　*　　　*

'Belgian chocolates? You go to Belgium for six

88

weeks and the best you can come up with is Belgian chocolates?' growled Holly sleepily. She had been woken abruptly by Tom jumping onto the bed like an excited puppy and announcing that he was home. It was two-thirty in the morning.

'But look at the wrapping!' Tom replied loudly to make sure Holly was fully awake.

Holly blinked her eyes, still trying to adjust to the painfully bright bedroom light that Tom had just switched on. Her heart was thudding in her chest, partly from the shock of the early morning wake-up and partly from the joy of Tom's return. She looked at the large red chocolate box. 'It's not even wrapped,' she complained.

Tom undid the top buttons on his shirt and slipped the box inside. 'How about now?' He was kneeling with his legs on each side of Holly, pinning her down. He leant over and kissed the tip of her nose.

'You smell,' she teased. 'It would be like peeling a clove of garlic.'

'Peel away, Mrs Corrigan.'

She kissed him, softly at first and then with a hunger that came from deep within. In her mind, she chased away the shadows of the past and more importantly the shadows of the future. Everything she needed was in the present. All she needed was Tom.

The box of chocolates disappeared beneath a sea of bed linen and eagerly discarded clothing. 'I missed you,' she whispered as she lay in his arms. She curled her fingers through his unruly hair and pulled his head back to look into his eyes. They were the same eyes she had looked into during her moonlit nightmare, only now they glinted green and held no hint of the grief that had consumed the man her warped mind had created. Try as she might, Holly couldn't shake the picture she had now created of Tom in her mind. The fear for the future that Holly had tried to ignore sparked into life and doubt crept in. What if the moondial had summoned the vision? What if it really had shown her the future?

Tom frowned as he recognized the look of sadness in Holly's eyes. 'You must hate me for doing this to you,' he told her. 'Uprooting you to the country and then abandoning you. I'm a lousy husband.'

'You're the best husband I could ever have. I'm blessed to be loved so much, never forget that.' Holly wrapped Tom tightly in her arms and squeezed away the tears and the doubts. Fully awake and thinking only of the present, Holly's mind did a double take and she pushed Tom away from her again so that they were face to face. 'Hold on, why are you here? You were supposed to be staying over in London tonight, ready for the showdown with the studio tomorrow. What's happened?'

Tom sighed and closed his eyes. He leaned forward and rested his head on Holly's as if the weight of the world was bearing down on him.

'It's bad, isn't it?' Holly said, her heart hammering.

Tom lifted his head and tried to smile. Holly knew he wasn't about to put her mind at ease. 'I've still got a job, or at least I will have,' he said, but Holly sensed that he was softening the blow.

'Tell me,' she demanded softly.

'Peter Richards is retiring at the end of the year

and they want me to be part of the new line-up.'

'A news anchor? They want you to be an anchorman?' Holly was almost laughing, partly with relief and partly at the thought of Tom behind a desk in a slick, smart suit reading the news. 'And that's bad?'

Tom grimaced. 'Well, can you picture me in a shiny suit every day? Ah, I see by the wicked smile on your face that you're already imagining it. But no, that's not the bad news, not really.'

Holly stopped smiling as she realized there was something else that Tom was trying to tell her. 'So that's at the end of the year. What do they have planned for you in the meantime?'

'The merger has meant joining forces with a couple of other production companies and I'm being seconded. It means more special assignments and they're going to involve quite a bit of travel. The first assignment is investigating the Canadian oil sands and I have to leave in a couple of weeks. Environmental impact of oil extraction, that kind of thing.'

'You're going to Canada?' Holly knew it was a stupid question and Tom had the good grace to bite his tongue rather than make a smart response.

'So how long?' Holly continued.

'At least a month.'

'And after that?' Holly could feel her heart wrenching in her chest.

'More travelling. I'm sorry, Holly.'

Tom's eyes were glistening and Holly's heart pulled some more. She didn't want to see Tom hurting, not again. She leaned over to kiss Tom on each of his eyes. 'Kiss me,' she told him sternly.

'Even when I smell of garlic?' Tom asked with a

weak smile.

'It just makes me hungry.'

'So eat me.' The smile on his face had now reached his eyes.

Holly giggled and the sound of laughter eased her disappointment. They had each other, they would always have each other, she told herself. She savoured every kiss and every caress and when they made love Holly held onto Tom like she was never going to let go.

Later that morning, when they had worn themselves out and had nothing to sustain their appetites other than a box of very squashed chocolates, Tom and Holly dragged themselves out of bed and down to the kitchen to raid the fridge.

'So when do I get to see your fabulous new studio?' Tom asked.

'As soon as you're dressed and decent. This is a respectable village and I can't have you going out in nothing but a pair of boxer shorts and risk frightening the locals.'

'We're not overlooked,' replied Tom, 'and anyway, if your friend Jocelyn comes calling it would probably make her day.'

'Jocelyn won't be calling, not today. Everyone knows to keep away for a day or two. Even Billy.'

'Ah yes, Billy. I wouldn't mind speaking to him.'

'So he can finish your half-hearted attempt to landscape the garden, by any chance?'

'My new job is going to mean more money. If I can't be here to do the work myself, the least I can do is spend my hard-earned cash on making a beautiful garden for my wife. And I might just be able to afford another project I've had in mind,' Tom answered cryptically.

Holly recalled standing beneath the full moon, standing on the well-manicured garden and looking towards the house. 'What kind of project?' she asked as the now familiar sense of fear crawled up her spine. She held the vision of the conservatory in her mind's eye and willed Tom not to make the suggestion.

'That's going to be between me and Billy.'

Holly shrugged her shoulders. She didn't want to hear something that might give more substance to her hallucination. 'Suit yourself, then,' she told Tom.

Tom looked at Holly open-mouthed, shocked and a little disappointed by her quick submission. He wasn't used to winning so easily. 'I will, then,' he said, his bottom lip turned out in boyish petulance.

Feeling guilty at bringing Tom's little game of words to a sudden end, Holly set about distracting him. 'Well, if you want to size up Billy's expertise, let's go take a look at the studio. I'll even let you visit half-naked. Let's live dangerously.'

The weather was warm and there was a damp, earthy smell in the air. June was blooming and in the garden the spring daffodils had made way for the summer blooms. 'The dandelions are doing well,' Holly commented as they slipped out of the house barefooted towards the studio. She was only wearing a vest top and knickers and hid as best she could behind Tom.

'Ooh, ouch, so are the nettles,' he said as he led the way carefully along a narrow and overgrown path that marked the boundary between the house and the studio.

The entrance to the studio faced the road and was the only place where they risked being seen.

'Morning, Mrs Davis!' Tom shouted casually.

Holly gasped and crouched further behind Tom. Then she peeped over his shoulder before thumping him. 'You don't know a Mrs Davis,' she said. 'Now open the door before someone really does see us.'

Nowadays Holly spent most mornings in her studio and the bright airy space was a second home to her. Tom, on the other hand, had last seen the studio when it was still a building site. She looked at his face intently to savour the reaction. His eyes were wide in amazement as he took in the white walls and the sunlight that danced brightly across the walls and floor. Against the starkness of the white, Holly had hung a mixture of her own artwork and an eclectic selection of photos and other images to inspire her. Some pictures had been pinned to the walls and others hung on wires from the ceiling, creating small clusters of colour scattered around the outer edges of the room.

Tom walked around the studio as if stepping through an enchanted forest. 'It's amazing,' he said at last. 'I never imagined it would be like this.' He touched a picture frame which seemed to be floating in mid air. It was a photograph of Tom and Holly laughing. A neighbouring photo was one of them on their wedding day, another was of Grandma Edith. 'She would be so proud of you,' he told her.

Tom's attention was next drawn to Holly's ongoing projects. Workbenches lined one full side of the room and a few pieces of work in progress were stacked up waiting for completion. The main work area, taking full advantage of the sky lights, was the centre of the studio and here a dust sheet hung over the sculpture Holly was working on. There was an easel next to it with some of Holly's sketches taped to it.

'So this must be the sculpture for the dreaded Mrs Bronson,' Tom noted.

'It's a scaled-down version and I'm still not one hundred per cent happy with it. I've got another month to get her to sign off the final design and then up until Christmas to complete it. And then I'll finally be free of her.'

'Can I take a look?' Tom asked. He knew very well that Holly hated him looking over her shoulder while she worked and often refused to show him any of her works in progress, not until she was sure in her own mind what the finished article would look like. She didn't want to risk being swayed by other people's opinions, as she always seemed to lose her way if she did. Holly decided to take a chance and pulled off the dust sheet to reveal the sculpture. It was about three feet high and was standing on a wooden box to raise it up to eye-level to work on it more easily.

The bottom section was made from plaster of Paris but painted black to represent the marble which would be part of the final piece. Above the swirling, black figures that formed the base emerged the white figure of the mother, or at least that was what the current mess of twisted chicken wire would eventually become. Holly had made better progress with the figure of the baby held in its mother's arms. The baby's face was smooth and white, the Cupid's bow lips perfectly formed and its plump cheeks perfectly round. Holly had drawn inspiration not from Mrs Bronson's photographs of her son, which were discarded somewhere on her workbench, but from the baby she had seen in her vision.

Tom traced its tiny face with a gentle stroke of his finger. 'She's beautiful,' he said.

Holly smiled but the treacherous wings of guilt fluttered across her heart. She felt awkward as she watched Tom look in wonderment at the beautiful contours of the baby, not least because her own mind had already created a vision of him holding and feeding the very same child.

'I can't wait to have a baby of our own,' Tom said, as if reading her mind. He looked at Holly and saw the shadow of doubt in her eyes. 'Now that I know what's happening at the studio, we can start on that five-year plan of yours.'

Holly didn't want to have this conversation right now. Her resolve to have a baby and prove her vision wrong, to prove Sam wrong, had withered and died when Tom had cast doubt about his job and their future. She stood in front of Tom speechless, unsure what to say.

'You've changed your mind, haven't you?' he said, almost as an accusation.

'I don't know. Everything is so unsettled at the moment, maybe we should put off making plans for now.'

Tom's body tensed and there was anger in his voice. 'For God's sake, Holly, when is the time ever going to be right?'

Holly wasn't surprised at Tom's frustration, but the anger shocked her. 'What's wrong?' she asked, knowing Tom well enough to know that his reaction was about more than Holly's usual prevarication over having children.

Tom sighed and the anger left his body with a

low hiss like a deflated balloon. 'I'm taking the anchorman job because it means I can give you and any children we may have a stable, secure life. If I had the guts, I'd tell them to stuff their job and go freelance, but I haven't because I want what's best for us—us as a family.'

'Well, why don't you go freelance? I'm sure you'd find enough work, we'd manage. My work at the gallery is selling well. Tom, we could do it if you really hate the thought of being a news anchor so much.'

'It's a good job and I can't look a gift horse in the mouth. And if it means I can be at home more when we do have a family then I really do want to do it. I just want you to want it too. Yes, it's going to be unsettled for a year, but after that, we'll know what's going to happen and we can plan.'

Holly laughed but it was tinged with suppressed hysteria. 'Do we? Do we really know what's going to happen? What if we can't have everything we want, Tom? What if everything comes at a price?' Holly was conscious that she was teetering on the edge of a precipice and, with a little more nudging from Tom, she was ready to tell him about her vision.

Tom lifted his hands in despair. 'I love you, Holly. I love you with every beat of my heart, with every breath that I take and with every bone in my body. I couldn't love you any more and I will never, never love you any less. But you drive me mad sometimes. You drive me mad because I can't seem to convince you that you're not going to repeat your mother's mistakes. What could be so frightening about creating a baby? Look at the sculpture you're working on. If that's what you can make from a load of chicken wire and paste, imagine what you can make from love. What do we have to lose?'

Holly knew exactly what she could lose, but she really did need to hold onto reality. The Tom standing in front of her was real and the baby they could make together would be real too. 'She is beautiful, isn't she?' Holly told him. She looked intently at the sculpted image of the baby and the orange embers of maternal feelings that she had all but extinguished burst into flames. 'I think I'm ready to put that five-year plan down in writing. Five years for me, you and whoever comes along.'

Tom stepped towards Holly and leaned down to kiss her forehead, then her nose. Hovering over her lips, he waited for her to come to him.

'Don't tell me, more practice?' she asked in a whisper. She needed Tom to hold her more than ever and she leaned up to kiss him. They tumbled onto the dust sheet which was lying abandoned on the floor and their gentle caresses transformed into an urgent, passionate rhythm that chased away Holly's fears for the future and replaced them with hope and anticipation.

*   *   *

Jocelyn was ready to forego her usual Sunday brunch with Holly while Tom was home but Holly insisted. It might have been only days before Tom would be jetting off for Canada, but Holly was looking forward to introducing her to Tom. It felt just like she was introducing a new boyfriend to her parents, not that she had ever experienced that before, or even contemplated it, for that matter.

'What time will she be here?' Tom asked

nervously as he came out onto the patio, which was bathed in sweet summer sunshine.

Holly was laying out napkins and cutlery on the garden table. 'Oh, she usually gets here about eleven. It depends how long it takes her to loosen up her joints and get walking.'

'You should have said, I'll go get the car and pick her up,' Tom said, turning on his heels to head back into the house.

Grabbing Tom by the arm, Holly pulled him back. 'Oh no, you don't. Jocelyn would be livid if you started treating her like an invalid. She's a firm believer in mind over matter and she won't even think about slowing down yet. Believe me, I've tried already.'

'Good grief, I'm going to have another iron lady to deal with. If I'd known, I would have invited Billy over to even out the numbers.'

'You've been meeting up with Billy quite enough as it is,' Holly accused him.

'Well, you'll be seeing a little bit more of him while I'm away,' Tom replied. He looked ready to slope back into the house, but Holly still had hold of his sleeve.

'Tell,' commanded Holly. She ignored the flow of adrenalin surging through her veins. She knew what was coming but she had a new talisman to ward off any doubts about the vision of the future. She and Tom had committed their five-year plan to paper just as she had promised. She had written it down with Tom sitting beside her at the kitchen table, in full view of the full moon and fully aware that the moondial was vying for her attention. The plan recorded that the rest of the current year would be set aside for Tom's travels, in the following year they would plan for baby number one, by year three Tom was supposed to start writing the book he'd been putting off forever, and then by year five, maybe, just maybe, baby number two. Five years, all planned out, and Holly was there in the future with Tom. It was written down in black and white and nowhere did it mention dying in childbirth. It simply wasn't in the plan.

'Well, see this patio table,' Tom explained as he guided Holly further away from the house so they could visualize his plans. 'Say, from over there, just before the kitchen door, right across the back of the house in front of the living room and then out, say this much.' Tom was now pointing excitedly to an imaginary line that reached past the current patio area and across the garden. 'Imagine, if you will, a beautiful structure of glass and steel, perfectly placed to catch the warmth of the sun with the right amount of shade at the end of the day to take the occasional evening aperitif in our brand-new . . .'

'Conservatory,' Holly said blankly, finishing his sentence. She didn't need to visualize the conservatory, she had already seen it first-hand.

'So what do you think?'

Holly wanted to tell Tom to rip up his plans, but she looked at his puppy-dog expression and couldn't say no. That didn't mean, however, that the vision she had seen would come to pass and Holly was about to make sure it didn't. 'I think that's a lovely idea, but there is one suggestion I'd like to make before you finish off your designs.'

'Suggest away, you are the artiste of the family, after all,' conceded Tom.

'I don't know where you were planning on putting the door, but I'd really like French doors coming from the front of the conservatory. Just in case you were thinking of putting them on the side next to the kitchen . . .' Holly held her breath. Not only was it where she had seen the doors in her vision, it was also the logical place to put them. But Holly was willing to sacrifice practicalities to prove that the future she had seen had been and always would be restricted to her imagination. If her mind could play games, so could she.

'But that way, you'd have to walk back around to the patio, which would be in front of the kitchen,' argued Tom.

'You've just said I'm the creative one. Trust me, it'll work better. It creates a continuous flow from the living room, through the conservatory and then out to the garden beyond.'

The explanation sounded so good, Holly almost believed it herself and Tom didn't have a chance to question her because at that precise moment the doorbell rang. Jocelyn had arrived.

*　　　　*　　　　*

'I can't imagine another family living here,' Tom mused. He had used his journalistic skills to extract almost as much information from Jocelyn as Holly had and Tom had known her for less than an hour.

'I can barely imagine you living here, Tom,' Holly added pointedly, unable to resist the urge to tease him.

With the sun in his eyes, he squinted at Holly with what was possibly meant to be a hurt look. 'Distance makes the heart grow fonder.'

'Well, your travelling seems to be taking you so far around the world you're practically coming back on yourself. How far do you need to go to prove to your wife that you love her, anyway?' countered Holly.

'Oh, all the way,' smiled Tom, before realizing Jocelyn was sitting quietly watching them. He coughed with embarrassment.

'Don't mind me,' Jocelyn encouraged, 'it's been a while since I saw such love in this house.'

'So what happened to your cruel excuse for a husband anyway?' Tom asked her. Holly's jaw dropped. She couldn't believe how forward he was being, but before she could scold him, to her surprise, Jocelyn replied.

'He killed himself,' she answered candidly.

The silence that passed between them left a chill in the air despite the sunshine. 'I'm sorry, Jocelyn,' Tom said to fill the space that had opened up an unwanted connection to the past.

Jocelyn looked at Holly and seemed to read her mind. 'No, it wasn't in this house,' she assured them. 'When I left with Paul, Harry had nothing left to live for. If you want the honest answer, it was always going to be him or me. For Paul's sake, I'm glad I left, but I carry the guilt with me too.'

'Guilt? What on earth do you have to feel guilty about? You've told me enough to know what a horrible man he was. He made his choices, you made yours. Don't ever feel guilty,' Holly told her firmly.

'You have a good wife there,' Jocelyn told Tom. 'Don't you ever let her go.'

'I don't intend to,' Tom replied.

Holly couldn't help but think how easily things could change. Life was so precarious and nothing could be taken for granted. She glanced nervously towards the moondial which was now half hidden beneath the new summer's growth of grass and weeds. Jocelyn followed her gaze.

'It came from Hardmonton Hall—the moondial, that is,' she told Holly. 'There was a massive fire that razed the Hall to the ground in the seventies and the moondial was amongst the few things that survived it.'

'I read up on that. The family actually died in the fire,' added Tom.

'Lord and Lady Hardmonton perished, but their young son was away at the time. He never returned and what little was left of the estate was sold off.'

'And that's how you came by the moondial,' concluded Tom.

'I can see why you make a living from your enquiring mind,' laughed Jocelyn. 'Yes, Harry spotted the dial and just had to buy it, not because he liked it but because he knew I wouldn't. We'd been married a good while by then. I think Paul would have been about ten and life wasn't good, wasn't good at all.' She turned to Tom before she continued, ready to make a point. 'Hard as it is to believe, the garden was beautiful back then. It was the one part of my life I still felt I had some control over, a form of escape, but Harry tried his best to spoil that too. He set up the moondial in the middle of my beautiful garden just because he thought it would sully it.'

They all stood up without prompting and walked over to the dial. Tom did his best to stamp down the overgrowth to make it easier for Jocelyn to get to the dial. 'I will make it good,' he promised her apologetically. 'Once I'm done with all of this travelling, it'll be restored to its former glory, and that's a promise.'

'Well, make sure you do,' Jocelyn answered.

Holly stood in front of the dial but was reluctant to touch it. She had purposely avoided getting close to the dial since her fall, and seeing the stone up close, watching the quartz glinting menacingly in the sunlight, she could almost feel the electric shock she had received from the dial course up her arm.

It was Jocelyn who tentatively reached out and touched the surface of the dial first. 'You found the mechanism,' she whispered. Holly thought she detected a slight tremor in her voice.

'Yes, but it doesn't seem to do anything. We tried putting the glass ball thing in the claws but it didn't fit properly,' explained Tom.

Jocelyn visibly relaxed. 'It doesn't work, never has,' she told Tom. 'Still, it makes a good bird table.'

'I've never seen a bird land on it yet,' Holly said, almost to herself, as she realized how strange it was that she hadn't actually seen a bird anywhere near it.

'So what else do we know of the moondial?' Tom asked her, his eyebrow raised in suspicion.

Guilt flushed Holly's cheeks. 'What do you mean?' she stammered.

Tom turned to Jocelyn. 'My wife here has been doing her own research. I've been waiting patiently for her to reveal the murky history of the moondial, but so far she's keeping her information to herself. She hasn't even apologized for spilling coffee all over my computer.'

Tom turned back to Holly. Her mouth opened to speak but she couldn't quite find the words that would help her wriggle out of a conversation that was making her decidedly uncomfortable.

'You switched the screen off, but you didn't close down the computer,' he explained.

'I was just trying to find out where the moondial came from,' she confessed. 'Sorry about the coffee.'

'What did you find out?' Jocelyn asked tentatively.

'There was a Lord Hardmonton in the nineteenth century who was an explorer,' Holly explained. 'He discovered something called a Moon Stone in Mexico and it went missing on the return voyage to England. I think maybe he kept the stone for himself and made the moondial from it.'

Jocelyn's eyes didn't flicker. If she knew any more about the moondial, Holly thought, she was hiding it well.

'Not only that,' added Tom, eager to share his own discoveries, 'there was a legend that the stone could summon up visions. I found some suggestion that the Aztecs actually believed these were visions of the future, although, if you ask me, it had more to do with the hallucinogenic drugs they would have been taking back then. Still, it's made me look at the dial in a new light.'

Tom ran his fingers across the etched words on the outer edge of the dial. 'I read it wrong,' he told the two women, who both seemed to have turned to stone, with complexions as grey as the moondial. 'Reflection is the key to travelling in time.'

They all fell silent and the only thing Holly could hear was the hammering of her heart in her chest.

'All stuff and nonsense,' sniffed Jocelyn, breaking the spell.

'I think you might be right there,' agreed Tom.

'After all, if it had worked, then why didn't Lord Hardmonton know that the electrical rewiring he'd just had installed at the Hall would raze it to the ground?'

An electric current of her very own making coursed up Holly's spine and sent stars glittering across her vision. She was sure she was going to faint so, despite her best intentions, she put her hand on the dial to steady herself. The stone felt cold and Holly felt an almost imperceptible tingling between her palms and the dial. As her vision settled, Holly looked across to Jocelyn, but Jocelyn was looking just as intently at the dial and didn't meet her gaze.

'I wonder if this thing could tell me if my wife will burn our supper tonight?' Tom asked mischievously.

'Bread and water is all you deserve until you get this garden in order, young man,' scolded Jocelyn. 'These nettles are stinging the backs of my legs.'

It was only when their laughter filled the garden that Holly felt the moondial loosen its grip on her.

'Time for another cup of tea, I think,' Holly told Tom, who led the two women carefully back to the safety of the patio.

*　　　*　　　*

Tom seemed more relaxed as the time approached for him to set off on his travels again. Meeting Jocelyn had obviously eased his guilt and allayed any fears he might have had about leaving Holly alone and isolated in her new surroundings.

'There's going to be a major time difference this time around,' he warned Holly, as he started to cram clothes into his suitcase for the early start the next day. They were in the bedroom and the open window was easing in the summer night's breeze and the sweet smell of the overgrown honeysuckle that had clawed its way out of the neglected garden and along the back of the house. 'I think we're only going to manage to speak once a day.'

'Without exception,' Holly warned him. She was leaning over the open suitcase, plucking out the crumpled clothes and then neatly folding them and placing them back in the suitcase.

'Speaking of phone calls . . .' Tom started.

'Speaking of phone calls, are you finally going to tell me what your long conversation with the studio was about this morning?'

'I told you, it's nothing bad. It's still the same plan. I'll spend a month in Canada, then come home briefly before setting off again. It's looking like the next assignment will definitely be in Haiti and I could be away for longer this time, maybe a couple of months.'

'So I knew that anyway. What's new?' Holly asked suspiciously. Tom had already broken the bad news about his next assignment days earlier. Although Holly wasn't happy about the travelling, or where he was going, for that matter, their future was there, written down in their five-year plan, so all was well in the world and Holly had reluctantly accepted the news.

'They were saying how happy they were with my front-of-camera work,' continued Tom a little sheepishly.

'But?' Holly demanded.

'They want to work on my image.'

It was no secret that Tom preferred writing at

107

a desk to presenting behind one and part of that reluctance was the pressure for him to conform to certain standards when it came to image. It was inevitable that the studio would want him to smarten up his appearance at some point.

'Well, I could see that one coming,' laughed Holly.

Tom gasped in mock horror. 'Thanks for the vote of confidence! So go on, say it. Tell me I've got the perfect face for radio.'

'You have a perfect face,' Holly told him. 'Your hair, on the other hand . . .'

'I know,' Tom said, self-consciously pulling at a wayward curl that was sticking up on top of his head.

Holly suddenly burst into laughter. 'They want you to cut your hair, don't they?'

'It's not funny,' Tom said seriously, but then started laughing too. 'The studio wants me to have my new image sorted before they start filming my pieces over in Canada.'

Pushing the suitcase out of the way, Holly crawled over the bed towards Tom. She wrapped her arms around him and lovingly began to caress his dark locks. 'Then I think I'm going to have to kiss every last one goodbye,' she whispered.

As Tom joined her on the bed he barely noticed the fraction of a second when Holly's whole body froze. She had just remembered the broken-hearted Tom in her vision. His hair had been cropped short. Holly was tiring of the game the moondial seemed to be playing with her mind and, in that split second, she knew she had to put that particular nightmare to bed once and for all.

108

5

On the day that Tom set off for Canada, Holly couldn't wait for night to fall. The evening was warm and wet as Holly scrambled through the long grass and stood in defiance in front of the moondial. Above her, the waning moon shone down on her and sought out the reflected surface of the glass orb that Holly clasped in her hand. She didn't want any more time to think about what she was doing so she dropped the orb hastily into the dial, taking care not to let her fingers make contact with the brass mechanism or the stone dial itself.

The orb rattled into place and then remained as still as the night that closed in expectantly around Holly, feeding on her growing tension. She strained her ears for the telltale ticking of a clock, the sound that had accompanied the violent flash of moonbeams the last time she had used the dial, but the only sound that greeted her was the rustling of the tall grasses as they scraped against each other in the gentle breeze. The orb sparkled innocently as it reflected the moonlight but it held no power of its own, nothing that existed beyond the realms of her own imagination.

In the distance Holly heard the occasional hooting of an owl, and she imagined it was laughing at her. She didn't blame it. She lifted up her head to the skies to expel a huge sigh of relief, but the smile on her face faltered as she stared at the skies above her. On the night of her vision, there had been a full moon, not the partially hidden face that peaked out behind the shadow of the earth. The images of the moon etched on the surface of the dial were all perfect circles. Reluctantly, she understood in that moment that if the moondial really did hold any power of its own it would be by the light of the full moon. Cautiously, using her finger and thumb, she prised the glass orb from the weak grasp of the dial and returned it to its box.

Holly felt defeated and deflated. There were three whole weeks to wait until the next full moon at the end of July, and Holly felt like her life had been placed in limbo. Dealing with the emotional fallout from this latest separation from Tom was bad enough, but living with the nagging doubts and the growing possibility that she had seen a vision of her future and one where she had already died, was just too much to bear.

That night, Holly tossed and turned in bed, trying to make sense of everything she had seen or thought she had seen during her hallucination and the connections she had made to this vision since then. Perhaps the bang on her head when she had fallen in the garden had caused a long-term problem. Perhaps she hadn't seen a conservatory in her original vision. Perhaps she hadn't seen Tom with short hair. What if her mind had just altered her memory of the vision when Tom told her about his plans? Didn't that make more sense? Holly knew this didn't explain away the parallels between her own experience and the legend of the Moon Stone, but the link between the moondial and the Moon Stone was still a tenuous one. 'Reflection is the key,' that was what the inscription said, but what did it mean? The moon reflected the light of the sun into the darkness of the night. The moondial took that light and reflected it where?

Into the future?

Holly wondered if she should speak to Jocelyn about the dial. Had she simply imagined Jocelyn's uneasiness as they stood around the moondial? Did Jocelyn have more secrets to reveal? She couldn't share her thoughts until she had unravelled the puzzle a little more and she couldn't do that until the moon was full. Holly shook her head to free herself from the spider's web of theories that tangled up her thoughts into a silken mess.

It was no surprise that during each and every night that followed Holly seemed to sleep less and less as the moon shrank into a crooked smile that seemed more of a smirk, before beginning to open its wide yawning mouth, ready to swallow up her fading hope that everything could be explained away by a simple bump on the head.

*   *   *

While the moondial occupied her thoughts during the night, it was Mrs Bronson's sculpture that occupied her days. The baby figure was faultless, its smooth, soft curves had just enough echoes of Libby to tug at Holly's heart every time she looked at it, which she often did. The mother figure was nearing completion too, cradling the baby in her arms in a way that made Holly's own arms ache for the weight of her child. The mother's arms were wrapped around the tiny figure as if it was the most delicate of flowers, but there was also something about that pose that suggested the mother had a grip of iron.

Holly stepped back to review her work. Her hands were covered in dust from sanding and

111

chipping away at any imperfections to reveal smoother lines and refined curves. It was almost finished, but still Holly frowned. She stepped slowly around the sculpture, surveying every inch of the spiralling form and the transition points where the black stone would meet white. It didn't have the finesse that would be reserved for the final version, but otherwise everything looked as it was supposed to. Still not satisfied, Holly took a few more steps back until she was practically at the door, checking the work from a distance. There was something about the pose that Holly felt was wrong even though it was precisely as she had drawn it in her initial sketches.

Her eyes drifted towards a chisel but she stopped herself from going and picking it up. Instead she released a deep sigh. 'It's good enough for Mrs Bronson,' she told herself with a touch of annoyance.

It was mid July and, although she had until the end of the month to sign off the sample piece, Mrs Bronson couldn't wait and had been pestering her for days. Holly knew she had to take a leap of faith and accept that this was the best she could produce. She went to lean against the studio door in resignation. Unfortunately, at that precise moment, the door opened outwards and Holly's body met nothing but thin air.

'Watch yourself,' Billy shouted, catching Holly mid fall.

Hovering no more than a foot from the ground and relying on Billy's arms to keep her from hitting the floor, Holly looked up into the builder's eyes as he leaned over her. He gave her a sympathetic smile as he shook his head. 'You women really can't be trusted on your own,' he told her with a sigh.

'I can look after myself perfectly well,' said Holly with a growl.

'Women,' he replied with a mischievous glint in his eyes.

'You can let go of me now, Bill,' Holly suggested.

'You're the boss,' he said, letting go of her.

Holly landed on the floor with a clatter of jarred joints. 'Thanks, Billy!' she said, rubbing her elbows as she struggled up. 'What are you doing here, anyway?'

'Reporting for duty, ma'am.' Billy saluted her. Holly stared at him vacantly so he continued, 'Your husband has commissioned me to build you one conservatory.'

'Hmm,' frowned Holly. 'Just what I need.'

'Ooh, wait until you see it. It's going to be spectacular,' gushed Billy.

'Ooh, I can just imagine it,' sighed Holly, mirroring Billy's enthusiasm with an added sprinkle of sarcasm that only she could appreciate.

'Well, imagining is all you can do. I agreed the plans with Tom but I'm not to show you. You've done enough meddling by messing about with the position of the doors. Tom wants the finished product to be a surprise.'

'That might be more difficult than you think,' Holly replied.

'I suppose there's no chance that you could stay out of the garden for the next couple of weeks?'

'No chance,' confirmed Holly. 'I tell you what,' she added when she saw Billy's shoulders sag in disappointment, 'I'll avert my eyes whenever I go past and promise not to go snooping.'

'It's a deal. We'll start work after the weekend.'

'Great, I'll see you next week,' replied Holly.

Billy looked over towards the sculpture and was obviously about to give Holly his expert opinion.

'See you Monday, Billy,' Holly told him before he had a chance to speak.

'Could it do with . . .' he began.

'Go away, Billy,' Holly said a little more forcefully, but with a suppressed laugh tickling the back of her throat.

With Billy out of the way, Holly picked up the phone and called Mrs Bronson. If she could arrange for her client to visit the studio next week then she would be ahead of schedule and able to spend some time working on the other pieces she had promised Sam for the gallery. That was, of course, assuming Mrs Bronson was happy with the scaled version. Holly stared at the sculpture as she made the necessary arrangements with Mrs Bronson over the phone. The frown returned.

She just hoped it was her own self-doubt and insecurities that made her look at the piece differently. The mother-and-child theme was always going to be a challenge, but even Holly couldn't have suspected how challenging.

Holly sighed, chasing away the ghosts of the future. Hopefully Mrs Bronson would have an uncomplicated view and see the sculpture as Holly had intended: a simple and idealistic portrayal of the bond between mother and child.

*   *   *

Holly's separation from Tom had grown and not just in terms of distance. The emotional effects were wider than the Atlantic Ocean that now lay

114

between them. She had been prepared for the impracticalities of their long-distance relationship caused by the time zone differences, but what she hadn't factored in was the chaos Tom had left her to face on her own, thanks to the moondial.

She realized it had been naive to think that she could handle the bizarre situation which she found herself in on her own. She had been cast adrift by her loveless parents, but when Tom came along, he had become her anchor. Her original five-year plan had set the course for her adult life, but it was Tom and only Tom who had given her the stability that she had craved for so long. The next five years were supposed to be plain sailing and, for Tom, having a baby and a wife was fundamental to that plan.

With the full moon only days away, Holly needed him more than ever. She wondered how he would react if she were to tell him about her hallucination and how she was even vaguely willing to accept that she had seen a vision of the future. He would probably book the next flight home. He would be supportive, of course, but he would never understand her fears. He wasn't the one who had walked into a house where the air was leaden with grief. He hadn't felt his heart break at the sight of the one he loved falling apart, and he hadn't see the vision of Libby, with the most perfect, beautiful green eyes staring back at him, and then been unable to hold her, not then and perhaps not ever, if the vision was as portentous as Holly was starting to believe it was. So when Holly picked up the phone and made her usual international call to Tom, she let the sound of his voice ease her fears and gave away no clue to her growing anxieties.

'So how's Billy getting on with my project?' Tom

115

asked eagerly.

It was mid afternoon in Fincross and the sun was high, breaking record temperatures for the year. It would have been a beautiful day for sitting out in the garden if Holly had been allowed outside in what had now become a construction site. The patio, where Holly, Tom and Jocelyn had enjoyed their Sunday brunch, had been ripped up and the foundations had been laid for the conservatory.

'I'm under strict instructions from Billy not to look out of any of the windows or go into the garden, so how would I know how it's going?' complained Holly.

'But everything's going to plan?'

'Billy's still complaining about the position of the conservatory doors and won't stop bending my ear. I've had to recruit Jocelyn to use her influence over him just to stop him changing the design behind my back.'

'Well, he has a point. I'm still not convinced it's the right place for the doors.'

'I told you, I'm the creative one. I know what's best,' Holly assured him.

'So, speaking of creativity, have you seen the dreaded Mrs Bronson yet?'

'She's not long ago left,' Holly told Tom as she sat at the kitchen table picking at a sandwich.

'And?' he demanded.

'And she loved it, thank God.' Holly leaned back in her chair and let the sense of relief wash over her. She couldn't stop grinning.

'I'm not surprised. It looked amazing even when I saw it only half-finished. Can you send me a photo now, please?'

Holly had refused to show him the completed

article until Mrs Bronson was ready to sign it off. She knew Tom would love it but Mrs Bronson was the client and she was the one that needed to be pleased.

'I will,' she promised.

'So she didn't want any changes, then?'

'Well, I didn't get off completely scot-free. She was keen to point out that her dearest child has a longer face and a dimple on his chin. I had half a mind to tell her she should be grateful I've based it on a far prettier baby, but the client is always right.'

'So of course the final sculpture will look more like her son,' added Tom.

'Of course,' Holly said with a wicked grin.

'Really?'

'How could you doubt me? If she wants her baby's ugly features immortalized, why would I do anything else?'

'Because it's your work being immortalized maybe?'

'Now I never thought of it that way. I might need to have a rethink.'

'Like you haven't already,' laughed Tom. 'Well, I hope you won't abandon our babies if they're ugly.'

Holly's smile faltered and she was just glad that Tom was on the end of the phone and not in front of her.

'Our babies will be beautiful,' she said before the pause became too noticeable. She closed her eyes and a familiar face came to mind.

'They will be if they take after you.'

'As long as they have your eyes,' she told him. A vision of Libby looking up at Holly hovered behind her closed lids and she had to squeeze her eyes tightly to chase away the ghost of her image.

117

'My eyes, but your nose. And your mouth. And your hair. Beautiful babies who will grow up to be just as gorgeous as their mum,' Tom went on with absolute certainty. 'Well, the girls will. I'm not so sure about having sons with long blond hair though, call me old fashioned.'

Holly giggled and the sound chased away the tension that had been building up inside her. This was why she needed Tom in her life, to make everything normal and safe and simple. 'You've got it all planned out, haven't you? You've probably even picked the names,' Holly accused him.

'Me? You're the one with all the plans! Although, now you mention it, I had been toying with some ideas for names,' admitted Tom.

'Don't tell me you've picked out a bunch of weird and wacky names now you're aspiring to celebrity status.'

'Hmm, don't remind me. I've got an appointment with the stylist soon. I can't believe what the studio is putting me through. But no, no stupid names. I was kind of toying with the idea of calling one of our boys Jack after Dad.'

'OK,' Holly replied sceptically. 'And I'll ignore the reference to having hordes of children yet again.'

'And I'd really, really like it if we named our first girl after Grandma.'

'Edith?' Holly grimaced at the very idea.

'No, I wouldn't be that cruel. Grandma's second name was Elizabeth. We could call her Beth or Eliza or even Lizzy for short.'

'Or Libby,' added Holly, the tension returning to her body with all the subtlety of a knockout punch in the chest.

118

'Hey, that sounds perfect. Our little Libby. I can just imagine her now.'

'Me too,' whispered Holly.

As they said their goodbyes and Holly put down the phone, she desperately wished life could be as simple as it used to be. She wanted to believe once more that tomorrow was a blank page ready to be filled and that while it remained blank their love could make up a whole new world ahead of them. With any luck, the full moon was about to prove that the moondial was just a garden ornament and, more importantly, that her future was written only in their five-year plan and not captured within the reflections from the moondial.

*　　　*　　　*

'You look different,' Holly told him as she stared at the photo Tom had sent to her phone. In the safety of her bedroom, surrounded by a sea of pillows and wrapped in her duvet, Holly had insulated herself from the fear of the full moon which was already creeping across the night sky.

'Different in a good way or different in a bad way?' pushed Tom. The tinny echo of his voice seemed more noticeable in the night time and emphasized the distance between them.

'Just different,' repeated Holly. The photo wasn't great quality and Tom had obviously taken it himself, arm outstretched with the bland hotel-room decor as the backdrop.

His face looked thinner and his features sharper without his usual halo of curls. Although Holly could vaguely recall the image of Tom with short cropped hair from her vision, it had been the hollowness in his eyes that she had focused on then. In the safe realms of reality, Holly was clear headed and able to take a more critical view of his new hairstyle.

She hadn't doubted that Tom would look as handsome as ever with a slick hairdo and suit to match, but seeing him with his cropped hair, she felt an unexpected wrench. She had become accustomed to the dishevelled Tom, that was her Tom and he had gone away in more than one sense. 'It'll grow on me,' she added hesitantly.

'You don't like it,' moaned Tom. 'And to think you always used to nag me about getting my hair cut.'

'I have, in the past, suggested you keep it tidy and trimmed. I did, on occasion, drag you to the bathroom to wash it. I accept that once, and only once, I chopped off a couple of knotted tats when you were asleep.'

'You practically scalped me!'

'You look dashing. You look suave. The viewers are going to be enthralled.'

'Now you're just being nice. Tell me more,' encouraged Tom.

Holly soothed and reassured Tom, who, like Samson, felt emasculated by the simple act of a haircut. As she tucked in the covers around her, Holly's gaze occasionally lifted towards the bedroom window. She had all the lights on in the room to neutralize the moonbeams that were trying to invade her peace of mind.

She had been counting the days until the full moon, but now she was tempted to rely solely on her rational thinking to dismiss the idea of its latent power. Did she really need to put it to the test?

Still chatting to Tom, Holly reluctantly peeled herself out of bed and crept towards the window. She pulled back the curtains and tentatively opened the blind. The enigmatic face of the moon beamed at her and Holly let out a sigh of resignation.

'Are you tired? Do you want me to go?' asked Tom, interpreting her sigh as a repressed yawn.

'Not yet,' answered Holly, and a spasm of fear and anticipation gripped her chest.

But she couldn't keep Tom talking all night so with the pretence that he was guiding her towards a peaceful sleep, Holly said her final goodnight with the acrid taste of guilt on her tongue.

The walls closed in around her as soon as she put the phone down. The air seemed to have been sucked out of the room and Holly succumbed to the urgent need to flee the house, grabbing a fleece and slipping on her trainers along the way. Retrieving the wooden box from the kitchen, Holly pushed onwards. It was only when her hands touched the cold stone of the dial that she realized that it wasn't the house she was running from but the dial she had been running to.

*   *   *

The summer rain during the day had left the July evening damp and humid, and as Holly caught her breath in front of the moondial the sweat was already tickling the back of her neck. She had wrapped the fleece around her waist and hoped that she wouldn't need it.

A host of fluffy clouds were scattered across the sky, with the biggest hiding the perfectly round face of the moon. Holly dropped the orb cautiously into

121

the brass claws of the dial and squeezed her eyes shut, waiting for a dazzling light show and hoping against hope that it wouldn't arrive.

After a second or two of anxious waiting, Holly prised an eye open and looked around her. She took in the comforting sight of the long grass standing to attention at her feet. In the distance, the branches of the trees in the orchard were gently weighed down by the burden of their emerging fruits. The breath that Holly had been holding escaped as a relieved sigh.

'See, Holly, no magic, no voodoo.' Holly reached out to retrieve the orb just as a gust of wind whipped across the garden and the long grass rustled around her. The cloud that had been hiding the moon's face was also swept away and moonbeams stretched out greedily towards the dial.

Holly's fingertip had barely made contact with the orb when it glowed into life and thin lines of light trickled onto the surface of the dial. Her finger trembled and she pulled her hand away as an explosion of moonbeams danced across the garden. She squeezed her eyes shut and held on tightly to the sides of the dial to steady herself just as her grip on reality seemed to slip away and she felt herself being sucked into an abyss.

She could feel the dial almost buzzing with electricity beneath her grip, but she held on for dear life. The sound of a ticking clock thudded against her ears and then slowly receded into the distance.

It wasn't just the shock from the dial that took Holly's breath away or the dazzling light show as moonbeams danced around her, it was the sudden plummeting temperature as the warm breath of summer transformed into the harsh gasp of winter.

Slipping into her fleece, Holly felt the sweat on her neck turn to icicles. She desperately tried to blink away the light shadows and look around, but she didn't need full vision to confirm the changes in her surroundings. Long grass no longer tickled her legs and her feet felt like they had been plunged into buckets of ice. As her vision struggled to clear, she realized why she felt so cold. She was standing in over a foot of snow and the remaining light shadows that plagued her weren't shadows at all but fluffy snowflakes swirling around her.

Holly was frozen within seconds and couldn't stay where she was, no matter how much she wanted to. She had no choice but to seek refuge in the house and face whatever horrors awaited her. Across the virgin white blanket of snow, the kitchen window sent out a beacon of light towards her. The only other lights on in the house came from the living room, its warm glow partially hidden by the conservatory. Holly was too intent on reaching the safety of the house and its promised warmth to deal with what was happening or take in the detail of her surroundings. It was only as she reached the partial shelter offered by the side of the house that Holly finally took a moment to collect her thoughts.

There was absolutely no doubt that, whatever Holly was experiencing, it was the same thing that had happened to her before. Holly didn't want to use the term time travel, but whatever was happening couldn't be explained away by something as simple as a hallucination. There had been no blow to the head or other physical trauma. She knew where she was, she just wasn't sure when. It certainly wasn't a balmy summer's night.

Her glance shifted to the conservatory and the first thing she noticed was that the French doors that had been to the side of the structure on her last visit were no longer there. From this vantage point she couldn't see the front of the conservatory, but she didn't really need to see it. She knew that was where the doors would be; after all, that was where they were on the partially completed structure Billy was still working on. Holly's mind still fought to find a rational explanation. If this was a vision of her future then she had changed it in some way, but equally, if it was a vision created by her own imagination, then of course the doors would have moved. The position of the doors proved nothing.

Holly took one last look across the lawn to the moondial as she prepared herself to enter the house, challenging the dial to give her some clue as to its powers. The dial refused to face her glare, having retreated beneath a blanket of snow. She was just about to turn away from the dial when something caught her attention and it took a few seconds to work out what it was. The snow lay thick between the house and the dial with a single set of footprints showing the path she had trodden towards the back door. Holly peered into the flurry of snowflakes to take a closer at the footprints, particularly the ones furthest away near the dial. Although the snow was falling heavily, it shouldn't be enough to cover up her tracks so quickly, yet before her eyes the trail was slowly being erased. The footprints closest to the house were the last to disappear and Holly looked on in disbelief as the snow filled out the foot-shaped holes with perfect precision. In no time at all, the layer of snow on the lawn looked untouched, as if she had never walked across it.

Turning quickly, Holly pushed down the handle on the back door, but her hand slipped. Remembering the effort she had needed to open the door last time, Holly gripped the handle with renewed urgency. She had to get away from the snow storm which was invading her brain as well as her surroundings.

The kitchen felt warm, safe and was thankfully empty. Holly closed her eyes and leaned against the door. She could feel the snowflakes melting from her hair and dripping down her face. They felt like tears trickling down her cheeks, but Holly knew better than to cry. She needed to steel herself for what lay ahead.

Holly shivered and shook away the tension that was threatening to paralyse her. Opening her eyes, the kitchen was exactly as she had feared, a chaotic mess of dirty dishes and baby equipment. The kitchen table was cluttered and there was a half-opened newspaper teetering on the edge of it. Holly picked the newspaper up and looked for the date. It was January 2012, a full eighteen months into the future. Holly knew she couldn't keep pushing away the idea that she had travelled in time, but her main objective at the moment was simply to keep functioning and get herself through this nightmare and hopefully out the other side.

She was about to replace the newspaper when she noticed a dark, circular scorch mark on the table. She stroked her finger across the grain of the wood but the mark seemed to be a permanent war wound—one that she had never seen before. Although the sound of the ticking clock that marked her arrival had disappeared, Holly still sensed time ticking by. She needed answers and her only hope of understanding what was happening, or perhaps more correctly, what could happen in the future, was if she kept moving and kept exploring.

Leaving the kitchen, she paused just outside the living room. The door was slightly ajar and although there was very little sound coming from the room, the shadows that danced across the walls belonged to Tom, Holly was sure of it. Her heart was hammering in her chest but she knew she had to enter the room. Whether it was the workings of the moondial or her own mind didn't matter. She was here for a reason and she had to face her future.

Holly stepped silently over the threshold and stayed as close to the wall as she was physically able. Tom was facing away from her, kneeling down over a changing mat. Libby was lying on the mat with her legs kicking furiously in the air and Tom was struggling to lever her into a pink babygro suit. Holly was thankful she had stayed so close to the wall because when Libby twisted around and smiled directly at her, Holly's legs turned to jelly and she had to lean against the wall for support.

Following Libby's gaze, Tom turned to look in her direction, but he only frowned in puzzlement. Holly's heart fell as once again he didn't acknowledge her presence at all.

'What are you looking at, you little monster?' cooed Tom, tickling Libby's tummy. Libby gasped and gurgled in delight.

Libby's smile alone had warmed Holly's insides and she longed to kneel down next to Tom and join in the fun. She knew in her heart that Libby really was her daughter and she desperately wanted to hold her baby, more than anything. The thought that her desire to hold Libby was greater than her need to free herself from this nightmare actually startled her.

'Now you stay there while I go get your bottle ready,' Tom told Libby, who was now all buttoned up.

As Tom stood up and turned, Holly was relieved to see a glimpse of her old Tom, not the haunted man she had seen last time. His hair was still short and neat although his clothes, jeans and T-shirt, were more creased and torn than ever before. It was his eyes that gave Holly most relief; they were green and bright, a little red-rimmed perhaps, but there was no emptiness, no abject despair.

Unable to deal with him completely ignoring her, Holly closed her eyes as he slipped past. With Tom out of the room, Holly launched herself onto the floor next to Libby to take a better look at her. She had grown since the first time Holly had seen her, although her eyes were just as green and her cheeks just as chubby. Holly didn't know enough about babies to even hazard a guess at how old Libby was. It had been three months since Holly's last vision and she could easily believe that Libby was three months older, but whether she was four months or nine months old, Holly couldn't even begin to guess. Out of the corner of her eyes, she noticed a pink teddy. It was the one she had bought during her visit to London to meet Sam and Mrs Bronson.

A frown of concern creased her brow. 'You shouldn't be playing with that. I don't know much, but I know you're not two years old,' she told Libby. Libby gasped and wriggled with excitement at the sound of Holly's voice. Holly stroked her cheek and the baby reached up and grasped Holly's finger with a smile.

Holly lifted the tiny hand and kissed it softly. 'Hello, beautiful,' she told her. Libby started to kick her legs again in excitement and Holly copied Tom, tickling the baby's soft tummy as Libby fiercely held onto her finger.

Twisting her finger free, Holly slipped her hands beneath Libby. She wasn't sure how Tom would react to see his daughter being carried in mid-air by an invisible woman, but Holly didn't care, she desperately needed to hold Libby. Libby's body, however, seemed to be glued to the floor; struggle as she might, and in a repeat of her previous vision, Holly couldn't hold her baby in her arms. Tears of frustration stung her eyes. 'I'm sorry, I'm so sorry. I wish I knew why, but I just can't hold you,' she whispered.

The smile on Libby's face faltered and was replaced by a frown as she looked up at her mother. Holly forced a smile and stuck out her tongue, to which Libby blew a wet raspberry in response, and the baby's smile returned.

Holly stroked her soft blonde hair, but behind her, she heard Tom returning from the kitchen. 'I love you, Libby,' whispered Holly, planting a kiss on her forehead. The words had come out before Holly had time to think about what she was saying, but it felt right. Whether Libby was a figment of her imagination or not, Holly knew she was experiencing pure motherly love for the first time.

When Tom came back she scuttled over to a corner of the room and watched as he picked up Libby. 'Beddie byes for you, my little pumpkin,' he said. With a feeding bottle in one hand and Libby balanced over one shoulder, Tom turned to leave. As he headed out of the room, Libby stretched her hand towards Holly, trying to grab hold of her before disappearing from view.

'Night night, sleep tight, my angel,' Holly called out in a hushed whisper.

Left on her own, Holly felt lost and scared once more and she wondered what to do next. She looked around the room, which seemed remarkably similar to the room she was used to. There were a few additions that could be accounted for by Libby's arrival, not to mention new scatter cushions and a rug, which were in exactly the right shade of green that Holly had already been scouring the shops for. There was also a pile of abandoned greetings cards on the shelf next to the smiling China cat that Tom had bought her from Covent Garden on their first official date.

Holly tried and failed to return the cat's smile as she turned her attention to the pile of greetings cards. Picking up the uppermost card was almost as difficult as picking up Libby and when she finally had it in her grasp, she realized with a shudder that it was a sympathy card and let it drop. A cloud of dust billowed up and wrapped itself around Holly like a shroud.

She quickly stepped away and moved towards the fireplace, running her finger along the top of the mantelpiece as if she was a matron inspecting the cleanliness of a ward. It too was covered in a sheet of dust. Tom obviously had more on his mind than housework; still Holly couldn't help but think it wasn't a good thing for Libby to be in such a dusty room. Unable to help herself, Holly pulled at the sleeve of her fleece and used it as best she could to

129

wipe away the dust. She stood back to admire her work only to watch in growing horror as a new layer of dust settled on its surface within moments.

Holly sensed she didn't belong here, but she was determined not to be frightened off. Perhaps her life depended upon it. There was little else in this room to offer any clues, so Holly decided to extend her exploration to the study. She crept out of the living room and listened out for Tom. He was now upstairs, feeding Libby, and Holly resisted the urge to go up and watch them go through their bedtime routines. Instead, she headed past the stairs and entered the study, which was draped in shadows, lit only by the moonlight seeping through the window. She took a risk and switched on a lamp, surprised this time by how easy it was to flick the switch. Perhaps her presence was growing stronger along with her determination to make sense of everything.

Tom's desk looked far more used than she had ever seen it. Leafing through the debris of his work, she spotted various research notes and scripts which fitted in with the news anchor position he would now have started, if this really was eighteen months in the future. There were pencilled notes at the edges of some pages in Tom's familiar scrawl, although the sharpness of the postscripts and the harshness of the comments didn't feel like Tom's writing at all. It had a tangible anger to it.

Propped upright on a bookshelf, Holly found what she was looking for. It was a box file and it had one word handwritten on its spine. It simply said, *Holly*, and in contrast to his notes, Tom had obviously taken his time writing each letter perfectly. Inside the box there were official documents and letters, all relating to Holly's death, but there was only one document that would point her to her destiny.

Her hands trembled as she held aloft her death certificate. The certificate recorded the cause of her death as an aneurism on 29 September 2011 following childbirth complications. Holly took a deep breath and focused on the sensation of her blood flowing through her veins and her heart beating rapidly in her chest. She was most definitely alive. 'Can't believe everything you read,' she told herself, forcing a smile and ignoring the weight that this knowledge had placed on her shoulders.

Hearing soft footfalls coming down the stairs, Holly quickly put away the papers and switched off the lamp. She entered the hall just as Tom disappeared into the kitchen. He was back out in a matter of seconds with a glass in one hand and a bottle of whisky in the other. Holly followed him into the living room, although it was with some reluctance. There was something about the look on his face that had given her a sense of foreboding.

Tom sat down heavily on the sofa and stared at the bottle in his hand. He looked deflated, less like the man who had left the room with Libby bouncing on his shoulder and more like the ghost of her previous vision. Holly watched from the safety of the doorway, unsettled by the sense of desolation creeping across the room towards her and feeling the need to keep an escape route clear in case she had cause to use it. Tom poured himself a generous measure of whisky and swirled the golden liquor around his glass, staring into its depths.

He suddenly gasped as if suppressing a sob and Holly jumped out of her skin. She hit the door behind her and the half-open door closed slightly. Tom looked straight at her and for a second Holly felt his gaze upon her, but the connection didn't last. Tom's face lifted imperceptibly with expectation, only for a tidal wave of grief to sweep away all remnants of hope.

Tom shook his head and turned his attention back to the glass. 'Hello, Holly,' he whispered. 'I know you're watching me. I know you're shaking your head at me and telling me to pull myself together. So why don't you come through that door right now? Why don't you march in and tell me to tidy up all this mess?'

'Tidy up this mess, Tom,' ordered Holly. Although she spoke in hushed tones, Holly willed Tom to hear her.

Tom made not the slightest sign that he had heard her speak, but still he answered her. 'I can't. I can't even wipe away the dust, because I keep imagining your fingerprints there on every surface, on everything you might have touched, and I can't bear to wipe them away just like you were wiped away out of my life.'

Holly gulped back her pain and she was torn between running towards Tom and running away from him. Instead she did neither. She stood transfixed to the spot as he carried on talking to her ghost.

'I should have been an actor, I'm so good at making people believe I'm OK. I'm back at work and as long as someone's there to watch me put on my act, I've got the stiff-upper-lip thing down to a tee. But that's not the real me, Holly. Only you could see through to the real me. Oh, Holly, God, how I love the sound of your name. You wouldn't believe the lengths people go to just to avoid saying it. They must think I'll turn into a blubbering wreck if they say your name. Me, blubbering? Now that's a joke.'

Tom laughed but it sounded hollow. Holly had edged closer to him as he carried on talking, as he tried to reach out to her. She sat down gently beside him and put her hand on his shoulder, moving her fingers to gently stroke the back of his neck. His neck felt rigid with tension and as she tried to soothe away the pain, Tom leaned fractionally towards her hand and his body relaxed.

He closed his eyes. 'I still won't cry,' he told her, gulping back his words, and then a faint smile trembled on his lips. 'You know how that feels, don't you, Hol?' The smile was fleeting and the despair quickly returned to his features. 'I won't let go. I can't let go.' He leaned forward, almost as if he was trying to curl himself up into a ball. His head rested against the glass in his hand and he rolled it across his forehead as if trying to soothe his thoughts. 'No,' he whispered through clenched teeth. 'No!' he repeated, his words coming out as angry sobs. 'I won't cry.'

Holly wrapped her arms around Tom tighter and tighter, holding on to him, willing him to feel her next to him. His whole body shuddered and the first tears that fell, fell softly, silently marking the breach in the dam that he had built against his grief. Then the heaving torrent of tears came, tears that even Tom couldn't hold back.

His body was wracked with pain and the untouched drink in his hand slopped around him, spilling onto the floor. 'I can't even drink myself into oblivion!' he cried, discarding the glass on the floor next to the bottle.

'You're going to be all right, Tom,' Holly told him, rocking him in her arms as she too, felt a huge wrenching in her chest. She felt the pressure of a lifetime of tears building inside her and each of Tom's sobs felt like a hammer blow against her own emotional walls. 'Let out the pain, don't hold on to it. Let it go,' she said, giving Tom advice that she had refused to take herself.

'I love you, Holly,' Tom stammered. 'I never told you enough how much I love you. I wish I could go back and tell you how much I love you just one more time, just once. I still love you, Holly. I always will.'

As the sobs slowly subsided, Tom's grief spent for now, there was the sound of a ticking clock echoing across the room. Holly was still holding onto Tom, rocking him gently as if he were the baby that she hadn't been able to hold. Her chest felt heavy and her body felt drained. Then Tom's body froze as another sound cut through the air. Libby was crying. She had been woken up by her father's sobs.

Holly felt her heart tug at the sound of Libby's cries, but the wrenching in her chest was also the moondial pulling her backwards in time. Her precious baby's cry echoed in her ears until all that was left was the soft whisper of a summer night's breeze.

6

In the days that followed the full moon, Holly surprised herself at how well she managed to function. She was so completely overwhelmed by the raft of emotions that had left her reeling after her latest vision that she was numb with shock. She couldn't begin to make sense of her implausible and impossible journey into the future, so she didn't even try. Phone calls with Tom were as sweet and carefree as they had ever been and for once Holly felt no guilt. She was in utter denial and, if she was lying to anyone, it was to herself. She was doing fine and she didn't need to make sense of what had happened to her, she had her five-year plan and one day she would have the list completed and would look back and laugh at her brush with insanity.

For the most part, Holly was left to her own devices. Billy had already finished the main construction of the conservatory and had moved on to other jobs while the plasterwork dried out. Sam Peterson had been in touch, desperate for Holly to complete the artworks she had promised him for the gallery, and she assured him she could supply him with new stock. In fact, Holly was more than willing to spend time in her studio, concentrating her mind on her work and especially work that didn't have anything to do with motherhood. Mrs Bronson's commission was left untouched.

It was only on the Sunday morning after the full moon that Holly's blessed isolation came to an end. Jocelyn was due for their usual brunch date.

Holly didn't even consider putting her off and instead went out of her way to make the morning picture-perfect. She decided to bake Jocelyn a cake. What could be more normal than baking a cake? she thought to herself with a fixed smile that was starting to make her cheeks ache. Holly suspected she wore the false mask even in her sleep.

Half an hour before Jocelyn was due to call, the cake was in the oven and Holly was making the toffee sauce. She had made this cake before under the watchful eye of Tom's mum and, if Holly was being honest, Diane had done most of the work. It had looked simple enough, but as soon as Holly took her eyes off the stove, the toffee sauce began bubbling over and after that, all hell broke loose.

By the time Jocelyn arrived, Holly was cowering in a corner of the kitchen, with her knees drawn up to her chest and her head buried. She had spent days retreating from the future and now she couldn't even deal with the present, so she withdrew even further.

Memories of her childhood came flooding back, taking her to a time when cowering in a corner had been the norm. Sometimes it was to block out the alcohol-fuelled arguments between her parents, but there were other times too. Holly had learnt quickly to hide away once one of her mother's parties was in full swing, but sometimes the parties lasted days and she would have to leave the safety of her bedroom to sneak downstairs to find something to eat. Mostly she was lucky, but if her mother caught sight of her, the party atmosphere would freeze around them and she would lurch drunkenly towards her daughter. To her guests she would appear the caring parent, taking her daughter to

136

one side to check on her welfare, but the loving hands she placed on Holly's arms dug deep into flesh and the enquiring look on her face could not hide the scowl. In a barely audible snarl she would hurl abuse at the terrified child while Holly begged to be released. But her mother wouldn't let go, not until Holly was crying like a baby, only then would she leave her daughter to cower in the nearest corner. Her mother would walk away laughing, telling people around her that her child had developed a fault, proclaiming that it was leaking and asking if she could send it back for a replacement. The room would erupt into laughter and Holly would curl herself tightly into a ball and try to staunch her tears. There she would stay until someone would take pity on her, usually a stranger, never one of her parents, and take her hand, giving her the briefest escape route from the crowd. Holly would scurry upstairs to her room where she would bury her head beneath her pillows in an attempt to block out the noise, especially the laughter.

It wasn't laughter she heard now but the sound of a familiar, friendly voice as a hand reached out towards her to help her to her feet.

'Holly? Are you all right? What happened in here?' Jocelyn asked anxiously.

Holly looked up helplessly and as she met the old lady's eyes she couldn't help but feel safe, at least for the moment, and she brought her thoughts back to the present. She even managed a smile as she looked at the proffered hand, knowing that the gesture was more likely to result in Jocelyn being pulled down with her than it was going to help Holly to her feet.

She stood up without assistance and took a deep

breath. 'I burnt the cake,' she told Jocelyn. Her hands were curled into fists and her fingernails dug deep into her palms. The pain was a good pain in Holly's mind because it stopped her brain from trying to think too much. Tears sprung to her eyes but she refused to let them fall.

Jocelyn frowned but then gave Holly time to collect her thoughts by turning to the kitchen door and opening it wide to drive away the smell of smoking sugar and incinerated sponge cake.

'Well, it's a good job I brought some scones from the teashop with me,' Jocelyn said once the room had cleared of acrid smoke. She picked up her shopping bag and took out a cake box before turning back to Holly. 'What happened?' she said, repeating her question but expecting a proper answer now.

Holly lifted a dishcloth up from the kitchen table to reveal a circular scorch mark.

'Oh, I see,' replied Jocelyn cautiously. She knew even this disaster wasn't enough to justify Holly's near catatonic state, but she said nothing else. Instead she bided her time and busied herself tidying away some of the mess left in the aftermath of Holly's culinary disaster. With the ease of an expert homemaker, Jocelyn managed to clear away the chaos and brew up a strong pot of tea in a matter of minutes.

Lifting a trembling china cup to her lips, Holly took a sip of the sweet tea. She looked at Jocelyn over the rim of her teacup and wondered not just where to begin but whether she had the guts to begin at all. How was she going to explain why a scorch mark on the table had filled her with such terror?

'I need Tom to come home,' whispered Holly.

'You're missing Tom? Oh, sweetheart, he'll be home soon. He is due home soon, isn't he? Or has something changed? Is that why you're upset?'

Holly shook her head. She had so far refused to allow herself to make sense of her visions. Every time something in her present life had created a link with her visions, she had explained it away. The conservatory, Tom's haircut, the doors changing position, even the pink teddy bear, she had dismissed them all as coincidences and mind games. But the scorch mark was something else. The scorch mark, it would seem, was the final nail in her coffin. Amidst the chaos of the burning toffee sauce and the thoughtless act of transferring the hot pan from the stove to the table, Holly hadn't changed her future, she had confirmed it.

Still trying to push away her thoughts, there was only one constant. 'I just need Tom with me right now,' she told Jocelyn.

'His travelling won't last for ever and you've said yourself how it will help his career. It'll be worth it in the end when he's got a good job based back in London. You'll have the rest of your lives to make up for lost time then, and you'll look back and long for the peace and quiet once you've got a house full of kids,' added Jocelyn with a jovial laugh, which was meant to lighten Holly's mood but sent it spiralling down further into the murky depths of despair.

Holly went to put her teacup back down on the saucer but with her hands trembling so much, the handle slipped from her grasp and the remnants of her tea splashed across the table. 'Why do I make such a mess of things?' cried Holly, leaping up to

139

grab the dishcloth before the spillage reached Jocelyn's side of the table.

As she turned back around, Jocelyn was already standing there beside her. She took the cloth from Holly's hand, discarded it on the table and then wrapped Holly in her arms.

'Tell me what's wrong,' Jocelyn pleaded.

'I can't,' whispered Holly. 'I'm so scared, Jocelyn! I've never been so scared in all my life.'

Jocelyn squeezed Holly tighter to her as she felt her friend's body shaking with fear. She started to rub her back. 'It's all right, I'm here. Whatever it is, it's going to be all right, I promise.'

Holly looked up at Jocelyn. How different her life would have been if she'd had a mother like Jocelyn. But at least she was with her now, and Holly didn't have to deal with her living nightmare on her own, not any more. 'I'm going crazy, but I know if I say it out loud it'll just make it real and I don't want it to be real,' she explained, fighting the suppressed tears that were burning the back of her throat.

'Oh, sweetheart, tell me what's wrong. You can't keep it all to yourself. I promise you I won't judge.'

Holding her breath in an effort to bring her shaking body under control, Holly hiccupped back a suppressed sob. She looked into Jocelyn's eyes and the steeliness in her gaze gave Holly the strength to speak the unspeakable. 'I'm going to die,' she whispered. 'I'm going to die and I don't want to. I don't want to leave Tom in such a mess. I don't want to leave Libby without a mother.'

Finally she took a breath, but as she paused, she noticed that Jocelyn had tensed her body. Jocelyn released her grip and took a step back to look Holly in the eye.

'How do you know all of this?' she asked hesitantly.

'I've seen it. I don't know how,' Holly hiccupped. 'I don't know how it works, but it has something to do with the moondial. It isn't broken at all. It works and I think it showed me my future. I'm going to die in childbirth on September twenty-ninth next year.'

'You need a glass of water for those hiccups,' Jocelyn said as she unravelled Holly from her arms and turned towards the kitchen sink.

'Did you hear what I said? I've either gone completely crazy or the moondial has helped me travel forward in time and it showed me that I'm going to die,' whispered Holly, horrified that she might have just made a fool of herself. Of course Jocelyn would think she had lost her mind, what else was she supposed to think?

Jocelyn's hand trembled as she handed Holly a long glass of cold water. Holly was too upset to notice. She took the glass but, rather than sip it, she put it to her forehead to cool her brow. She couldn't look Jocelyn in the eyes.

'Would it help if I told you that I died too?'

The glass in Holly's hand slipped between her fingers but she saved it just in time to prevent the table from being damaged further. She sat down again when she felt her legs about to give way. 'I don't understand,' she said, stumbling over her words but in her heart a spark of hope ignited.

'I used the dial too, Holly.' Jocelyn sat down on the chair next to her and grabbed her hands. 'I'm so sorry, I'm so sorry. I should have said something when I saw that you'd resurrected the dial, but I

141

hoped you wouldn't work out how to use it, that you wouldn't need to use it.'

'You saw your own death and you changed it?' Holly squeezed Jocelyn's hands, holding onto the hope that was now glowing brightly. It was almost enough to know that she wasn't going mad, that the whole thing wasn't just her mind unravelling. Yet Jocelyn wasn't simply telling her that the moondial really did have the power to look into the future, but that the future could be changed.

Jocelyn nodded and Holly felt a sense of control she hadn't felt for days. 'Tell me, tell me what happened.' She bit her lip and waited for Jocelyn to explain.

Jocelyn let go of Holly's hand and visibly sagged in her chair. She was quiet for the longest time and Holly wasn't sure if she was going to speak. When she did, it was in a barely audible, trembling whisper.

'I've already told you about Harry, what he was like and why I left. Well, that was only partly true. Harry was bad enough, but it was only through the moondial that I saw how things would get worse, so much worse . . .' Jocelyn's head was bowed down and she sat staring at her hands as she recalled her time in the gatehouse. 'That was why I left him, you see, to avoid the trouble that would come.'

Holly sat mesmerized as she watched Jocelyn lift her eyes towards the kitchen window. It may have been the height of summer, but it seemed a cold, mournful day outside. Jocelyn couldn't see the moondial from where she was sitting, but she obviously felt its presence bearing down on her.

'It's been such a long time and I tried to convince myself it was just a weird and complicated dream,'

142

offered Jocelyn. 'It was so much easier than living with the guilt.' Jocelyn glanced at Holly and gave her a weak smile before returning her gaze to the window.

'What happened?' Holly asked.

'I was horrified when Harry plonked the dial in the middle of the garden, which was just what he wanted. The garden was my escape, the only part of my life that I felt I could control, and he wanted to destroy that too.'

'Why did you stay with him?'

'I was an unskilled, unloved housewife and Harry had spent more than enough years eroding my self-confidence. I just didn't believe I could fend for myself and, more importantly, provide for Paul.'

'And the moondial showed you that you could?' Holly asked.

'No, the moondial showed me what would happen if I didn't.' Jocelyn paused, still trembling with fear. 'To cut a long story short, I saw a future where I hadn't been able to endure any more of Harry's mental and physical torture. I took my own life, Holly. It was the ultimate act of selfishness, not least because, without me to deride and humiliate, Paul became Harry's new target.'

Despite the horror of the story Jocelyn was revealing, a story that had been played out in this very house, Holly felt her heart lighten. 'So you can change the future that the moondial shows you?' Holly was aware that she was repeating herself, but she had seen a flicker of hope and she needed to hold onto it.

'It's not easy; everything comes at a price.'

Holly shook her head, dismissing Jocelyn's warning. 'I'd do anything to change what I saw.

In my vision, I walked into this house and had to watch Tom suffering so much, grieving for me. The worst part about it was that I was standing there, right in front of him, and he couldn't see me. The thought of him looking straight through me still sends a shudder down my spine.'

'Ah, reflection is the key, remember. That's how the moondial works. The light from the sun is reflected onto the surface of the moon and it's this borrowed light that is reflected further into the future through the moondial. But you are a reflection, you're not really there.'

'So that's why Tom can't see me. But I still don't understand—because Libby could see me, I'm sure of it.'

'Libby? Is she the baby you had?'

'Oh, Jocelyn, she's beautiful. You should see her. In fact you already have, she's the baby I based my sculpture on,' added Holly proudly.

Jocelyn smiled. 'Then yes, she is beautiful. Holly, I wish I could explain why she could see you but I don't know everything. Even Charles Hardmonton never understood exactly how it worked.'

'He was the explorer I read about, wasn't he? So he did make the moondial from the Moon Stone.'

Jocelyn nodded. 'I know your presence will be stronger when you're in direct moonlight, but I think sometimes it doesn't matter how strong the reflection is, people will refuse to see what's right in front of them. An adult in particular can't accept what shouldn't be there, but a child just might.'

'Did Paul see you?'

Jocelyn shook her head. 'He was older and very, very angry.'

'Because you abandoned him?'

144

It was Jocelyn's turn to stifle a sob. 'He was right to hate me; still is.'

'Why should he still hate you? You saved him, didn't you?'

'It's complicated. There's so much more you need to know about the moondial and its rules.' The tears were flowing freely down Jocelyn's face.

In a reversal of roles, it was now Holly who was comforting Jocelyn. She went to the cupboard and fetched her a tissue. 'Right,' Holly said, 'I'm all ears. Tell me everything. Tell me everything I need to do to change things.'

'There's just so much. Where to begin?' Jocelyn said, almost to herself. She was staring down at the paper tissue in her hands, which she twisted furiously with trembling fingers. 'There's the journal, of course. It was given to me not long after Harry bought the dial and it explains as much as anyone has ever learnt about how it works. I haven't looked at the journal for nearly thirty years, haven't wanted to. When I left this house, I never wanted to see the dial again or anything to do with it.'

It was now Holly's turn to reach out and steady Jocelyn's shaking hand. 'I need to know. I have a five-year plan to keep, remember? How can I become a mum if I don't live long enough to even hold my baby?'

Holly's tone was meant to be light-hearted to ease Jocelyn's sobs, but it simply intensified them. Jocelyn looked up desperately into Holly's face and shook her head in despair. 'I'm sorry, Holly, I'm so sorry. I should have destroyed the dial or at least the mechanism. We weren't meant to meddle with our futures, it's too much of a burden.'

145

'Please, don't cry,' soothed Holly, determined not to let the old lady's fear invade her own thoughts. 'We have each other now, we can each share the burden.'

'I want to. Oh, Holly I want to help you, and I will,' Jocelyn promised between heavy sobs.

Holly stood up and hurried to Jocelyn, who was crumbling before her eyes. She put her arms around her, frightened that her friend might be on the verge of collapsing, or even worse.

'It's all right, Jocelyn. I understand, you don't have to say any more. By my calculation, I'm due to conceive Libby at the end of December, so I've still got a good few months to get my head clear and decide, with your help, what I need to do.'

Holly had spoken with a generosity that she didn't feel. She wanted all the answers and she wanted them now, but she couldn't put Jocelyn through any more pain, not today at least. Her words seemed to do the trick. Slowly, Jocelyn's sobs started to subside and her body relaxed a little.

'I take it you haven't told Tom?' sniffed Jocelyn.

'I couldn't tell him before because I didn't know what was really happening and I didn't want him to worry. I still don't think I can tell him, not yet at least, not while he's travelling so much, not until I know everything I need to know.'

'At least he'll be home soon,' Jocelyn said. 'You just enjoy your time with Tom, and in the meantime I'll dig out the journal. It's in one of the storage boxes that I kept at my sister's house—no room in my flat, you see. Lisa lives there now, so she can help me get to it.'

'And then?'

'And then, I promise we will talk. Only next time

I won't turn to jelly. I'm sorry, Holly, I feel like such a wimp, I've let you down. I thought I was made of sterner stuff.'

'You haven't let me down and you're the strongest woman I know,' smiled Holly. 'And now I have you, this whole thing doesn't seem so daunting any more.'

'I'm glad. But please promise me you won't do anything to try to change your future until we've talked things through.'

'I promise,' beamed Holly. 'Well, nothing major anyway. There is just one thing I'd like to sort out.' Holly picked up a carrier bag at the side of the table and pulled out a pink teddy bear. 'Can you donate this to the next jumble sale? And make sure it doesn't go to someone with a child under two. I'd hate it to get into the wrong hands.'

*　　　*　　　*

'Do we have to go out?' complained Tom. 'I can see just as much of the outside world as I could possibly want from here.'

Tom and Holly were standing in the middle of their new conservatory. The walls were still bare plaster with delicate swirls of pink and cream. Holly dug her bare toes in the cold, hard concrete and she smiled blissfully. Tom's voice echoed across the room and chased away the distant sound of early morning birdsong. The room smelled deliciously of dust and stale summer air. Holly was ready to savour every detail, paying closest attention to her husband, who was standing behind her, his bare arms wrapped tightly around her waist.

'You smell of sweat,' she told him.

147

'Well-earned sweat,' Tom replied, kissing the back of her neck.

'Did I say I was complaining?' she whispered. 'And yes, we have to go out. You've proved perfectly well that you're over your jet lag.'

'Hmm, perfectly.'

'Yes, it was perfect,' agreed Holly. 'But we've been in the village almost six months now and you still barely know anyone.'

'As I told you, I can see everything I need to see from here, and I can also see everyone I want to see.'

'I need to call in at the doctor's surgery to make an appointment,' Holly told him, ignoring his wandering hands, which had reached up beneath the T-shirt she had stolen from him. His fingers traced every curve of her stomach before finding a spine-tingling path up between the curve of her breasts.

'Why, there's nothing wrong is there?'

'No, I just think we should both have a pre-baby check-up.'

'If you want a thorough checking-over, I can always oblige,' Tom offered.

'A proper medical check, if you don't mind. They must have something like that, don't you think?'

'Holly, I'm the picture of health and so are you, we don't need a doctor to tell us that. Besides, I've already been having all kinds of medical checks in preparation for my stint in Haiti. I don't think I could take any more prodding and poking,' he complained sulkily.

'If I'm going to start planning a family, I'd like to plan it properly,' Holly replied sternly.

Since speaking to Jocelyn, she had finally found

the strength and the hope to think about her future, and in particular what she needed to do to save herself. In fact, she had thought of little else. The obvious answer would be to avoid getting pregnant in December, which sounded simple enough, but what if the aneurysm she would die of were to happen at another time? And then of course, there was Libby. If she put off conceiving, then she would be erasing Libby from their future. Other children might come along, but they wouldn't be the daughter she was already falling in love with. Her first plan of attack was to look at reducing the risks of childbirth complications.

'Couldn't we just phone up for an appointment?' Tom pleaded. 'I do believe there's a phone in the bedroom.'

'Morning!' Billy bellowed cheerfully from outside the conservatory.

Holly pulled her T-shirt down to a respectable inch below her bottom and Tom went to open the conservatory door to greet Billy. They hugged each other like long-lost brothers.

'Sorry to intrude, but I heard Tom was home and I was just passing,' explained Billy by way of an apology to Holly.

'I swear,' she said, 'I think Billy misses you almost as much I do when you're away.'

'You know you're welcome any time, Billy,' Tom told him. 'You've done a great job on the conservatory, I love it.'

'Aw, thanks, I knew you'd like it. We've only got the walls to paint and the flooring to put down and then it'll be perfect. Shame about the doors though,' Billy tutted, giving Holly a disapproving look.

'Women,' tutted Tom. Holly took Billy's disapproving look, upgraded it to menacing and passed it on to Tom, who smiled sheepishly.

Billy coughed to get Holly's attention. 'I hope you're not going out dressed like that, Mrs C,' he told her.

Holly narrowed her eyes at him but otherwise ignored his comment. 'So what can we do for you, Billy?'

'Well, now you have the doors all wrong and no choice but to step out into the undergrowth rather than the patio, I was thinking maybe Tom would like to discuss widening the extent of his renovations.'

'So is someone going to tell me what you're talking about?' Holly asked.

'Erm,' replied Tom. 'Don't you think you might want to go and get dressed? We've got to get into the village soon, remember?'

Holly eyed the two men suspiciously. 'Men,' she tutted, turning on her heels. 'But whatever you're planning for the garden, do not touch the moondial.'

'Does she always interfere with your plans?' Billy whispered loudly as Holly stepped through the new patio doors and back into the living room.

'I can hear you nodding, Tom Corrigan,' Holly called back as she left the men to their secret plans. After all, she had secret plans of her own. She had more than one reason to visit the village. She was hoping that by now Jocelyn would have found the journal she had spoken of.

*   *   *

150

Jocelyn's teashop was busy and there were a few curious looks as Tom and Holly squeezed through the diners to the last available table. 'Morning, Mrs Johnson,' Holly said as she leaned over a diner to ease herself into the gap between two tables. Mrs Johnson was rather large and the little space that wasn't filled by the elderly lady was occupied by all her paraphernalia, including a thick woollen cardigan, an umbrella and a collection of shopping bags. 'How are things at the farm?' groaned Holly as she squeezed through the gap.

'Ooh, the lambs are coming on fine, dear. I couldn't ask for better after such a hard winter.'

'Don't forget you promised me that lamb shank recipe,' Holly added as she popped out of the gap and edged closer to the table they were aiming for. Tom was following behind but tripped over a bag and practically threw himself on top of Mrs Johnson.

'This must be him, then,' Mrs Johnson said, looking suspiciously at Tom, who was practically nose to nose with the woman.

'Pleased to meet you,' grinned Tom sheepishly.

Mrs Johnson pinched his cheek, shaking his head from side to side as she did so. 'Sweet little lamb, he is,' she said to Holly. 'Quite a dish himself.'

'Hands off, he's mine,' laughed Holly, pulling Tom to safety.

After a few more good mornings and introductions, Holly and Tom finally made it to the table. Lisa was busy working behind the counter while a younger girl Holly hadn't seen before was waitressing. The girl was in her early twenties with dark, short-cropped hair that gave her an elfin look. She had deep brown eyes that reminded Holly of

151

Jocelyn. Looking from Lisa to the girl, there were other family resemblances and Holly guessed that this must be Patti, Lisa's daughter, Jocelyn's great niece. From what Jocelyn had told her, Patti was at university studying literature. Her gap year had turned into three years travelling around Europe, but she had finally taken the plunge and settled back down to her studies. She was the first in their family to go to university and both Jocelyn and Lisa were very proud of her.

'What can I get you?' the girl asked with a bright cheery smile.

'Two cream teas, I think,' Holly said, looking at Tom for agreement. He nodded on cue. 'Is Jocelyn in today? I was hoping to catch her,' Holly continued with a flutter of anticipation.

'She's away, visiting her son. She won't be back for a few weeks. You're not Holly, are you?' the girl asked, a note of recognition in her voice.

Holly's heart sank as she nodded politely in agreement. 'She didn't leave anything for me, did she?' she asked hopefully.

'Sorry, but Auntie Joss did leave you a message. She said to say sorry she wouldn't get a chance to see Tim, but she'll catch up with you when she gets back.'

'Ah, so you must be Patti,' Holly replied, ignoring the mistake in Tom's name. 'How's it going at university?'

'Long story, but I've kind of thrown in the towel. I'm due back for my final year but I'm not sure it's the way I want to go. I'm trying to convince my mum I could just work here and take up writing in my spare time, make my way as a writer on my own instead of slaving away to get some piece of paper

152

that won't guarantee me a job anyway.'

'You shouldn't give up,' interrupted Tom.

'Sorry, this is my husband Tim, I mean Tom,' grinned Holly. Tom gave her a warning glare and Patti's cheeks flushed pink.

'I'm a journalist and it's a tough world out there. A degree might just get you in the door, even if it doesn't guarantee the job. You'll regret it if you give up now, especially when you're so close to finishing. I promise, if you get that piece of paper and you're looking for a job, I can help out with some contacts.'

Patti was almost awestruck by Tom's credentials and she hung on every word with enthusiasm. When she returned to the counter to get their order, Holly watched her out of the corner of her eye. Mother and daughter were deep in conversation. 'Aren't you the helpful one?' Holly said to Tom.

'I like to help along fledgling careers where I can,' Tom said proudly.

'I hope you don't go around offering your services to all the pretty girls you see on your travels.'

'I only have eyes for you,' Tom said, and his intent stare sought solace from Holly.

'I know, I'm only teasing. I trust you with my heart and my soul, no matter how far away they send you.' She reached over and pulled at a tiny lock of hair at the base of his neck. 'And no matter how polished and appealing they try to make you.'

Tom took hold of Holly's outstretched hand in his. 'Does it sound too wimpy to say I miss my curls?'

'I miss your curls too,' soothed Holly. 'But you have to get the viewing public swooning over you

153

if you're going to become an anchorman.' She paused, a mischievous glint in her eye. 'I did mean the female viewing public, by the way.'

Tom tried to smile but his lips couldn't quite complete the manoeuvre. 'I was happy in my comfort zone, I am happy in my comfort zone,' he tried to explain. 'This new persona the studio is trying to create just feels . . .' He seemed to be lost for words for once.

'Uncomfortable?' offered Holly.

'God, it's like squeezing into a suit that doesn't quite fit.'

'Too tight around the shoulders?'

'Too tight in the crotch,' replied Tom, just as Patti returned with their cream teas. If she heard his last comment, she didn't let on.

'These are on the house,' she told them. 'Mum insists.'

'You're going back to university?' Holly asked excitedly, knowing how pleased Jocelyn and Lisa would be by the news.

'Hmm, I'm not quite ready to decide just yet, but I have agreed to sit down and talk it through properly with Mum. And if I do give it another try, I'll be back looking for those contacts,' she told Tom.

'My word is my bond,' he agreed.

As Patti left, Tom sighed. 'Oh, to be that young and hopeful.'

'So, back to you. When do I get to see your new image in action?' Holly asked. Tom's reports on the Canadian oil sands were currently being edited and hadn't been aired yet.

'Next week; the day before I leave, as a matter of fact.'

'I'd better spread the word. Your mum and dad are dying to see you too. Now eat up, we've still got to call in at the surgery, remember.'

'Yes, Mum,' Tom replied, before stuffing half a cream scone in his mouth.

*   *   *

It didn't seem to Holly that she had to wait long to see Tom's reports as the days slipped by at an alarming rate. On the night that Tom's first report was being aired, they cuddled up on the sofa, ready to watch the broadcast with a bottle of wine and popcorn. Holly was relieved that Tom was still home. The summer nights were drawing in as August moved closer to September and whilst Holly sat in the relative safety of her living room she knew the full moon was casting its borrowed light across the surface of the moondial. Tonight its lure was no match for the safety of Tom's arms, her Tom, the man whose heart hadn't been broken by the loss of his wife.

It was a strange experience, sitting on the sofa, watching the new improved Tom in professional reporting mode on screen while her real-life Tom gave a commentary on what had been happening behind the scenes. Stranger still because the image on screen didn't match the man sitting next to her, who, despite his lack of hair, was still the old, dishevelled Tom she knew and loved. She wasn't sure she liked the polished, pristine version on screen. He was too slick for her liking. He was interviewing an oil company spokesperson and he sounded different, harsher.

'So what do you think?' Tom asked tentatively as

soon as the programme had finished.

'You looked . . .' Holly started, but then couldn't think of the right words. 'You looked very professional.'

'You didn't like it, did you?' Tom asked. There was a note of disappointment in his voice that made Holly's heart ache.

'It's different,' she tried to explain. 'It's just not quite you.'

Tom sighed. 'I know, you're right. I'm trying my hardest to adapt. Everyone in the studio has been singing my praises, but it still doesn't quite feel right. It's strange how people react differently to you just because you're wearing a suit and you have that slick look. The career politicians and the experienced press officers I've been interviewing still look down their noses at me, but some of the people on the sidelines, I think I kind of intimidated them.'

'So is that what the studio really want from you? For you to go around intimidating people?' asked Holly. She kept her tone light, but she really didn't like the idea that Tom was being forced to move away from the approachable reporter he used to be.

'I'm not in the anchorman job yet. Maybe when I am, I can relax the style a little. At least they're not insisting I wear a suit when I'm in Haiti.'

'I'm going to miss you,' moaned Holly.

'I haven't gone yet and I will be back. All this pain will be worth it when we think about what it will mean for us next year. Next year I could have a little baby who'll love me no matter what kind of silly suit I have to wear. And now we've been given a clean bill of health from the doctor, there's nothing to stop us.'

156

'I know,' Holly answered, trying hard to hide her disappointment. She had mentioned her bump on the head, expecting that the doctor would send her off for an MRI, hoping that the aneurism might be an existing condition that could be treated and that she could then go on to have Libby, free from any risk. But he had given her only the basic health checks and so the risk remained. It seemed that the only thing Holly could do to avoid dying in childbirth was to avoid conceiving Libby. 'Just as long as we get to spend the rest of our lives together.'

'You don't get rid of me that easy,' Tom said, kissing the top of her head.

'And you don't get rid of me that easily either. Just don't go getting all celebrity on me and running off with the first airhead you meet.'

'You know I won't do that,' Tom assured her.

'Yes, I know you won't,' Holly answered. The moondial had at least provided her with that certainty.

'Anyway, I've got a long journey tomorrow,' Tom said, raising his arms and yawning loudly. 'Fancy an early night?'

'Can I bring my popcorn?' teased Holly.

'As long as your crunching doesn't keep me awake,' Tom warned, still yawning enthusiastically.

'Oh, it won't be my crunching keeping you awake,' countered Holly. She wiggled her eyebrows suggestively at Tom, a trick she had learnt from Billy.

'Mrs Corrigan, I don't know what you mean.'

'Then let me explain further,' promised Holly, climbing onto Tom's knee. 'I don't think we need to go to bed to have an early night.'

157

By the time Holly and Tom made it to their bedroom, the moonlight that had shone through the open window had faded and failed. Holly's path lay firmly in the present.

7

Jocelyn arrived at eleven o'clock prompt with a wicker basket full of hidden treasures. 'I thought we might make the most of the Indian summer and have a little picnic, if you're up to it?' she challenged.

'If I'm up to it? So what's put a spring in your step?' answered Holly, genuinely surprised.

'Well, I believe I have your Tom to thank for persuading Patti to return to university.'

'She's decided to go back? Jocelyn, that's fantastic news, but please don't go giving Tom all the credit. I'm sure she would have made the same decision eventually,' Holly assured her.

Jocelyn had only recently returned from her visit to see her son and this was the first chance they'd had to catch up. Holly had been impatient to find out all there was to know about the moondial, but now the time was here, she was suddenly very nervous about bringing the subject up and she knew Jocelyn shared her reluctance.

Holly had managed to call a truce on all the thoughts and theories that had plagued her ever since she had crossed paths with the moondial. She hadn't found all the answers, she hadn't even worked out all of the questions, but she still held out hope that the answers were in her grasp and, most importantly, that there may be a way to secure her future and Libby's too. She wasn't about to give up on her daughter just yet.

But no matter how positive she was trying to be, she couldn't dispel all her fears. Her experiences of the moondial had been to the extremes of bitter and sweet. For every ounce of hope it had revealed, it seemed to add a pound of pain. Jocelyn had already said there was a price to pay for changing the future and Holly wasn't sure she was ready to hear the secrets that her friend had promised to reveal.

'I hope you have something better in mind than the garden for our picnic,' grimaced Holly. Although Holly had tried to keep the garden under control, if only so that Tom's hard work wasn't completely undone by another year's summer growth, it was hardly the lush landscape she knew it could be and she still felt guilty about the state it was in every time Jocelyn visited.

'I was thinking we'd take a trip to the ruins of Hardmonton Hall.'

'Really? I didn't know we could drive up there,' asked Holly. To her shame, she had never visited the ruins close up and had seen no more than the crumbling walls that skirted the outside of the old estate boundaries and which lead right up to the gatehouse. Even then, the extent of the estate wasn't as grand as it used to be with most of the land having been sold off, redeveloped or reclaimed for farming. Only the areas immediately surrounding the ruins had been left untouched.

'We can't drive up there,' scolded Jocelyn. 'Kids these days want to be ferried around everywhere. These joints of mine are feeling well oiled today

159

and if I can make the trek, I'm sure you can.'

'You want to show me where the moondial was originally sited, don't you?' Holly asked, and her stomach did a flip simply saying its name out loud.

'It seems the ideal place to debate the pros and cons of time travel,' chirped Jocelyn, but Holly sensed a tone of false bravado in her voice.

'Well, what should I bring?' asked Holly in a panic. She started to randomly open kitchen cupboards. 'I've already made a pot of tea. There's a flask here somewhere. Have you brought food? I've got some bits and pieces in the fridge. And cutlery. Have you got cutlery?' Holly was gulping air at the end of every sentence as panic set in.

'I've got a flask,' soothed Jocelyn, 'and enough food to feed an army.' Holly went to say something else but Jocelyn stopped her. 'And I've got a blanket and all the utensils we could possibly need.'

'You're sure?' replied Holly meekly.

Jocelyn took hold of Holly's shaking hands to steady her. 'We're not about to carry out brain surgery here,' she told her. 'Just talk, that's all. Just as much as both of us can bear.'

'Maybe I should get changed,' suggested Holly.

Jocelyn sighed. 'You're fine as you are.'

'Umbrella?'

Jocelyn raised an eyebrow, silencing any further prevarication.

'Let's throw caution to the wind, shall we? Life's all about taking risks,' she told Holly.

*   *   *

Holly and Jocelyn began their walk in silence as they followed the overgrown path that had once been an impressive drive leading up to the Hall. The disused road was hidden beneath years of decay and neglect. The only sound breaking the silence was the occasional snapping of twigs underfoot and sweet birdsong that brightened the morning in spite of the growing tension between the two women.

The ancient trees that had guarded the approach to Hardmonton Hall loomed overhead, growing more dense as the women made their pilgrimage. The September sun glinted occasionally through the canopy and the dappled sunlight lit the way ahead for Holly and Jocelyn. Holly tried to enjoy the mixture of light and shadow and the contrast between the rotting vegetation underfoot and the sparkling greenery above. The leaves were yet to show the onset of autumn, but as the breeze whipped them into a frenzy Holly could hear their telltale death rattle.

'So how was your visit with Paul?' Holly asked, eager to break the silence.

'As well as could be expected.'

'That doesn't sound good,' quizzed Holly.

Jocelyn sighed. 'Paul hasn't let me into his life for a very long time, ever since his father died really,' confessed Jocelyn. 'He was a teenager when I left Harry and he never knew what I'd been subjected to—and he certainly didn't know what I'd seen of the future. I'd protected him as much as I could from Harry's cruelty and, perversely, so had Harry. Harry was incapable of love but he could put on a good act. He found it entertaining to engender Paul's affection and use that against me so when I decided to leave, Paul never really understood why.'

161

'He blames you for Harry's suicide?' Holly asked, although the answer was clear.

Jocelyn laughed. 'Oh, Holly, yes. Yes, he blames me, and he has every right to.'

'But you know that's not true. He would have driven you to suicide. He killed himself instead of you. How could you even begin to feel guilty about that?'

Jocelyn looked into the distance where the canopy of trees had started to thin and the full light of day could be seen in all its glory, marking their arrival at the ruins. 'Ah, the light at the end of the tunnel,' she told Holly, avoiding the question.

'Or an oncoming train,' sighed Holly.

Jocelyn took Holly's hand and gave it a squeeze. 'I'm here to help. It'll be all right,' Jocelyn assured her but the sadness in her eyes told a different story.

The ruins lived up to their name. The Hall itself was nothing more than a series of lonely, half-demolished walls covered in ivy and lichen. Holly could almost believe she was wandering through an overgrown cemetery with giant headstones.

'Do you remember when the Hall was in its heyday?' she asked Jocelyn.

'Lord Hardmonton—the old Lord Hardmonton, that is—used to hold annual garden parties and the whole village was invited. They were glorious affairs and we'd spend all year looking forward it. When he died, his son Edward, the one who was lost in the fire, carried on the tradition, but I was married by then, so I never went.'

'Harry?' guessed Holly.

Jocelyn simply nodded.

'So why did it burn down anyway? Tom was

162

right, even though he didn't know it. If they had the moondial and could see into the future, why didn't they see it coming? Didn't Edward Hardmonton use the dial?' Holly knew Jocelyn was leading her slowly to the revelations of the moondial and she felt herself trying to sprint to the finish line. She needed to know everything and the questions just kept coming.

'Oh, Edward Hardmonton used it,' Jocelyn told her, but offered no further explanation. 'Now, the site for the moondial is right over here, as I recall.'

Biting her lip to hold back questions, Holly let Jocelyn lead her towards what would have been the ornamental gardens. The gardens were still magnificent despite the neglect. The mixture of exotic shrubs and grasses had fought for supremacy over the abandoned and partly demolished architecture and had secured a glorious victory. The red, orange and yellow hues of autumn had arrived early here and the view was breathtaking. Holly wished she had seen the gardens earlier in the summer at the height of the flowering season.

Holly recognized the site of the moondial from the architectural plans she had already seen. The outer edge of the circle was made from grey stone, although most was now hidden beneath the shrubbery that had bordered it. In the plan, each of the four segments of the main circle had been planted up with a different mix of plants and shrubs, possibly chosen to depict the four seasons. Over the years, the more delicate specimens had either been consumed by their more dominant bedfellows or had simply withered and died. In contrast to other parts of the garden, the landscaping here looked bleak.

163

'What's this?' asked Holly as she stepped onto one of the four paths that led to the stone centre circle where the moondial had stood. Kicking away thick layers of moss underfoot, Holly revealed writing that had been etched into the stone.

'There are inscriptions on each of the four paths,' Jocelyn told her. 'A poem with four verses. This is why I wanted to bring you here. They explain how the moondial works and, if I remember correctly, the first one is over here.'

As they crossed the centre of the circle, Holly put down the wicker basket she had been carrying.

'Wait, I need something from in there,' Jocelyn said. She rummaged in the basket and took out a wire brush.

With a little careful brushing, Holly revealed the wording on the first path:

Beneath the fullest moon
If only for an hour
Reflection is the key
To the moondial's power

'Well, that's nothing I couldn't have worked out for myself,' Holly said sulkily, unable to hide her disappointment that this verse hadn't revealed any hidden secrets. 'I'd already noticed that the vision only lasts about an hour, and I'd worked out the need for a full moon too. I tried using the dial once when there wasn't a full moon and the orb barely flickered.'

'Let's read the next verse,' Jocelyn suggested.

There was no moss growing on the next path so the second part of the poem was relatively easy for Holly to read.

164

A timepiece like no other
Moonlight will point the way
A shadow cast by moonlight
Reaching out to an unborn day

The reference to a timepiece triggered a memory. This time, Holly did have a question. 'The moonlight reflected from the centre of the glass orb created what looked like hands of a dial spinning around and I could hear the ticking of a clock too. But if it's a timepiece, how does it work? How does it dictate how far its reflection is cast into the future?'

'I think that's the one thing that will always remain a mystery. The journal shows how the brass mechanism was engineered, but the timepiece was an instrument to count down the hour, not dictate where the reflection would lead to. It's clear from the notes that it can only be the dial that makes the choice. How it does that, I don't honestly know, but it does seem to choose a critical point in the traveller's life.'

'Or death,' added Holly morosely. 'Have you brought the journal with you?'

'Don't worry, it's in the basket. Once we've finished with our picnic, you can have it. I don't want it any more.'

'How did you get hold of the journal, anyway?'

'Mr Andrews, the old gardener at the Hall, came to see me not long after Harry bought the moondial. Though he had never used the dial himself, he had been a close confidante of Edward Hardmonton. I'll tell you all about it later, but I think you need to read the poem in full first. Ready for the next verse?' insisted Jocelyn.

165

This path too was practically clear, with pretty clusters of lichen around its edges, though not enough to conceal the engraving.

Like a hand upon the water
No imprint shall there be
Like a drop of rain on glass
The choice of path may not be free

Holly stared at the words and tried to make sense of it. A shiver passed through her body as she remembered her footprints in the snow and the dust on the mantelpiece during her last vision and she realized that the first part of this verse fitted perfectly with her own experience. She had visited the future but left no imprint, any impression she made disappearing just like the poem said, like a hand upon the water. The meaning of the second part, however, eluded her, or perhaps she was simply evading it.

'The choice of path isn't free? What does that mean? Does it mean I have no free choice or does it mean something else? You said there was a price to pay.'

'A little of both, I think. The best way of explaining it is to picture raindrops on a window like the poem says.'

Holly wasn't convinced that picturing a pane of glass would ease her confusion, but she did as she was told and let Jocelyn guide her through the image developing in her mind.

'Have you ever tried to follow a particular raindrop as it makes its way down the glass?'

Holly nodded in agreement but said nothing. As a child she had spent hours watching the rain trickle tears down her bedroom window.

'As it hits the window,' continued Jocelyn, 'you would think it's setting off on its own journey. But at some point, it will cross the path of another raindrop. You may not be able to see that path and you may think that there's not even a trace of it there, but then suddenly, your raindrop veers in a new direction. It's following its predecessor, no longer on its own journey but one that has already been laid before it.'

Holly hadn't realized but she had her eyes closed as she followed an imaginary raindrop on its path down her old bedroom window. When she opened her eyes, Jocelyn was watching, her gaze infused with sadness.

'Life, it seems, demands a certain balance. Even when you think you're choosing a new path, it can sometimes lead you to the same place.'

'Oh, my God,' gasped Holly. 'It means no matter what kind of health checks I have, if I get pregnant with Libby then I can't avoid dying in childbirth. That's what you're trying to tell me, isn't it?'

'I'm sorry, Holly. I wish I could say the last verse will give you hope, but I can't. The moondial's rules are cruel, there's no way of softening the blow. Just remember that the dial is giving you a chance to save your life. Try not to lose sight of that. Try to see it as a gift.' Her voice had the hushed tones befitting a funeral parlour.

'A gift? How can this horror that I'm being forced to go through ever be called a gift?' Holly demanded, anger burning the back of her throat.

'If it keeps you safe, and I know it will, then yes, it is a gift. Come on, let's read the last verse,' Jocelyn said, her tone still soft and unnervingly sympathetic.

The last path was covered in a thick carpet of moss and as Holly scrubbed away the stone's living shroud, she felt her heart sinking.

> *If evading death you seek*
> *Then the dial shall keep the score*
> *A life for a life the price to pay*
> *Never one less and not one more*

'A life for a life,' Holly repeated. 'What does it mean, "keep the score"?'

She had asked the question, but Jocelyn wouldn't answer her. She just looked at Holly and waited for her to interpret the poem for herself.

'My life for Libby's? I have to erase my beautiful baby's life for the sake of my own. Please, Jocelyn, please tell me I'm reading it wrong.'

When Jocelyn's continued silence gave Holly the answer she hadn't wanted to hear, a crushing weight knocked the wind out of her and she let herself sink to her knees. 'Oh, Jocelyn, I don't think I can bear this any more!' she cried out. Then she did something that she had never done before in her entire adult life. She let herself cry without restraint. In a matter of moments, she was howling sobs that had been a long time in the making.

*   *   *

Jocelyn laid out the picnic in the rose garden, picking the location because it was out of sight of the moondial circle. The food remained untouched but Jocelyn had insisted that Holly drink some tea, which was, as always, sweet and hot.

168

Holly had quelled her tears and, despite the shock, she wanted to hear more about the dial. She needed to understand how it had been used in the past. She had to be sure that there were no other options before she gave Libby up completely. 'Tell me what happened to you, Jocelyn,' she asked. 'You told me how you were going to be driven to suicide, but how did the rules apply to you?'

Jocelyn played with her teacup, swirling its contents as if she would find a path back to the past. 'I think I need to start at the beginning. Is that all right?' Jocelyn asked, her eyes already glistening with unshed tears.

'Take your time. I'm here for you too,' offered Holly as she leaned over and squeezed the old lady's hand.

'Mr Andrews didn't mention time travel the first time he visited me at the gatehouse. He had simply come to hand over the wooden box and the journal—with some reluctance, I'd have to say. I think he was torn between letting the secret of the moondial die with the Hardmontons, or leaving it to its new owner to decide. He warned me to read the journal first and not to resurrect the moondial unless I was prepared to accept the consequences. By the time he returned a few months later, I hadn't just read the journal but I'd experienced the power of the moondial first-hand.'

'The dial chose to take you to that point in time when you'd committed suicide.'

Jocelyn nodded. 'I went through the same nightmare you probably did, questioning my own sanity. The journal seemed to confirm everything I'd experienced, but I was more than willing to dismiss it as fantasy. When Mr Andrews realized

I'd seen my future, he helped me accept that what I'd seen could really happen. We took this exact same walk to the Hall and the stone circle where he helped me interpret the poem exactly as I've done with you.'

'The raindrop on the window pane,' confirmed Holly.

'When I realized that the "life for a life" rule meant that someone else would have to die in my place, I simply resigned myself to my fate and for two years, I did nothing.' Jocelyn shrugged her shoulders by way of any further explanation.

'But then you used the dial again and saw what Harry would do to Paul. That's why you changed your path. But the life for a life rule?' asked Holly, but she was already working out the answer as the words came out of her mouth. 'Oh, I see. It was Harry. Harry took his own life. That's why you feel so guilty, isn't it?'

'That isn't the half of it,' confessed Jocelyn. 'When you avoid death, the life that will be sacrificed in your stead isn't necessarily yours to choose. The life taken is always a close family member, not necessarily a blood relative but within the family circle. You can't just go out and randomly kill a stranger and expect the score to be settled.'

'You said the moondial's rules were cruel, but, Jocelyn, cruel doesn't even begin to describe it!'

Both women were staring in the direction of the moondial site, unable to meet each other's haunted gaze. Morning had slipped silently into afternoon and as the determined September sun fought through the gathering clouds there was still just enough warmth left in the day to heat up the gentle breeze. Holly shivered nonetheless.

'I couldn't avoid death without risking another member of my family. The moondial demanded a life and my worst fear was that it could be Paul's life I was risking. That's why I did nothing for two years, not until I saw what would happen to Paul if I didn't try to change the future.'

'Please don't say you killed Harry,' gasped Holly, half jokingly, but with a fear that there were yet more unpleasant surprises to be revealed amongst the ruins of the Hall.

Jocelyn smiled but as she wrinkled her eyes a tear began its solemn journey down her cheek. 'As good as,' she confessed. 'I saw what he would do to Paul and I felt a rage growing inside me that perhaps only a mother can feel. I had never fought back against Harry's abuse. I couldn't have been more submissive if I'd tried. But when I saw Harry's cruelty being directed at Paul, destroying him as surely as it had destroyed me, that rage consumed me and I think I would have been capable of murder if it had come to it.'

Holly did her best to concentrate on Jocelyn's experiences. Though she was trying hard not to think about how all of this knowledge would dictate her own path, she could feel those familiar insecurities about motherhood returning to haunt her yet again. She thought she had been learning to be a mother, but she wondered if she could even begin to imagine the burning rage that Jocelyn described.

Jocelyn was trembling as she resurrected the spectres of her past and she seemed to have reached the point where she couldn't go on. Holly desperately needed to hear more to help her understand. 'If you didn't kill him, how did you make sure the life that would be taken was Harry's?' asked Holly softly.

'I started fighting back,' whispered Jocelyn, as if she were afraid to wake up the ghosts that seemed to be crowding around them. 'Harry had unwittingly given me the skills to undermine him. Of course, unlike me, Harry wasn't in the least bit submissive, so when I started to stand up to him, his reaction was explosive. The abuse and cruelty he inflicted on me escalated and the physical abuse became more frequent, more intense.'

'Oh, Jocelyn, I'd never imagined it had been so bad,' replied Holly, genuinely shocked by the horrors Jocelyn must have faced in the house that was now Holly's home.

'I think the saying, "What doesn't kill you, makes you stronger" certainly applies to me. And through it all, Harry still managed to keep the abuse hidden from Paul. My secret shame would have remained just that if I hadn't realized that I could use it to my advantage. I made certain other people knew. Slowly but surely, Harry's work dried up as people refused to deal with him. The people in the village became my silent allies and, with the help of my sister, Harry was ostracized. He was close to breaking point, but then I started to wonder if I'd gone too far, if maybe I would still die but at Harry's hands instead of my own. It was only the intervention of a dear friend, my knight in shining armour, who tipped the balance back in my favour and really set the path of my future on its new course.'

'And who was this knight in shining armour?'

'Someone you already know,' answered Jocelyn,

cryptically. 'He's still a regular visitor to the gatehouse.'

'Billy?' gasped Holly.

Jocelyn nodded. 'He was a young man in his prime back then. He had called around to the gatehouse to chase Harry for money that he owed him. It was the middle of the day and Paul was at school so Harry was making the most of the time we had to ourselves by beating me to a pulp. One minute I was cowering in a corner and the next, Billy was there and it was Harry who was nursing bruises and broken ribs at the end of the day.'

'Well done, Billy.' Holly was smiling with a newfound admiration for her builder.

'It wasn't so much the beating that Harry found so hard to take but the humiliation, and I reinforced his shame every chance I got. It broke him, and when he was at his lowest, I knew it was time to leave.'

'And that's when the moondial showed you it would lead Harry to suicide?' asked Holly in disbelief. Holly had always known that Jocelyn was much, much stronger than the frail body that ensnared her, but it was still difficult to imagine Jocelyn taking her husband's cruelty and using it as her own.

'There was just one more thing I had to do first. The moondial needs a specific event as a catalyst to switch from one vision of the future to another and, for me, it was sitting down and writing Harry a letter, telling him that I was leaving him. I told him how he had failed at everything and the world would be a better place without him, although I think I might not have put it quite so subtly. With the letter written and my bags packed, I used the

173

moondial one last time. It confirmed that everyone I loved would be safe, that it would be Harry and not me that would commit suicide and that it was safe for me to leave.' Jocelyn lifted her head high and looked directly at Holly. 'So going back to your original question, yes, in a way I did kill Harry.'

'And you never told Paul.'

'No,' confirmed Jocelyn. 'I couldn't tell him before Harry died in case it changed the future, and afterwards, I was wracked with guilt. I couldn't justify what I had done even to myself, let alone justify it to Paul.'

'You let Paul believe his father was the innocent party.' Holly shook her head and tried to suppress her anger.

'When the gatehouse was cleared out, Paul found the letter I'd written to Harry. I was officially divorced by that point so had no rights to the property, everything went to Paul. As soon as he was old enough, he left me and left the village. He joined the army and travelled the world, travelled anywhere that would take him as far away from me as possible.'

'It must have been hard for both of you, but you're all right together now?'

Jocelyn shook her head and a tear trickled down her face. 'I tried. For years I tried to get back in touch with him, but he was intent on wiping me out of his life as surely as if I had been the one that had died. Every single letter or card I sent to him was returned unopened. Up until last month, I'd not managed to speak to him for years.'

'I just assumed you went to visit him regularly. You did stay with him, didn't you? You were away for over a week,' Holly asked, confusion adding to the raft of emotions brewing up inside her.

'You gave me the jolt I needed to try one last time. I tracked him down through an army friend who's also from Fincross. I practically took up roost on Paul's doorstep until he couldn't ignore me any longer.'

'What did you tell him?'

'I didn't tell him about the moondial, if that's what you mean. I think that would have been a step too far. But I told him his father had driven me to the point of suicide. I told him that I'd left Harry to protect him as much as for my own sake.'

'Did he listen?'

Jocelyn smiled and the weary lines on her face softened. 'He listened enough, I think. We've not mended all our fences, but some.'

Jocelyn smiled as her tears dried, but the ghost of those tears remained and Holly knew the old lady wouldn't let go of the guilt she had carried with her for thirty years.

The clouds gathering overhead were leaching the colour from the sky and the warm breeze had developed a sharpness. The gloriously overgrown gardens that surrounded them had lost their lustre and Holly needed no persuading when Jocelyn suggested they head home.

'I don't think this picnic was a very good idea, was it?' sighed Jocelyn. 'We've both lost our appetites and, I hate to say this, but I think my joints have seized up. I'm not sure I'll be able to get up off the ground.'

Holly smiled as she picked herself up and put her arms out to help pull Jocelyn to her feet. 'Well, I can't leave you here and I can't make it back without you.'

This was Holly's way of reaching out for help and Jocelyn found enough determination to make it to her feet and give Holly a hug. 'I won't leave you to face this on your own,' she assured her.

*   *   *

The journey home was slower and it was also darker. The dappled light that had lit their way to Hardmonton Hall had been replaced by a cold murkiness. Holly's journey to the ruins had been undertaken with a mixture of fear and hope but on her return, she carried back with her only the fear and a sense of emptiness that had seeped into her body once her tears had been spent.

'What if there's an exception to the rule?' she asked Jocelyn as they neared the gatehouse. It was the first time they had spoken on their bleak journey home, other than the occasional expletive from Jocelyn as her hip joints failed her.

'There's no bargaining with the moondial,' Jocelyn warned. She stopped and turned to look at Holly. It was hard to tell if the grimace on the old woman's face was from the pain or from the thought of Holly taking risks with her future.

'So why use it!' Holly blurted out, not sure if her sudden anger was directed at Jocelyn or the moondial. 'Why didn't you destroy it, or at least the mechanism? Why did you leave it so some poor fool like me would come along and start putting it back together again?'

Fresh guilt weighed down heavily on Jocelyn's shoulders and she suddenly looked very frail and old. 'I don't know why, Holly, I really don't. Just like Mr Andrews, I suppose I didn't think I had the right to destroy the moondial. I hid the box in one of the walls in Harry's workshop and I thought it would be safe there. It was certainly the last place Harry would ever look. And I kept the journal with me, remember. I didn't think anyone would be able to work out how to put the mechanism together on their own.'

As soon as Holly saw the pain in Jocelyn's face she immediately regretted her outburst and her anger vanished as quickly as it had arrived. She knew she was being unfair and besides, she couldn't ignore the fact that the dial would be instrumental in avoiding her death in childbirth. 'I'm so sorry, Jocelyn. I shouldn't have said that. You're as much a victim of the moondial as I am.' She slipped her arm into Jocelyn's and started walking once more towards home. 'So tell me everything you know about the journal,' she said, easing the conversation away from her ill-conceived accusation.

'It was written by Edward Hardmonton and it describes in harrowing detail how he resurrected the dial and the decisions he was forced to take. He knew tragedy was coming, but there was still only so much he could do to change future events.'

' "Like a drop of rain on glass, the choice of path may not be free," ' Holly recited.

'You've remembered the poem perfectly.'

'It's not something I'm likely to forget,' sighed Holly. 'It's the only thing I have to get me through this nightmare.'

'Not the only thing. I'm here to help you—unless you're ready to talk to Tom about it?'

It was Holly's turn to feel guilty. She was coming to realize that she was going to have to make some life-changing decisions and Tom had a right to be involved. 'I need to have everything clear in my own mind first. I will tell him, one day.'

'Just not today,' suggested Jocelyn.

'Or tomorrow,' added Holly. 'Perhaps not until all of this is over and there are no decisions left to take.'

The trees started to thin out and Holly sensed Jocelyn's relief as the gatehouse came into view.

'I'll drive you back home,' insisted Holly.

'I've told you before, I won't give in to these joints,' Jocelyn said with a warning glare.

'Then at least let me escort you home. No arguing.'

'Who's arguing?' asked Jocelyn with a pained smile.

*   *   *

Although Jocelyn was relieved when they stopped in front of the teashop, she was less eager to say goodbye to Holly. She didn't want to leave her on her own to dwell on the future. They both knew there was only one path Holly could take if she was going to survive and that meant a future without Libby. Her daughter might not exist in the present time, might never exist at all, but Jocelyn could see the pain of loss in Holly's eyes.

'I could always pack a bag and come stay with you until Tom gets back,' Jocelyn offered. She had taken the journal out of her basket, but seemed reluctant to hand it over.

'I'll be fine, don't worry,' Holly assured her, reaching out and taking the journal from Jocelyn's protective grasp. 'I've got this to read and then there are lots of other things to keep me busy. The marble for Mrs Bronson's sculpture is finally being delivered next week and Billy has promised to come back and finish off the conservatory. Besides, you're busy too.'

'Yes, it's always busy at harvest time in the village, but I'm sure they could do perfectly well without me.' Jocelyn still wasn't making a move to go inside the teashop.

'Jocelyn, am I going to have to drag you up the stairs to your flat?' warned Holly with a mischievous smile. Even though Jocelyn was the only person that she could talk to about the moondial, Holly desperately needed time on her own.

*   *   *

When Holly returned home, the gatehouse felt empty and barren. She had been given a glimpse of motherhood, had seen the face of the child she and Tom would create, and then she had been lulled into believing that she still could have it all. She had assumed that the moondial in its mystical benevolence had shown her the dangers that lay ahead so that she could avoid them, so that she could survive, so that they could all survive.

She put the journal down on the kitchen table and stared at it. It was bound in dark brown leather with the monogram E.H. stamped in the top left corner. There was a leather strap tied tightly around it to keep in place ragged bits of paper which had been inserted between its unkempt pages. Holly was tempted to leave it unopened, especially now that Jocelyn had described its contents as harrowing; she had already heard

179

enough harrowing stories for one day. But the journal demanded her attention and she knew she wouldn't rest until her torture was complete.

8

Edward Hardmonton had been intrigued by the moondial ever since he was a small child. To the rest of his family, the dial was nothing more than a garden curiosity in the grounds of Hardmonton Hall, half-forgotten for almost a century. But young Edward had been irresistibly drawn to the stone circle where it stood proud and glistening in the sunshine and he would spend endless summer days playing there. He knew every inch of the dial's engraved surface and every word of the poem that encircled it, but without the mechanism to unlock its power, the moondial had kept its secrets from him.

When Edward left for university, he was too excited with the world that awaited him to give any thought to what he was leaving behind and soon he forgot all about the moondial. After completing his degree in agriculture, Edward travelled the world to do what many of his peers were doing in the sixties: to find himself. He knew he was fortunate, not just because he had the financial means to flit from one country to the next, but also because his father wholeheartedly supported his wanderlust. They both knew that Edward, as an only child, would one day take over the running of the estate from his father and, while he fully acknowledged and accepted that duty, in the meantime Edward was intent on enjoying his freedom, with his father's blessing.

Edward's soul-searching came to an abrupt end when his father died unexpectedly from a heart attack. Edward was touring Italy at the time and the news was devastating. He deeply regretted not being there at his father's side and while there was no question that he would return home to Hardmonton Hall, it wasn't a decision he found as easy to take as he had expected. He had met someone. She was a young woman from a small village in Italy, more beautiful than anyone Edward had ever met before, with olive skin and the darkest brown eyes. He had known her for barely a month but he already knew that Isabella was the one. He couldn't bear the thought of leaving her behind, so he took a leap of faith and asked her to marry him on the eve of his return to England. They would never be parted again.

It was five years later when Edward's attention was drawn once again to the moondial by a twist in fate. By this time Edward and Isabella had a two-year-old son, Lucas, and with his family's future established for the next generation, Edward had turned his thoughts to the past. Trawling through the family archives, he came across a collection of handwritten notes and drawings in the inky scrawl of the eighth Lord Hardmonton. The records documented his great, great grandfather's explorations of the ancient worlds, and Edward was finally able to piece together the history of the dial and its link to the infamous Moon Stone.

Edward's renewed interest in the dial took on a life of its own and he started the journal to keep track of his findings. As well as his own notes, Edward included extracts from the original archives. His research proved, amongst other things, that the rumours about his predecessor had been correct. When Charles Hardmonton had been ostracized by the scientific community on suspicion of stealing a precious artefact, the evidence Edward uncovered showed that, on the face of it at least, his punishment had been deserved.

The missing item was the Moon Stone, a sacred altar which was the centrepiece of an Aztec temple in honour of the moon goddess Coyolxauhqui. Charles had already made public his disapproval of the systematic ransacking of ancient worlds and the Moon Stone proved to be the last straw. Charles secretly removed the Moon Stone from the cargo shipment that would bring his reputation into question and diverted it onto another ship.

After a lifetime committed to scientific discovery, Charles had been willing to sacrifice everything he'd worked for just to have that one treasure in his possession. Why? Because during the course of his last expedition he had not only uncovered the legend of the dial but he had come to believe in its power.

It was Charles Hardmonton who had transformed the Moon Stone into the dial. The process of engineering a mechanism that could harness the power of the full moon and bring the dial to life appeared to have taken him many years: drawings in the archives showed various incarnations of the brass cogs and claws and the orb at its centre. Once the mechanism was perfected and the power of the Moon Stone had been harnessed, he had used it to see into his own future and, with the discipline of a seasoned scientist, he had collected the evidence that would establish the extent of the moondial's power as well as its limitations. He had used his knowledge to write the poem which would eventually be etched into paths that surrounded it.

The poem had been his way of providing a user guide to the moondial for future generations, on display in the gardens for all to see. His records, however, gave no clue as to why Charles had then left instructions for the orb he had created for the centre of the dial to be buried with him. The whereabouts of the rest of the mechanism were never recorded and so the dial fell into disrepair.

Edward's first task, therefore, was to locate the mechanism and find a suitable replacement for the orb. The mechanism had been relatively easy to track down once Edward knew what he was looking for. The wooden box that contained the assortment of brass cogs and brackets had been stored amongst a collection of timepieces gathering dust in the Hall's vast attic space. Whilst his forebears may have assumed it was a useful box of spare parts, the etchings carved into the surface of the box had led Edward straight to it.

Finding a replacement for the orb proved a little more difficult because raiding Charles Hardmonton's grave was an option Edward refused to consider. His initial attempt was to use a topper from a crystal decanter, adapted to fit the claws of the dial. The dial had worked in a fashion, but the vision of the future that had been revealed to him was a ghostly impression of the world around him, a barren world with barely recognizable features. It gave Edward valuable evidence that the legend of the dial had substance, but he realized that he was going to need a more powerful device to replace the orb.

Edward developed the idea of a prism and he eventually commissioned an orb to be made to his own design. As he waited for the orb to be constructed his excitement mounted, only to be reduced to abject despair when his first use of the dial with the new orb revealed, in perfect clarity, why on his previous visit the world around him had seemed so desolate. The Hall had been razed to the ground, wiping out centuries of his family's history. The entire estate looked as if it had just been abandoned to its fate, although to Edward's horror, there was one particular area that looked like it was still being tended with care. The family cemetery had been cleared and there was a new grave. The headstone bore the names of his wife and his son, the dates of their death the same. It was less than one year into the future.

Consumed by fear, over the following months Edward tried desperately to discover how the fire started. His initial efforts were frustrated as, again and again the moondial returned him to an abandoned site, devoid of life, offering no clues that would allow him to avoid the tragedy. He realized that he would need help, someone who would be there in the future, waiting for him at the site of the moondial to provide a crucial link between the present and the future. Of course, he himself had survived the fire and could be there to lead the way, but Edward could not and would not face his future self. Instead, he chose as his confidante Mr Andrews, the gardener whose family had worked on the estate for generations. Mr Andrews was able to meet Edward, or at least Edward's reflection revealed by moonlight, on his next foray into the future. Mr Andrews had survived the tragedy and could explain to Edward that the fire had been caused by an electrical fault in the Hall's ancient wiring.

By this time Edward was well acquainted with the moondial's rules. He knew the path on which his family were embarked would prove difficult to change, but still he tried. He took every precaution he possibly could to prevent the fire, having the entire Hall rewired and even installing fire alarms and sprinklers. He funded the work by using well placed bets on horse races, again using information provided by Mr Andrews, who continued to meet him on his moondial visits, armed with any information the loyal gardener thought might help save the Hardmontons.

Each visit into the future confirmed that all his precautions were futile. His meddling had created subtle changes to the ruins that had become a familiar backdrop to his moondial visions, evidence that the source of the fire had altered though the ruins remained the constant. To make matters worse, the fortune Edward had accumulated to fund his renovation works was wiped out by an unexpected tax bill. Future attempts to raise money also managed to be lost by some unforeseen calamity. The moondial would not allow those who used it to alter their fortunes easily, and that included financial fortunes. There was a path to be followed and the dial would not allow any deviation from that course.

Refusing to accept defeat, Edward began planning to escape with his family, fleeing to another country. The Hall was destined to burn to the ground and Edward would let it, but he and his family didn't have to be there when it happened. Again, Edward's attempts to save his family seemed doomed to failure. Each time he went back to the moondial, Mr Andrews would appear in his vision, telling him that some new tragedy had befallen his beloved wife and son.

The dial's rules held fast and they haunted Edward. A life for a life was to prove the cruellest of rules. Destiny was about to take two lives from him and he only had one life to give in return. He was never going to be able to save both his wife and his son.

Edward's growing anger consumed him and his rage was directed at the moondial for bringing him to the brink of insanity. He was determined to destroy it, smash it into pieces, but despite his loathing for the device, he couldn't bring himself to do it. Instead, he entrusted Mr Andrews with the task of deciding the dial's own destiny. Meanwhile, Edward clung to a desperate hope that the vision was a false one.

It was only in his last entry, the day before the fire, that Edward finally accepted his fate:

I had often wondered why my great, great grandfather had allowed the device for which he had sacrificed his career and his reputation to fall into wrack and ruin. Now I know what Charles Hardmonton must have known on his deathbed. We are not meant to meddle with destiny. It is too heavy a burden for any man, to have the ability to see into the future and then to accept that the path we take is not all of our own choosing. Like a drop of rain that trickles down

186

a window pane, the future we see will leave a trace that our rewritten destinies will inevitably be drawn back to. Charles had hoped the secret of the dial would be buried with him and my dying wish is that it should now die with me.

I regret the day I ever resurrected the dial, but I have to accept that there will be some good to come from my torment, my son Lucas will be a testament to that.

My only relief is that my burden has now been shared, a selfish act but also a necessary evil. Isabella was distraught and it broke my heart to see her in such pain, but time is running out. I needed to prepare her for what lies ahead and I also needed her help in making all the arrangements to ensure that our beautiful Lucas would be safe and secure.

I should have known Isabella would be the strong one. Once she knew, once she shared my conviction that our fates were doomed, she didn't wallow in her grief. She has one single purpose in mind and that is to make every possible provision for Lucas and by doing so she has eased my guilt, my fears. I am blessed and I am loved. What is more, I am ready to face tomorrow and to lie in the arms of the woman I would have gladly given my life for, if it hadn't already been promised to our dearest Lucas.

Closing the journal, Holly carefully, almost reverently, retied the leather strap around its tattered pages. She felt completely drained. The story of Edward Hardmonton had sapped what little strength she had left, what little hope she had left. She hadn't moved from the kitchen table for

187

over two hours and when she stood up, her joints screamed their disapproval. The pain was almost a relief from the numbness that had taken over her body and her mind.

Holly walked out of the kitchen almost in a trance but there was a new sensation welling up inside her. From the pit of her stomach, Holly could feel an anger starting to build and as she stepped into the living room, the room where she had shared precious moments with Libby, the first shout of rage escaped. She looked beyond the empty space on the floor and saw Libby, lying on the changing mat, kicking her legs. She looked beyond the empty space on the sofa and saw Tom feeding his daughter. Everywhere she turned, she saw the ghost of her unborn child.

'You can't make me do this!' she screamed. 'You can't make me choose my own life over Libby's!'

She scanned the room, looking for answers to the questions that were flooding her brain. She spotted the China cat smiling at her from the shelf. It had survived in a future where Holly had not, it would survive in a future where Libby would not and all the while it was smiling.

'If Libby can't survive, then why should you?' she shouted at its cheerful face. In a blur of crimson fury, Holly grabbed the cat from the shelf and flung it across the room. She could hear the snap of its head parting company with its body as it hit the wall and then fell out of sight behind one of the sofas.

Holly stood in the middle of the room, trying to breathe through her anger. Her thoughts kept spinning as she tried to make sense of everything, but there was only one thought that kept catching her attention. It was one particular line of the poem and she spoke the words out loud: 'A life for a life the price to pay, never one less and not one more.' If it wasn't her life that would be lost, then it would be someone else's, a family member, someone she loved. She closed her eyes as the words echoed through her mind. Her life for Libby's; there really was no other choice.

Eventually Holly's anger ran out of steam and there was only one refuge left.

'Hello. Are you busy?' Holly asked.

'No, I was just doing some paperwork. What's wrong, Hol?' There was a note of concern in Tom's voice. It might have been early evening for Holly, but it was midday in Haiti and Tom wasn't expecting her to phone until later.

Holly had put off the call as long as she could bear, but as she sat at the kitchen table and watched the sun setting, it seemed to her that the fading light was taking with it not only Holly's hopes and dreams but Tom's too, if only he knew it.

'Nothing's wrong, I just thought I'd surprise you,' lied Holly. 'If you're really busy then tell me to go, I can call back later. I only wanted to hear your voice and now I have. I needed to know you were all right and now I know.'

'No, don't go. I could do with a friendly distraction. I was thinking about having an early siesta now that I've finished writing up my notes from this morning's interviews, but I know I'll only end up lying awake, thinking things through.'

'I thought it was supposed to help empty your mind when you write things down,' Holly said, still staring at the journal.

'Well, it hasn't worked so far,' Tom told her. 'I love this job and I hate it at the same time. It's

189

really opening my eyes to another world, being out here. I wish you could meet some of the people I've met. Some of the stories they have to tell would just blow you away, but I can't help feeling so guilty. I'm surrounded by literally thousands upon thousands of homeless, desperate people, knowing all the time that I can go home at any point to my beautiful house and my beautiful wife. I have the kind of security that they couldn't even dream of. I won't go hungry, I'll get the medical care I need when I need it. When I have kids, I won't have to worry about them fighting for survival each and every day. I don't know how I'll be able to take things for granted ever again.'

There was a long pause as Holly wondered how to answer him. She wondered what plans and hopes Edward Hardmonton had had for the future before the moondial sealed his fate. 'You're right. We shouldn't take anything for granted. We should appreciate what we have now. I know we have a five-year plan, but I'm starting to see how arrogant that is. We should spend more time enjoying the things we have, appreciating what we have and not constantly looking for more.'

Holly knew she was laying the seed for a decision in the near future to put off having children but she stopped short of saying the words. If she spoke that thought out loud, it could change the future and erase Libby forever, and Holly didn't have the strength to face that yet.

'We're getting very philosophical in our old age,' observed Tom. 'I know I don't appreciate what I have, not enough anyway. I don't appreciate you. Look at me, I'm on the other side of the world from you, expecting you to put your life on hold. I don't

190

deserve you.'

'I want you to be happy more than anything in the world. I know I can't give you everything you want,' Holly paused, choking back the emotion. 'But the work you're doing is important and it's going to set you on the right path for the rest of your career.'

'Sitting behind a desk in front of a camera all my life, you mean?'

'Sitting behind a desk writing your book sounds better to me,' suggested Holly, already fully aware of Tom's resistance to becoming an anchorman.

Tom's tone picked up as he started talking about the kind of book he might write and the sound of his animated voice brought the life back into Holly's frozen heart. Her phone call to Tom had paid off. Listening to him reminded her that there were still so many things in life that they both wanted to achieve, things that weren't bound by the rules of the moondial. There was a long pause on the phone and Holly realized that she had lost track of the conversation.

'Am I boring you?' accused Tom.

'Sorry,' she replied. 'And no, you're not boring me, you're making me realize there's still so much to look forward to, not least you coming home in a few weeks. I miss you.'

'I miss you too,' whispered Tom. 'I love you, Mrs Corrigan.'

'I love you too. Come home safely.'

As Holly replaced the phone she stared out of the window at the moondial, which was glinting in the twilight. 'You're not going to beat me,' she said. 'You can't erase everything.' She had thought all hope was lost, but Tom had reminded her that they still had a future. There was hope, there had to be, and she wasn't going to let the moondial take it away from her, not completely.

9

The studio was a hive of frenetic activity and Holly was all but lost in the heat, dust and deafening noise of hard labour. The piece of marble she had picked for the base of Mrs Bronson's sculpture was beautiful, even before she started working on it. It was almost a pity to have to hack away at the multicoloured veins that threaded life into the blackest stone. But hack away she did. Three days had passed since Holly had taken that fateful walk to the ruins with Jocelyn. She had started to accept that she must surrender her dreams of holding Libby in her arms, of watching her grow and completing the family that Tom so desperately wanted, that she so desperately wanted. But the pain of the loss, the burden of guilt in taking the decision without Tom, the shame of sacrificing her daughter's life for her own, these were emotions she wasn't sure she would ever be able to come to terms with.

Dust billowed around her as she cut into the stone with a chainsaw, obscuring her vision. Slowly but surely, the spiral was taking form, to become a dramatic foundation for the mother and child figures that would emerge above it. Despite her progress, Holly found no joy in her work. She had a job to do, that was all.

Holly felt like the worst kind of hypocrite.

192

There had been no bond with her own mother, no foundation on which to build a future, and now there would be no Libby to build a future for. She had been right to doubt herself all along. She was never going to make a good mother. She was willing to forfeit Libby's life for her own. Holly had read and reread the poem, over and over again. She had scrutinized every page of the journal, hoping to uncover a secret that would help her avoid the life for a life rule, but her efforts were futile and she knew it. If there had been any way to avoid the sacrifice that had to be made then Edward Hardmonton would have found it.

As Holly chipped away great chunks of stone, she toyed with the idea of using the dial again. The moondial might have thrown her life into chaos but it still gave Holly a way in which she could spend time with the child she was sacrificing. Perhaps Jocelyn was right. Perhaps it was a gift and Holly shouldn't be so quick to turn away from it.

Not every lesson she had learnt about the dial's workings had been a harsh one. Holly now knew that her presence would be strongest under direct moonlight. She remembered leafing through Tom's papers in the study, with the full moon shining through the window. That had been why she had found it so much easier to move things in that room. Perhaps she could find a way to finally hold Libby. Every nerve in her body cried out just at the thought of cradling her baby in her arms. But then her thoughts turned to Tom. She would have to face his grief, his eyes looking through her again, and she didn't think she could do that.

There were other fears too. She couldn't be sure if the decision she had now taken, the decision not

193

to conceive Libby, had already rewritten her future. If that was the case, Holly wasn't ready to face what the moondial might reveal. She wouldn't use the dial, not yet. Reluctantly, however, she knew that it still had a part to play in her future. There was still one question that she would need an answer to eventually. If the dial was keeping score, was Holly sacrificing just Libby's life or her chances of ever being a mother?

The question at the moment was almost irrelevant. She didn't think she deserved to be a mother and she was tempted to smash up the moondial as surely as she was smashing away at the marble in front of her.

'Ever thought of taking up the building trade?' Billy was standing at the open studio doors and he had to shout over the din that Holly was making.

'Is it lunchtime already?' Holly asked. She was used to being dragged away from her work to feed the hungry horde of builders who were putting the final touches to the conservatory.

'Lunchtime? More like home time! It's three-thirty.'

'I'm sorry, Billy, I must have got carried away.'

'We thought as much, but don't worry. We've worked right through and we'll have an early start, if you don't mind. It's a glorious day out there, probably the last of the year. You should get out into the sunshine once in a while.'

'Well, if you hadn't disappeared for weeks and left me with a half-finished conservatory, I'd have been catching the rays in there,' scolded Holly. Billy had risen significantly in her estimation since Jocelyn's revelations, but she wasn't about to let him know that.

194

'It'll be worth the wait,' he said with pride.

'So when will you be finished?'

'Another couple of days and we'll be done. But you haven't seen the last of me. I'm still finishing the plans for the garden.'

'So Tom is getting you to do the garden!' exclaimed Holly.

Billy hit his palm against his head in despair and his cheeks flushed with embarrassment. 'What am I like? The cat is well and truly out of the bag. Your husband is going to be so annoyed with me.'

'Well, by rights, he should be home doing the work himself. But I suppose if he's running around the globe earning lots of money, the least we can do is spend it for him,' sighed Holly.

'When is that man of yours coming home? I keep telling him that he shouldn't leave you alone for so long. You need looking after, whether you think you do or not.'

'He's back in a couple of weeks, but not for long. He's got plans to go jetting off somewhere in South America next.'

Billy shook his head slowly in disapproval. 'You've never considered going with him on his travels?'

'Don't think I haven't been tempted,' Holly replied, and her body wrenched with a renewed sense of guilt. She wriggled her toes in her shoes, seeking the firmness of the floor to anchor her, but all she found was the painful crunch of stone debris underfoot.

She ached for Tom more than ever. Billy was right, she did need looking after and no one could do that better than Tom. But she wanted to spare Tom from the torment she was now going through.

195

Her decision to erase Libby from their future would be a matter for her conscience, not his. She wouldn't tell him until the new year, when he was home for good and the date had passed when Libby was meant to be conceived.

'Well, if you need company, you know where I am,' Billy said, shaking her from her thoughts. 'If you don't mind me saying, you don't seem yourself. You should get out more. It's not good for a person to lock themselves away.'

'I go to the village, I have Tom's parents, and then there's always Jocelyn,' Holly told him. 'Besides, I speak to Tom every day.'

'You can be in a crowded room and still be alone,' Billy answered.

'Sage words,' agreed Holly, taken aback slightly by the seriousness of Billy's warning. 'I'll bear that in mind.'

'And next time you speak to that husband of yours, you tell him his conservatory will be ready for a grand opening when he comes home.'

'Shall I tell him the garden will be fully landscaped too?'

'Hmm,' replied Billy with a stern look that turned into a smirk, 'the less said about that the better.'

*   *   *

Although the teashop wasn't bustling with customers at this time of year, Jocelyn was busier than ever. When she wasn't doing the day job, she had more than enough extracurricular activities to keep her occupied. She seemed to be on almost every committee or voluntary group for miles around. With harvest time in full swing, her schedule was so full that she couldn't get away from the teashop to visit Holly for their usual Sunday brunch, but she wasn't about to let Holly off the hook so easily, so she invited Holly over for brunch at the teashop instead. Holly suspected that Billy had shared his concerns about her frame of mind with Jocelyn and there was simply no way to turn down her invitation.

The atmosphere in the village felt as crisp and fresh as the late September air, a stark contrast from the dusty atmosphere of her studio, and Holly felt invigorated as she walked to the teashop. Holly just wished Tom was home to enjoy it too.

He was due home in a week and although she knew, thanks to the moondial, that Tom would return home in one piece, she still worried about him. Each time she spoke to him he seemed to be becoming more and more lost. He was passionate about his job and had stepped up to the challenge of reporting on global environmental and political issues, but that hadn't prepared him for the human tragedy he was witnessing in Haiti. Tom was becoming increasingly frustrated with his own inability to make a difference.

It was clear to Holly that this trip was going to be more than just another assignment. It was changing Tom's perspective on life and that would no doubt affect his career. Although Holly had glimpsed Tom's future, she had never really seen beyond his grief to understand what might or might not be happening to him on a professional level. He had obviously taken up the anchorman role, judging from the paperwork she had seen in his study, but she had also seen his scrawled notes on the scripts, their angry tone suggesting it wasn't a job he enjoyed—and now she was beginning to understand why.

As Holly arrived at the teashop, she had to put her fears for Tom to one side. He wasn't the only one causing concern.

'We're worried about you,' Jocelyn told her.

They were sitting at a table in the teashop, which was in a rare state of calm, midway between the breakfast mania and the lunchtime rush. Lisa was prepping some food in the back and the only customers in the place had already been fed and watered. The teashop was filled with the welcoming aromas of freshly baked croissants.

'Would that be you and Billy, by any chance?'

'If someone as socially inept as Billy can sense there's something wrong, then there's something to worry about,' Jocelyn replied.

'Well, we both know exactly what it is I have to worry about.' Holly was picking at a few crumbs around the Danish pastry Jocelyn was trying to force-feed her with.

'Have you decided what you're going to do in the next few months?' It was Jocelyn's turn to look worried.

'I have to avoid conceiving Libby, I know that and it's not going to be difficult. I have contraception injections every three months and my next one would be due in November. The plan I agreed with Tom was to stop the injections and start making babies at the end of this year. Now, thanks to the moondial, I have to keep that appointment, don't I?'

'The moondial gives you a window which looks out onto your future, but it's you that has to make

198

the life-changing decisions,' Jocelyn told Holly. 'It's a big responsibility, I know that, and I'm here when you need me, but I can't make those decisions for you. I won't make them for you, not when your own life is at stake.'

Holly knew that Jocelyn was the only person who could really understand the torture she was going through. For Holly, the options were somewhat easier to put into effect than it had been for Jocelyn, but the burden of the decision weighed just as heavily. 'Did you have to manage on your own? Was the gardener the only person who knew?'

'Even Mr Andrews didn't know everything; I was too ashamed to tell him exactly what I had seen. For a long time I kept the secret of my future to myself, but eventually I told my sister Beatrice. She helped and influenced where she could but it was still down to me to navigate my own way into the future. The burden was mine and mine alone.'

'I understand and I wouldn't let you take any of my burden either. You don't want someone's life on your conscience,' Holly concluded, but then blushed when she realized how thoughtless the comment was under the circumstances.

'I don't want anyone else's death on my conscience. One is enough.'

'I've spent the last week or so trying to find a way to wriggle out of this deal with the moondial. Don't look so worried,' Holly added, seeing the look of alarm growing on Jocelyn's face. 'I know I can't try to hold onto Libby without risking someone else's life. I wouldn't only be risking my life. I know I could just as easily be risking Tom's.'

'That's why I won't tell you what to do. I'm so sorry, Holly, you have to make your own choices

199

and live with the consequences. But don't go playing games with the dial and don't let your guard down. Please, Holly, not when you're playing with people's lives.'

'I wish I'd never uncovered the cursed thing.'

'If it gets to save your life, then it's a gift not a curse, but be careful. Don't forget about the choice of path not being free. Remember that raindrop on the window,' she warned.

'You think it's going to take more than simply making an appointment at the doctor's to avoid conceiving Libby?' Holly's frown matched Jocelyn's.

'Sometimes you change the circumstances around events, but then they still happen. Remember what happened at Hardmonton Hall? Edward went to great lengths to protect the Hall from a fire, but all it did was change the cause of it.'

'You're not putting my mind at rest, Joss!' laughed Holly, but the laugh was hollow and laced with fear.

Jocelyn sighed in quiet submission to the will of the moondial. 'I just believe that there's a universal balance and I know without a doubt that changing the future isn't easy. If the moondial has taught me anything, it's taught me that there's less chaos in the world than we might think. People spend so much time wondering whether they should turn left or right. They don't realize that they'll end up in the same place anyway.'

'But the future can be changed,' countered Holly, a familiar sense of panic rising in her chest.

'Yes, and that's why there's a price to be paid.'

'I'm scared, Jocelyn,' confessed Holly. 'I'm scared that I have to spend the rest of my life paying the price. I'm scared the moondial intends to take away not just Libby but any other child I may have. What kind of life am I going to lead if I can't ever have children? Will Tom still love me?'

'I may have met him only once, but that man will always love you, I'm sure of it,' replied Jocelyn firmly.

Before Holly had a chance to dwell on her fears the bell hanging above the door of the teashop tinkled, announcing the arrival of new customers. Lisa was at the far end of the small kitchen, still busily chopping vegetables.

'Duty calls,' Jocelyn said with a sigh as she pulled herself to her feet. Wincing in pain, she added, 'I think I'm still recovering from that walk of ours. I really shouldn't put myself through these long shifts any more.' Although she was in her eighties, Jocelyn worked just as hard as someone half her age and despite her creaking bones the teashop seemed to charge her energy levels rather than drain them.

'You should get more help in here,' Holly told her.

'If that's an offer, then I accept,' Jocelyn said with an air of triumph.

Holly opened her mouth to speak but did an impression of a fish on a line gulping for air, as she tried her best to think of a way to get herself out of the trap Jocelyn had set. 'If I didn't know better, Jocelyn, I'd say I'd just been set up.'

'If you didn't know better, you'd say no and go home to wallow in your misery.'

Holly's eyes narrowed as she thought about the offer and tried her best to ignore Jocelyn's exaggerated moans and groans as she shuffled along the table.

'I still need to keep my mornings free to work in the studio. And do you have any idea what a complete novice I am in the kitchen?' warned Holly.

'All the more reason to start putting in some practice,' retorted Jocelyn.

'Would you like me to start right now?' offered Holly.

'No, tomorrow afternoon will be soon enough.'

Holly was reluctant to move. She glanced at the young family who had settled at one of the tables and were scrutinizing the menu. 'I just have the full moon to survive tonight then,' she said.

Jocelyn sat herself back down with a thump. 'How stupid am I? Sorry, Holly, I didn't realize it was that close. Are you going to use it?'

'No, absolutely not. I've seen enough of my future for one lifetime.' Though she managed a brave smile, Holly's heart felt heavy and her stomach leaden. 'I've already wrapped up the dial in a dust sheet just to keep it out of sight. It can stay under wraps for the foreseeable future.'

They both chuckled at Holly's feeble pun.

'Are you sure you'll be all right?' Jocelyn asked.

Holly stood up. 'Of course I will. I'll see you tomorrow.'

Jocelyn rose from the table for a second time and gave Holly a bear hug. 'You'll be fine. You're a strong woman. Stronger than I ever was.'

'I doubt that. I'd be happy to have half your strength,' Holly said. 'You're a very special lady.'

'Don't be daft,' replied Jocelyn, wafting her out of the shop with a flutter of embarrassment. 'And don't think buttering up the boss means I'll be taking it easy on you. I want you here at one o'clock

202

sharp!'

As Holly left the teashop she was surprised to find she had a spring in her step. She practically sauntered back to the gatehouse with a sense of control she hadn't felt in a long time. She had been strong once and she could be again. She wouldn't drop her guard and she would get through this for her sake and for Tom's.

That evening, Holly won her first battle with the moondial and ignored its persistent pull from beneath its makeshift shroud.

*   *   *

Holly clattered pots and pans as she raced around the kitchen trying to juggle over-boiled vegetables and burning roast potatoes. She had insisted on inviting Tom's parents and Jocelyn around for Sunday lunch to welcome Tom home, but she was now seriously regretting the decision. It probably hadn't been a good idea either to open a bottle of wine to give her Dutch courage.

'Are you sure you wouldn't like some help?' Diane asked, peering around the kitchen door and doing her best not to show any visible signs of horror at the mess that Holly was in the process of creating.

'No, I'll be fine,' insisted Holly as she dropped a tea towel over the scorch mark she'd made on the kitchen table. She had already confessed her mishap to Diane, who had taken it well.

Diane looked at the tea towel and was about to say something but thought better of it. Holly was in no mood to be soothed. 'If you're sure?' she said, more as a question than a statement.

203

'I'm sure,' replied Holly through gritted teeth and with only the slightest hint of hysteria. 'You get back in there with Tom. I'm sure there's still plenty of catching up to do.'

'All right then,' Diane told her with an unconvincing smile. She still didn't look like she was going anywhere but then the doorbell rang.

'That'll be Jocelyn,' Holly gasped, looking around in panic and wondering how long she could leave the oven unattended before the whole kitchen imploded. Jocelyn hadn't met Tom's parents and she barely knew Tom. Holly would be a poor hostess if she didn't do the introductions. She did a little jig in the middle of the kitchen as she went to go one way and then the other.

'Are you all right? I can take over if you like while you get the door,' Diane suggested with enthusiasm.

For a split second, Holly really was tempted to escape the kitchen with her opened bottle of wine and leave the cooking in more capable hands. There must be something Diane could salvage from the chaos, but she was going to have a hard job recreating perfectly formed sprouts from the green mush bubbling in a pan hidden at the back of the stove. 'No, I'm the one who made this mess and I'm the one who has to cook my way out of it. Could you see to Jocelyn for me?'

'If you're sure,' Diane conceded reluctantly. She backed out of the kitchen as if she was too scared to turn her back on the bubbling bedlam.

Two minutes later, Jocelyn popped her head around the door.

'Diane said you're determined to do this on your own, but . . .' Jocelyn cast a wary look over the kitchen. 'Are you sure you don't want some help?'

'I'm fine,' Holly replied with a fixed grin that was starting to make her cheeks ache. It was difficult enough keeping track of the countless miniature disasters that were appearing by the minute without the constant battle of keeping out the good Samaritans. 'I'm just sorry I can't come out of here to do some proper introductions.'

'Oh, don't worry about us. Diane and Jack are lovely and I'm getting reacquainted with your gorgeous husband. You really shouldn't leave me alone with him.'

'I'll trust you,' smiled Holly. 'Now if you don't mind, I've got a dinner to bring back to life.'

'You know where I am if you need me,' Jocelyn told her as she too backed out of the kitchen. 'And you might want to check the oven. I think I can smell burning,' she shouted before disappearing from view.

Holly opened the oven door and a cloud of smoke hit her between the eyes. She was busily wafting the smoke out through the kitchen door when Tom appeared. 'How's it going?' he asked.

Holly was just about to scream at him to get out of the kitchen but he had picked up her wine and was refilling her glass.

'You look like you could do with a drink,' he told her.

'I really shouldn't,' she said, 'but one more glass couldn't do any harm. I think all the damage that could be done, has been done.'

'It smells delicious,' Tom said brightly. He was deliberately avoiding making eye contact with Holly or looking towards the billowing smoke coming from the oven.

'You're a big fat liar, but I love you for saying it. Is everyone all right in there?'

'Yes, they're getting on like a house on fire. Sorry, no pun intended.' Holly hit him with a tea towel before letting him continue. 'Jocelyn and my mum are chatting away like old friends.'

Holly knocked back the glass of wine and lifted up her empty glass for a refill.

Tom lifted up the wine bottle to show Holly that it was now empty.

'There's plenty more where that came from,' she replied, tipping her head towards the fridge.

'How long will dinner be?' Tom asked tentatively. He was probably calculating if she could serve dinner before she was totally trashed.

'By my guess, it was ready half an hour ago. It's now over cooked and burnt.'

'At least we don't have to clear space in here and can eat in the conservatory,' Tom commented. He braved a look at the kitchen table, which didn't have an inch of spare space.

Holly took a deep breath to clear her head. 'Oh, I give up,' she said. 'Give me a hand serving this up. Do you think I should stick a pizza in the oven just in case?'

'It'll be fine,' Tom assured her.

The smell of fresh paint in the conservatory was quickly beaten into submission by the aroma of stewed vegetable with the faintest hint of burning. It was early afternoon but the day was already fading fast. At least the subdued lighting made the food look almost edible, thought Holly. They had borrowed a long table and chairs from the teashop to seat them all.

'It's lovely,' smiled Jocelyn, taking her first

206

mouthful of Holly's roast dinner. Holly heard a distinct crunch as Jocelyn bit down on a roast potato.

'Delicious,' confirmed Diane sweetly.

'It reminds me of Diane's cooking,' Jack offered. Diane raised an eyebrow at her husband. 'In the early days, I mean,' he clarified.

'You mean to say Mum couldn't cook either when you first got married?' Tom was laughing but one look at Holly silenced him.

'It's awful, isn't it?' Holly admitted. She took a long swig of wine to wash away the bitter taste of disappointment.

There was a chorus of denials and compliments and everyone made a concerted effort to fill their mouths with food.

'It's nice to have a home-cooked meal. You don't know how much I've missed being home,' Tom told them all.

'And we've missed you,' Holly replied. She was staring intently at Tom but from the corner of her eye, she could see beyond him and into the garden. She could see the pale form of the moondial in its dustsheet glowing in the twilight like an ever-present ghost.

Holly sipped her wine, listening intently as Tom described his time in Haiti. The experience had left its mark and it was going to take a long time before he'd be able to put it all behind him, if he ever could. Holly was more certain than ever that putting off telling Tom about the moondial was the right thing to do.

'It's just so frightening to see lives and communities wiped out in one single event,' he was telling Jocelyn.

'None of us can take life for granted,' agreed Holly sadly.

Jocelyn gave Holly a guarded look but said nothing.

'I'm sure this chicken didn't see it coming,' Jack said, laughing at his own joke until his wife prodded him.

'It's a lovely conservatory,' Diane said, trying to move the conversation to safer ground.

'Yes, Billy's done a lovely job,' agreed Jocelyn.

'We came up with the design together,' Tom said proudly. 'Mostly Billy, I have to admit. And then of course there was my dear wife's interference. The doors were supposed to be at the side, but Holly changed the plans at the last minute.'

'Yes,' added Holly, 'you can always change plans or they can be changed for you. Makes me wonder why we bother with them in the first place.'

Her head was becoming a fuzzy mess, a mixture of too much wine and a growing realization that she really had so little control over her future. Tears were welling in her eyes and she became aware that the others had fallen silent and were all looking at her with growing concern. She hadn't cried since the fateful trip to Hardmonton Hall and she had hoped she had contained her tears once more, but they never seemed to be too far from the surface. 'If you'll excuse me, I think I need a glass of water,' she said, jumping up and quickly heading out to the kitchen.

She took a long drink of water as she tried to clear the fog in her head.

'Hol, what's wrong?' Tom had followed her out and he walked up behind her and wrapped his arms around her waist, resting his head on her shoulder.

208

'I just don't think I like plans any more. You can't always assume that you can have everything you want in life. Life doesn't work like that.'

'Is this about our five-year plan? Have you changed your mind?' asked Tom. He kept his tone light but his body had tensed.

Holly didn't answer him. She needed to be sober to have that particular conversation and preferably when they weren't in the middle of entertaining guests.

'Please tell me you still want a baby,' Tom persisted. He was used to Holly's reluctance but he had obviously assumed that all her doubts had been put to rest now their plans for the future had been committed to paper.

Holly turned to face him, a swell of anger in her throat as she sensed herself being forced into a corner. 'I want to be a mother, yes. I want that with all my heart. But why do we always have to want more? Why can't we just appreciate what we have now?' she hissed, trying to keep her voice low.

'Do you think I don't know that? After what I've seen?' Tom countered.

'Then you should know that you can't count on the people you love being around tomorrow.'

They stood glaring at each other for the longest time. It was Holly who broke the silence first. 'I'm sorry,' she gasped, 'can we not do this now?'

Tom sighed and gently kissed Holly on her forehead. 'You lead the way,' he said with a flourish of his hand, pointing the way back to their guests.

There was gentle laughter rippling around the dining table but Tom and Holly brought their awkward silence into the room with them.

'Are you all right, Holly?' Diane asked.

209

'A little bit too much cooking wine, I think,' Holly admitted. She lifted up her glass of water and tried to let go of her anger and fear, but once again the ghostly shroud in the garden caught her attention. If only the moondial would loosen its grip.

'I expect it's taking a while getting used to this lean and keen stranger who just appeared on your doorstep,' replied Diane.

'Hey, I'm no stranger,' challenged Tom.

'No stranger than usual,' Holly added. Their eyes met for the first time since returning to their guests. A wordless apology passed between them and as everyone laughed at her joke, Holly sensed the tension leaving the room.

Diane was next to have a go at Tom's looks. 'You have lost a fair bit of weight on this trip, but at least your hair's starting to grow back. I never thought I'd say this, but after years of nagging you about the knots and tats in your hair, I think I actually miss the long-haired Tom.'

'Me too,' smiled Holly. 'But any version of Tom is better than none.'

'Hear, hear,' Jocelyn said, raising her glass. 'He looks pretty tasty to me.'

'Tastier than this dinner anyway,' muttered Holly. 'But you'll be pleased to know that Jocelyn has provided the dessert. Anyone hungry?'

The afternoon ebbed away with no more cross words. Tom and Holly said their goodbyes to their guests as the final rays of sunlight gave up the ghost for the night.

'Tell me truthfully,' Tom asked as they closed the front door. 'Are you having doubts about our relationship? Is that what you meant

210

about not being here tomorrow? Because if you are, I won't give up without a fight. I love you, Holly, and if my being away is causing a rift between us, then I'll stop. I don't want to lose you.'

'I know you don't,' replied Holly with a truth that Tom couldn't begin to understand, not yet, hopefully not ever. 'I just think we spend too much time looking to the future, looking at what's missing, instead of appreciating what we have now. I don't want you to ever look back and think, hey, I was happy then and I didn't even know it, I had my wife, I had my dreams and it was enough.'

Tom looked at her with a deep intensity that made Holly feel uneasy, as if he was looking deep into her soul and was about to uncover the secrets she was keeping from him. He seemed to be struggling to find the words so he simply wrapped her in his arms and held on tightly. 'Right now, Holly, you're right. This is enough. This is more than enough.'

10

'Move your hand a little bit. Ooh, that's good. Now just a little bit more,' Holly said with growing excitement. 'No, no, not that much. Now move to the left a bit. Slowly does it, nearly there. That's it, that's it. Don't move!'

'I'm getting tired,' groaned Tom.

'Stop complaining, we've only just started.'

'This wasn't exactly how I imagined spending my time at home. Semi-naked, yes. Experimenting with lots of positions, yes. Standing in the middle of your studio, holding a plastic doll? Not exactly part of my plan.'

'We've already wasted a whole weekend in bed,' Holly reminded him.

'Wasted?'

Holly grinned and acknowledged every aching muscle in her satiated body. 'OK, not wasted. Trouble is, I may be able to take time off from the teashop while you're home but I can't afford to fall behind schedule with Mrs Bronson's commission. I love you and adore you and, if nothing else, this only gives me more time to stare at your gorgeous if not slightly undernourished body.'

Holly had practically completed the base. A dark, nebulous spiral had emerged from the large stone block and, unlike the scaled version, this one had the finer detail. There were eerie suggestions of figures which made up its curves, depicting the generations that came before, the foundations from the past that supported the future.

The upper section was going to be more of a challenge and Holly wanted to work up some additional sketches before she started constructing the wire skeletons which would support the mother and child figures that were to be moulded from clay. She had persuaded Tom to strip down to his waist and drape a dust sheet around himself, holding a baby doll in his arms. Tom wasn't exactly the figure of the mother she had in mind, but he was certainly less of the man she had waved goodbye to.

'Well, if you'd seen what it was like, you'd have come back half-starved too. It wasn't that we weren't well catered for, we were. But I couldn't switch off what was happening around me, none of us could,' Tom had told her.

When he had set off to Haiti he had been a highly polished, slick anchorman in the making with his cropped hair and shiny suit, but his transformation had shocked Holly. He'd appeared on screen reporting in Haiti and each time Holly had seen him, he had looked just a little bit less polished, a little less slick. In some ways, Holly had been glad to see him reverting back to his old dishevelled self, but he had gone beyond dishevelled and had acquired a look that was gaunt, tortured even. It was more than evident that the changes weren't only physical.

'Well, you're home now. I know you're not going to be able to forget what you've seen, but you can't fix it, not everything, not on your own. You are making a difference, Tom. It's a demanding job but it's the job you always dreamed of, and who knows where it will lead to?'

'Straight back to the studio, that's where. It's only a secondment, remember. What difference will I be able to make then?'

'You'll make a difference,' Holly said, in a weak attempt to reassure him. 'Now stop moving and keep your arm straight.'

'I know I shouldn't complain, it'll be worth it in the end. I can't wait to be a dad,' he said with growing excitement as he cradled the plastic doll in his arms.

'We'll see,' whispered Holly, desperately trying to focus on her sketch and not resurrect the drunken argument that had been so narrowly avoided at the disastrous Sunday lunch.

'What's happened, Holly? Last time I was home

213

you were so keen to start a family. Now, every time I raise the subject, you're freezing me out again.' Tom had kept to his pose so he wasn't looking at her, but still he sensed the sadness that was threatening to overwhelm her.

'What if we can't have children?'

'Of course we'll be able to have children. Just look at this baby-making physique.' Tom flexed non-existent muscles in a rather scrawny arm as if to prove the point.

'Would our relationship survive if we couldn't?' Holly's voice echoed across the studio. The photos hanging around the room swayed mournfully in an invisible breeze, their hopeful smiles mocking her. She wished she knew with absolute certainty the answer to the one question that was still haunting her. Would the moondial ever show her that she could be a mother and survive to watch them grow? Holly visualized rain trickling down a windowpane. Each raindrop represented an unborn child and, in her mind's eye, each one trickled towards the same path. Would there be no way to avoid paying her dues to the moondial for the rest of her life?

Tom finally broke from his pose and looked over to her. 'We'd survive anything, Hol, I promise. But it's not going to come to that. As long as it's still what you want. You do still want kids, don't you?'

'I do. You wouldn't believe how much I do now, but . . .' stumbled Holly just as the door to the studio swung open, bringing with it a blast of cold air.

'Whoops, am I interrupting?' Billy was standing at the studio door covering his eyes from the sight he'd just seen.

'It's all right Billy, you can look,' Holly said,

214

casually wiping the corners of her eyes in case either of them noticed her newly formed tears.

'I hope he isn't naked underneath that sheet,' warned Billy.

'It could be worse, he could be standing there without the sheet!' Holly laughed as Billy pulled a face of disgust.

'Hey, I take exception to that,' complained Tom, who was now trying to flex his muscles and hold onto the doll at the same time.

Holly and Billy stood staring at Tom's less than manly stance. 'I think you should pick your models a little more carefully next time,' suggested Billy.

'I thought us men were supposed to stick together,' replied Tom, indignantly.

Holly had a feeling this childish banter could go on all morning. 'Listen, boys, I've got work to do. Billy, you're distracting my model. What is it we can help you with?'

'I was only dropping by to say hello,' Billy answered sheepishly.

'So what's that rolled up under your arm?' Holly demanded.

'This? Oh, just a little plan for a job I'm doing. It's nothing much.'

'Hand it over.' Holly had assumed the tone of a parent chastizing her child and the irony didn't escape her.

Billy looked beseechingly at Tom, but Tom was looking equally uncomfortable.

'It's the plan for the garden, isn't it?' Holly asked when neither man made a move.

'Might be, then again it might not,' muttered Billy, again looking to Tom for help.

'I've just remembered, I need to phone the

215

studio,' Tom said, letting the sheet slip to the ground and tossing the poor baby doll onto the workbench some ten feet away.

Wearing nothing but boxer shorts, he headed for the door. Billy tried to follow suit, but Holly grabbed him by the shoulder.

'Oh, I don't think so,' Holly said. 'You've lost me my model and you're just going to have to take his place.'

'Me?' stammered Billy.

'Sorry, Bill,' Tom said, taking the plan from him and disappearing out the door.

'Didn't you know I was always after your body?' Holly told Billy with a mischievous wink.

*   *   *

Two weeks together was all they had and for that brief time Holly tried hard not to think about the future. Life was all about living in the present. Tom's next trip was to be his last assignment; he was going to South America to film a piece on the lives of young children who made their living scavenging on landfill sites. The subject matter promised to be as harrowing as he'd encountered in Haiti, and Holly worried how this new assignment would affect Tom. She wondered if he would be in any fit state to deal with the news that she would have to break to him when he returned. Part of her was looking for more excuses to put off her confession, but she knew that one day soon she was going to have to tell him about the moondial.

It had taken the full fortnight to get Tom looking like his old self, but the hollow anxiety etched around his beautiful green eyes had gradually

216

filled out after copious amounts of rest, relaxation and home cooking, even including Holly's burnt offerings.

'I'm glad your hair's growing back.' Holly was watching Tom run his fingers through his damp, freshly washed hair. It was the early hours of the morning and the taxi was already on its way to pick him up. Holly lay back on the bed watching him pack up the last few things that had actually made it out of his suitcase.

'You do realize that the studio is going to make me get it cut again as soon as I get back from South America,' warned Tom. 'While we were in Haiti, they tried to bribe the crew into cutting it while I was asleep.'

'So why didn't they?'

'I put in a higher bid. You'll spot a rather large payment at the duty-free shop on our credit-card bill.'

'Well, I hope the crew will be looking after you on this trip too.'

'They will, we'll look after each other, don't you worry.'

Tom sat down on the bed to put his socks on and Holly crawled up behind him and wrapped her arms around him.

'But I do worry,' Holly said, kissing the top of Tom's head.

Tom pulled Holly around so that she was sitting on his knee. 'I'm going to miss you.'

'You'll be back soon enough. It's not for ever.' As Holly wrapped her arms around his neck and felt her heart beating against his chest, she could also feel it ache. She reminded herself that the decision she was about to take was as much for him as it was for both of them and she tried desperately not to think of the one thing, the one person that made that decision so heartbreaking.

'We could just stay here,' Tom suggested, pulling Holly onto the bed and kissing her slowly and sensuously.

'Don't,' moaned Holly. 'I'll never let you go if you say that.'

'I love you, Hol.'

'I love you too,' Holly croaked, holding back the tears.

'The taxi will be here soon but, oh, how I wish we had more time,' Tom said, peeling himself from her and reluctantly getting up off the bed.

'We will have more time. One day soon we'll have the rest of our lives to spend together,' promised Holly, squeezing her eyes shut against the vision of Libby's beautiful green eyes staring back at her.

She lay where Tom had left her, watching him in silence as he quickly dressed and finished off his packing. A solemn knock on the door announced the arrival of the taxi. Tom leaned over and kissed the top of her head.

'By the way . . .' Tom said, kissing Holly gently on the lips.

'What?' she asked, looking up into his green eyes.

'Your breath stinks.' Tom smiled his beautiful mischievous smile.

'Well, you've got a bogie hanging from your nose,' countered Holly.

'And with those loving words of endearment, I'll leave you in peace. Go back to sleep.'

Holly wrapped her arms around Tom and held

onto him tightly. There was another knock at the door, firmer this time, but Tom didn't pull away, it was Holly who had to let him go.

The all too familiar sense of loneliness settled around her even before she heard the front door slam and the taxi pull away.

*   *   *

Holly had made little to no progress on Mrs Bronson's sculpture while Tom had been at home but she couldn't just blame her husband. She knew she had been deliberately prevaricating. The figure of the baby she was about to create would be based on Libby's image, not Mrs Bronson's son, whose photographs were now lost at the back of a drawer somewhere. She was torn between wanting to create an image of Libby and the fear of seeing her daughter's beautiful, trusting face looking back at her. But Libby wasn't the only reason she was prevaricating. Holly had been uneasy about the concept of the sculpture long before her embryonic maternal instincts had been crushed by the moondial and its rules. She couldn't start work in earnest until her belief in the design was firmly established. She needed a second opinion.

'I just don't know what it is that's missing,' Holly said, staring at the sculpture. She had been constructing the figure of the mother and child from chicken wire and steel poles drilled into the marble base and it was a true reflection of the scaled-down version Mrs Bronson had signed off.

'The base is absolutely beautiful.' Jocelyn was standing shoulder to shoulder with Holly at the far end of the studio, as far back from the sculpture as they could get. The biting October wind outside was making the withered branches of nearby trees scratch forlornly at the windows.

'Which means you don't like the top half,' Holly answered flatly.

'Now I can hardly make a fair assessment on a twisted pile of chicken wire,' scolded Jocelyn. She turned her attention to the scaled-down version and went over to trace her fingers along the figures of the mother and then the baby. 'It is beautiful and I know you're going to do justice to the full-size version. Is this Libby?'

Holly nodded, unable to trust herself to speak without her voice cracking with emotion.

'She's beautiful.'

'And I'm a terrible mother,' Holly added, voicing her guilt.

'You have no choice, we both know that.'

'I know. I just don't know how I can live without her. I know I've been given a chance to save my life and it's wonderful that I ever got to meet her at all, but it breaks my heart.'

'So this sculpture, then,' Jocelyn said, deliberately changing the subject. 'It's meant to represent the generations, each child becoming the mother of the next?'

'Yes,' Holly said with a sigh. 'What I'm trying to do with the base is show the link from one generation to the next—and believe me, I was tempted to slip in a broken link in there somewhere.'

'To reflect your relationship with your own mother, by any chance?' Jocelyn asked, knowing enough of Holly's past to understand why she had struggled with this aspect of the sculpture.

220

'The only foundation my mother laid for me was a foundation of doubt.'

'Libby has shown you how to be a mother and for that reason she'll always be a blessing in your life, even if she can't share it with you.'

'I know. That's why it's more important than ever to get this right. I'm the first to admit that I didn't put my heart into it at first, but now it's about the only thing in this whole mess that I still have complete control over. I just can't shake this feeling that something doesn't work. It's the pose that's wrong, I think.'

'Well, explain it to me. How does it make you feel?'

Holly concentrated on the scaled-down sculpture. She walked around it, following the spiral at the base, the vague images of the figures and then the upper section where the mother continued the spiral upwards. 'The linked figures don't just represent the connections between mother and child, they also show how each generation forms the base for the next. The spiral adds the dynamics to the piece. There's always a corner to turn, venturing into the unknown.' Holly paused and laughed. 'Quite ironic, as it turns out, don't you think?'

'Not everyone has the chance to see what lies ahead,' Jocelyn added, always the defender of the moondial.

'Anyway, the mother and baby represent the present generation.'

Jocelyn tapped her chin, deep in thought. 'So why is the mother holding the baby and looking down? Is that because it's in the present?'

Holly stopped still. She walked quickly around

the sculpture again. Then she rushed over to Jocelyn and gave her a big hug. 'You clever thing! That's it, that's why it wasn't working.' Holly released Jocelyn just as quickly and rushed over to her workbench to grab her sketch pad.

Scribbling away, she explained to Jocelyn what she was doing. 'I paid too much attention to Mrs Bronson's need to be centre of attention, so much so that I didn't follow the concept all the way through.'

'I'm still not following you,' Jocelyn said.

'The base is a perfect representation of the concept, the spiral, the links, one generation providing the foundation for the next. The top half, though, the mother and child, that was only my naive interpretation of the relationship between the two. The mother is turned in a way that continues the spiral but the way she's holding the baby, it's all wrong. Protective yes, but she's holding it like it's a possession. She needs to be holding the baby up, supporting it on its journey into the future, carrying on the theme of one generation being the foundation for the next.'

'Can you change the design now? Hasn't Mrs Bronson already signed it off?' warned Jocelyn.

'To hell with Mrs Bronson. It's my work and I struggled with this piece from the very beginning. I haven't been able to fully connect with it because I knew something wasn't quite right. I put a part of me in every piece I create, but with this sculpture I'm putting in a big piece of my heart and all of my soul. Now I know what's wrong, I have to change it.'

Jocelyn looked at Holly and smiled. 'It's been a while since I've seen that twinkle in your eye.'

Holly smiled back at Jocelyn. She was right.

222

For the last few months, Holly had seen each day as a battle with her emotions and working on the sculpture was a challenge. A piece of the jigsaw had now fallen into place and Holly was eager to demolish the chicken wire structure and start again from a new perspective.

Jocelyn told Holly that she would leave her to it, but she hovered by the door of the studio, reluctant to say goodbye.

'Is there something else?' asked Holly, aware that her friend still had something on her mind.

'It's a full moon tonight,' Jocelyn replied with an anxious smile.

'I know, and don't worry, it's still under wraps.'

'You won't use it again?'

'Not yet, at least. Perhaps one day, I don't know. I'm scared what the future now holds for me,' confessed Holly.

'It holds you and Tom,' Jocelyn assured her. 'You're doing the right thing.'

Jocelyn eventually left, believing, as did Holly, that her resolve was strong enough to resist the pull of the moondial and that she didn't need Jocelyn's help.

Left to her own devices, Holly threw herself back into her work. But if she had hoped that the new surge of creativity would help distract her, she couldn't have been more wrong. She had sketches of Libby's face scattered all over the studio and they all looked out to her, calling for her attention. She knew there was still a chance that the future hadn't been rewritten yet. She hadn't actually acted upon her decision not to conceive Libby. Her next appointment for the contraceptive injection wasn't until the following month. That would surely trigger the changes that would erase Libby from the future, but right now, as the full moon crept ever closer, Holly sensed that she was still travelling the same path.

She looked around her, her eyes moving from one image of her daughter to another. Then she looked at the new sketches she had drawn of the mother holding up her child. Her body tingled with excitement as she remembered what Jocelyn had said about her reflection being stronger in the moonlight. Tonight might just be the one and only chance she would have to hold Libby.

Holly was almost buzzing with anticipation and for the first time since the moondial had entered her life she was actually looking forward to seeing the moon's perfectly formed and hopefully benevolent face.

*   *   *

The cloudless sky had warmed the day with weak autumn sunshine but the moon that replaced it held no warmth of its own and a halo around its edges promised an early frost. The trees in the orchard rattled in the desolate wind, shedding leaves in grief for the lost summer, and the white dustsheet fluttered like a ghost as Holly uncovered the moondial.

The dial practically glowed in the moonlight and the brass claws of the dial reached out beseechingly, ready to grasp the glass orb that Holly held in her trembling hand. As she dropped the orb into place and waited for the shower of moonbeams to consume her, Holly focused on the orchard. It had been three months since she had last used the dial when it had taken her to a cold January night. If the dial continued to open a window eighteen months into the future, then the autumn landscape would be transformed into spring and the orchard would be the first sign of hope that the future she had seen still remained intact and that her seven-month-old daughter would be there waiting for her. If the orchard showed her something else, Holly knew she was opening a window to a world she wasn't prepared to see yet.

'Please don't take her from me, not yet. You can't be that cruel,' she whispered as she was forced to close her eyes against the shards of moonlight that spun across the surface of the dial and the world beyond.

As the dancing light faded, Holly blinked her eyes, desperate for that first glimpse of her new surroundings. The rambling chaos of her garden had been replaced by clean, manicured landscaping, but Holly held her breath as she looked beyond the garden towards the orchard. The apple blossom was only just starting to peek through the darkness but it was enough to give her hope.

Holly opened the back door with ease, her determination to see her daughter giving her the strength of presence she had struggled with in her earlier visits. The house was in complete darkness as Holly crept stealthily through the kitchen and into the hall, eager to reach Libby. It was only when she realized the house was completely still that she forced herself to stop and catch her breath and her thoughts. The occupants were either in bed or not there at all and a knot of fear caught Holly by surprise. She couldn't face going upstairs until she was sure Libby hadn't already been written out of her future. She took a breath, building up the courage to go into the living room, where she would find enough evidence to confirm whether or not her meddling had already taken her daughter from her.

In the eerie darkness of the room, Holly picked out some familiar silhouettes, the sofas, the TV stand, the fireplace and even the outline of the China cat on the shelf. She knew it was smiling at her smugly even though she couldn't see its face. Holly wondered how the cat could still be there when she had already smashed it, but she wasn't about to be distracted from her desperate search for confirmation that Libby was safe. Stepping deeper into the darkness, Holly accidently kicked something that rattled and rolled across the floor. She picked it up and smiled at the baby rattle in her hand. 'Thank you,' she whispered.

Before she left to search out Libby, Holly's curiosity got the better of her and she crept over to the shelf to peer at the China cat sitting proudly in front of her. In the dim light it looked in pristine condition but as she let her finger follow the curve of its body, she felt a telltale ridge at its neck. The shattered pieces of the cat which she had left to gather dust behind the sofa had at some point been retrieved and glued back together.

Holly took the stairs two at a time. She might now know that Libby still existed but she wasn't yet sure whether or not she was at home. Tom could be away somewhere with Libby, staying over with his parents perhaps. The gatehouse had only two bedrooms and Holly ignored the first door to the master bedroom with only a faint tug at her heart to see Tom. Holly knew if he was there she couldn't give him comfort, and she didn't think she could

226

bear to see any more of his pain. Besides, she didn't need to, she told herself. She was going to make sure that Tom would never suffer her loss.

The door to the second room was slightly ajar and there was the faint glow of a nightlight coming from the room. Holly knew in her heart that Libby was in there and she had to take a moment to compose herself before entering the room. Her body shook with raw emotion and anticipation, her heart hammering in her chest. She had used the dial with a single purpose in mind but as she paused at the doorway, her courage failed her and she fought the urge to turn and run. Holly had to face her daughter and she wasn't about to make it easy on herself. She had to tell Libby that she was sorry for what she was being forced to do, to choose who should live and who would never be born.

The room she entered was no longer a spare room full of junk. It was a beautiful nursery and Holly felt as if she was walking into a wonderland. It was decorated precisely as she would have liked it, in soft pastel tones but with a modern twist. The walls were painted in a delicate pale yellow but the accessories picked up deeper, contrasting colours and there was a beautiful fairytale tapestry hanging from one wall.

An ornate white cot was positioned against the far wall and a colourful mobile dangled above Libby, who was snoring softly beneath it. Holly leaned over and just breathed in her baby smell. Her racing heart slowed and warmth radiated through her chest and then spread across her entire body, relieving some of the tension in her muscles. She took in every detail of her baby's features, features she had tried so hard to burn into her memory since her last visit. The baby's face was heart-shaped with those perfectly chubby cheeks Holly remembered. Her rosebud lips were ruby red against her iridescent skin and her hair was a halo of soft, blonde curls.

As she reached out to stroke the sleeping baby's cheek with a trembling finger, Libby's eyes fluttered open and Holly gasped. 'Hello, sweetheart, did I wake you?' she soothed.

Joy was replaced by pure panic as Libby's lips trembled and Holly thought she was about to wail. She hadn't considered the possibility that the baby might actually be frightened of her. Holly's maternal instincts were fragile and she didn't think she could comfort a crying baby, not even Libby.

Fortunately Holly wasn't put to the test as the anxiety in Libby's face softened and the look of fear was replaced by a smile. Libby rolled onto her tummy and started pulling herself up towards Holly. 'Wow, you've grown,' gasped Holly in amazement, although her confidence was still dented and she wasn't at all sure what to do next.

Libby was by this time kneeling up against the bars of the cot, but then she leaned back to pick up a ragdoll that had been lying next to her. She looked up expectantly at Holly, waiting to be picked up. 'Mmm, nnn,' she babbled loudly and excitedly.

Still in a panic and now worried that Libby might wake Tom, Holly turned to the window and tugged desperately at the blinds. As moonlight seeped through the yawning window, the task became easier until at last, the bright face of the moon was revealed, surrounded by a million twinkling stars. Libby was still babbling impatiently behind her. 'Well, the plan's going well so far,' Holly whispered, her voice trembling. She was relieved to see the moonbeams lighting up the nursery and desperately hoped that the reflection of light from the moon would give her the strength of presence to do what she had failed to do in her previous visits.

She turned back to Libby and took a long, deep breath. The anticipation growing inside her was almost too much to bear. She had longed to hold Libby, to the point of obsession, and this could be the moment that dream came true, to feel Libby in her arms for the first and the last time.

When Holly reached out towards Libby, the baby lifted her arms towards her mother, her hands clasping and unclasping in excitement. Holly felt the softness of Libby's pyjamas, felt the warmth of her body as she carefully placed her hands beneath her baby's arms. Holly paused, preparing herself for the joy of lifting her up or the frustration of lifting nothing but despair. Libby looked up expectantly into Holly's eyes and the fragile connection that had formed between them took on a new strength that Holly believed could never be broken, should never be broken. As Holly's heart lifted, so did Libby, straight into her mother's arms.

'Oh my sweet, sweet, Libby,' cried Holly, holding her against her thundering heart. She kissed the top of Libby's head, her cheeks, her nose, her neck. Libby wriggled with excitement and grabbed at Holly's hair. 'Mmmm, mmm,' she said, hitting Holly in the face with her ragdoll.

'What is that?' asked Holly, trying to pull the soft toy from Libby's grasp but Libby held on tight and grumbled disapprovingly at her mother.

'OK, you keep hold of it,' apologized Holly. She could feel the full moon looking over her shoulder and she sensed it smiling down at her. In this moment at least, Holly was thankful that the moondial had given her this gift. She wished it could last forever.

Holly was only barely aware that she had been rocking Libby from side to side and as Libby yawned, she rested her head softly on Holly's shoulder. Slowly and gently, Libby was falling back to sleep and her eyes started to flicker whilst her fingers played rhythmically with the folds of her ragdoll. It was a strange toy, thought Holly. It had a soft ball head with a floppy hat and a square piece of soft cloth hanging down from its neck to form the doll's body. It had probably once been cream but now looked a worn shade of grey.

Holly continued rocking Libby long after she had fallen asleep. This was going to be the last time she held her daughter and, although she had thought about what she had to say to her, when the moment came, Holly struggled to find the words. There really was only one thing that she wanted to say.

'I love you, Libby,' Holly told her daughter, leaning down to place her lips on Libby's sweaty forehead. She didn't want to speak again and was tempted to leave her lips hovering on Libby's skin, silencing the confession that burned in her heart, but she had to speak the words if only to punish herself.

'I'm sorry,' she started as a sob escaped. 'I never realized before just how much I could love you, and I wish we had more time together. I wish I could get to be your mum properly. I wish life was fair. You don't know how hard this decision is for me.' Holly bit her lip to stifle the sobs that were painfully caught in her throat. 'I wanted to be a good mum, but I'm not. I'm sorry, Libby, I'm so sorry. You deserve a better mum than me, but I have to do this. For me, for your daddy.'

Her arms were starting to ache but Holly was determined to hold on to Libby for as long as she could. It was only when a muffled sob came from the room next door that Holly's thoughts were drawn away from her sleeping daughter. The sound of Tom's voice in the next room was too much to ignore and Holly's heart wrenched as she reluctantly returned Libby to her cot. She knew that she needed to see Tom to remind herself why she was willing to erase Libby from this world. Holly stroked Libby's face one last time. 'I will always, always love you,' she promised as she finally let the tears flow down her cheeks. Libby sighed and softly snored in blissful ignorance.

Tom's room was in complete darkness and it took a while for Holly's eyes to adjust to the light. She could hear Tom before she could see him. He was moaning and calling out her name, writhing between sheets that rustled in the darkness like dead leaves tumbling across a graveyard. In a fit of rage, Tom threw back the duvet and sat up in bed. Holly could just about make out his silhouette as he sat on the side of the bed, leaning over with his head in his hands.

'Holly,' he whispered, reaching over to switch on the bedside lamp.

The yellow light revealed a room that felt alien to her, a room that bore little resemblance to the bedroom she had left earlier to go in search of the full moon. The only part of the room that seemed to have escaped the chaos was Holly's dressing table, which, with the exception of a thick layer of

231

dust, looked identical to the one she knew.

It wasn't the room which drew Holly's attention but Tom. He had picked up a notepad from his bedside table and was now furiously writing. Holly crept over to sit next to him on the bed and her whole body shuddered as she realized that Tom was writing her a letter.

My beautiful Holly,
I can't bear this any more. I miss you so much
but I need to know why this is happening. I
need to know why you didn't stay with me. Why
couldn't you hold on? You didn't even get to
hold Libby. If you had just held her, just once,
you wouldn't have left. You wouldn't have given
up on us.

Tom paused, his pen pushing down into the pages of his notebook. The pen seemed to tremble under the pressure of his repressed fury. Holly was shocked. She had never seen him consumed by so much anger, especially not directed at her. Holly watched, frozen in fear as he began to write again.

It's my fault. I was the one who wanted kids, not
you. You didn't want to be a mum and I pushed
you into it. I didn't believe you when you said you
couldn't do it. I forced you into it and it killed
you, I killed you.

Tom's whole body was shaking now. The sobs that escaped him were gut-wrenching and Holly stood up to leave. She knew she couldn't reach him, she couldn't tell him it was going to be all right, but she couldn't stay either and witness the anger and frustration that was eating away at him, anger that he was now directing at himself. It was too much to bear, but even as Holly took a step back, she couldn't take her eyes from the notepad which was slowly revealing the depths of Tom's despair.

I thought I had it all planned. I thought I could be the perfect family man, take on a job that I loathe just so we could all be together, and look what happened. I've lost everything. I sit in front of the camera and the suit feels like a straitjacket—and so it should, because I don't know who I am any more. I put on this damned mask at work and then I come back here and I put on another mask.

Why can't I go back right now and change everything? I miss you so much, Holly! I just miss you so damned much it hurts and I can't live with the pain.

When Tom stopped writing, he looked so lost. Holly couldn't run away. Tom needed her and, whether he could sense her or not, she had to try. She stepped towards him again, determined to kneel down next to him and hold him in her arms. She needed to tell him it was going to be all right, whether he could hear her or not, whether he could feel her or not.

As she was about to step towards him, she heard Libby begin to cry, demanding attention. Holly was turning towards the nursery when she heard Tom call out Libby's name behind her, telling her he was coming. He stood up and as Holly remained frozen to the spot, Tom walked right through her.

Holly gasped in surprise, as did Tom. 'Holly?' he asked, as he too stood in shocked paralysis. But

233

then Libby's cries, now growing in intensity, shook him out of his trance and he stumbled out of the room.

Holly's body was shaking uncontrollably. At the moment that Tom had walked through her, she had felt his raw pain, his rage and his desperation. Holly feared for Tom and for Libby too. She didn't know how Tom could survive such pain. Taking deep breaths, Holly did her best to calm the worst of her tremors. Beyond the thump of her heart pounding against her ears, beyond the baby's cries, which were slowly subsiding, Holly heard another sound. The ticking of a clock as it counted down the last moments of her vision.

Holly moved fast, following Tom's trail and arriving in the nursery to see him standing with his back to her, looking out of the window and comforting Libby as she nestled against his neck. He may be an emotional wreck, thought Holly, but he's still a good dad.

'Daddy's here,' he was telling Libby in the softest, gentlest whisper. The rage that had consumed him had been spent and there was nothing left. His voice sounded devoid of strength, even of life. 'I just can't do this,' he said.

Holly could see Tom's gaunt face reflected in the window. He was looking up to the heavens but then his gaze fell to a point right in front of him, a point on the windowpane where Holly's face, lit up by moonbeams, was reflected against the darkness of the night. Their eyes locked and Holly watched Tom's eyes open in shock.

As the dancing moonbeams washed away her surroundings, Holly sensed rather than saw Tom turn towards her, and then he was gone and Libby

234

was lost to her forever.

11

It took Holly days to recover from her vision. She hadn't just seen Tom in abject misery, she had actually felt his pain as he had walked through her. Her body ached with his grief every time she thought about that moment. She could easily have spent the following week in bed, but she wouldn't rest, she daren't allow herself too much time to think. Fortunately, there was too much work to do anyway.

When Holly turned up for work at the teashop, Jocelyn was shocked to hear that she had used the moondial. She was eager for Holly to tell her all about it but, given that they were in a public place, Holly was spared any in-depth discussion and relayed only the basic facts. She wasn't quite ready to talk about it, there was simply too much to take in. In one short hour, Holly had had both the most exhilarating and the most harrowing experiences of her entire life. Holding Libby made her heart leap every time she thought about it, but then there was the memory of Tom. Thankfully Jocelyn didn't push her, but when the weekend arrived and they met up for Sunday brunch Jocelyn was more than ready for a full and frank discussion and was quick to ask the question that Holly knew had been eating away at her.

'You haven't changed your mind, have you?' Jocelyn asked. She wore a frown on her face that revealed a maze of weary wrinkles as she stirred

235

her cup of tea, looking deep into its swirling depths as if the cup would give the answer to her question and not Holly. They were sitting in Holly's kitchen, surrounded by the soothing smell of freshly made muffins which Jocelyn had brought with her.

Holly rubbed the back of her neck, still shaking off that Sunday-morning doziness. Sunday was the one day in the week she allowed herself to sleep in, getting up just in time to get dressed and brew the first pot of tea ready for Jocelyn's arrival. Despite the lie-in Holly was as tired as she had been all week. She had been sleeping fitfully ever since her date with the moondial.

'No, I haven't changed my mind,' Holly assured her.

'It's just that when you talk about Libby you don't sound like you're ready to give her up.'

Holly sighed. 'I think if I'd stayed in the nursery and hadn't seen Tom, then I might feel differently. You're right, I don't feel ready to give her up, but I have to remember what else I saw in my vision and I know what I have to do. I didn't simply see Tom being torn apart by grief, I actually felt his suffering too. I can't put him through that. I don't have a choice, I have to give Libby up. I know that.'

'Have you made your appointment at the doctor's yet?' Jocelyn asked.

'Yes, it's in a couple of weeks,' Holly told her. 'I was half expecting to be told you'd already made it for me.'

Jocelyn made a poor attempt at a smile. 'I know how the moondial works, that's all. I'm afraid it won't make it easy for you to avoid conceiving Libby.'

'I'll have the injection, I promise. And after that,

236

there will be no more Libby. No more chances to see her, to watch her grow. Oh, I wish you could have seen her, Jocelyn. She had already grown so much. She could sit up by herself and she was babbling, I think she could be talking soon.' Holly was stumbling over her words, her voice catching with emotion and then she froze as she realized what she had said. Jocelyn reached over the table and squeezed Holly's hand.

'Afterwards . . .' continued Holly, still struggling to find her words. 'After Libby's gone, do you think that will be it? Is Libby the only price I have to pay? Do you think I'll be able to have other children?' Holly had pushed the question to one side for too long, she wasn't sure how long she could carry on without knowing the answer.

Jocelyn still had hold of her hand and squeezed it fiercely. 'I wish I could answer that for you, but I can't. At least, I can't be certain,' Jocelyn replied reluctantly.

'Not certain, but you do have an idea?' pushed Holly.

Jocelyn paused, unsure how to or even whether to continue. 'If my theory's right about universal balance then I hate to say it but you were only ever destined to have one child.'

'So I'll never become a mother. Tom will never be a father, not if he stays with me, anyway,' Holly said flatly. 'So much for perfect order in the world. Is it too much to ask for there to be a future where the three of us could be together? Me, Tom and Libby, a proper family.'

'I said there has to be balance, not that it has to be fair. It's not fair. It's not fair at all, but please don't take my word for it. It's only a theory. When

237

the time is right, you need to use the moondial again, if only once more. Just to find out the answer for yourself.'

Holly shook her head. 'I don't want to even think about that. I hate that I have to live my life based on what the moondial shows me. I'm absolutely terrified when I think what might be in store for me once I've given up Libby just to save my own wretched life.'

Holly was now losing the feeling in her hand as Jocelyn's grip didn't loosen. 'Please don't take any chances,' Jocelyn told her firmly.

Holly felt the tears trickle down her face before she could stop them, each teardrop invariably following the path of the first no matter how much she wiped at her wet cheeks.

* * *

Life carried on as normal, or at least as normal as life was for Holly these days. She carried on helping out at the teashop but spent most of her time in the studio working on Mrs Bronson's sculpture. She now had her own experience of being a mother to draw upon and it was her beautiful and precious Libby who inspired her work. Although she wouldn't be allowed to give life to her daughter, she could at least immortalize her in the sculpture.

Holly had started wearing the same fleece she'd had on when she had held Libby in her arms, just so she could feel that connection with her daughter as she worked. She had convinced herself that she could still detect the faintest of baby smells where Libby had rested her head on her shoulder and fallen asleep.

238

It had taken many sleepless nights to come to terms with the promise she'd made to Jocelyn and to herself. She had to keep reminding herself that she wasn't just sacrificing her daughter's life for her own, but for Tom's too. Yet the bond that had been created between herself and Libby haunted her and seemed to be growing as the child form in the sculpture took shape. And as the bond grew, so did the guilt. At her lowest moments, in the middle of the night when she felt alone and isolated, Holly would pull no punches and accuse herself of destroying her daughter's life for the sake of her own. She would ask herself how she could hold that precious baby in her arms, knowing she was no better than a murderer. The only escape from those self-destructive thoughts came as sunlight filtered through the bedroom window to chase away the night's shadows. Holly would recall Tom's gaunt eyes staring back at her in the reflection of the window and she would strengthen her resolve. She would do what she had to do, but Libby would always be a part of Holly no matter what.

* * *

'Are you missing me?' Tom asked. 'Because I'm missing you.'

'Yes, I'm missing you, of course I'm missing you, although I think perhaps Billy is missing you more,' teased Holly.

'Has he started on the garden yet?' asked Tom.

'No, of course not. It may be lovely and sunny where you are, but here it's bitterly cold and the ground is frozen. Billy says he can't start work until the spring. By which point, you'll be home and can

239

help him yourself.'

'Hmm, speaking of coming home . . .' Tom said and Holly didn't like the tone of his voice. She knew he was about to impart bad news.

'You're not going to be home by spring?' she gasped.

Tom laughed. 'No, God, it's not that bad. It's just that the assignment here might last a little longer than we expected.'

'How long?' demanded Holly. Tom was due home early in December and Holly had already started counting down the days.

'Only a couple of weeks, but I will be home before Christmas. Although you might have to make do with a present from the duty-free shop,' confessed Tom.

Holly wanted to be angry with him but she remembered what her bereaved husband had said about hating the anchorman job he was going to take up in the New Year. She wasn't about to push Tom to give up so quickly the work he obviously enjoyed.

'It had better be a very big bottle, then,' Holly told him. 'And I mean perfume, not alcohol.'

'You're amazing, do you know that?'

Holly frowned, she knew she didn't deserve his praise. 'So why the delay? What's happening?' she asked.

'Some of the guys in the crew are freelancers and they've upped sticks to follow a breaking news story, there's been a mining disaster in the south and they're going to cover the rescue operation. It means more work for the poor fools who've been left here, so it's going to take a bit longer than we planned.'

'Don't you wish you could have gone with them?' asked Holly. She had wanted to have a long talk with Tom about his career when he came home, but there was no harm planting some ideas now. The moondial might have its rules but if she couldn't keep Libby she would be damned if it would stop her helping Tom make some important decisions about his career.

'I'm tied into my contract, even if it is a secondment. I can't go upsetting the studio now, can I?' Tom said submissively. It was clear that he had no idea where Holly was about to lead him.

'I can't believe they can look at what you've been doing these last six months and still think it's a good idea to stick you in a studio for the rest of your life.'

Tom laughed nervously. 'You make it sound like I'm being sent to prison.'

'Isn't that how you see it? I know you think you're doing your duty and that it's the right thing for us, but I can see how much you love what you're doing now, even when it's difficult, heartbreaking stuff you have to deal with. And I know you won't say it, so I'll say it for you. You were never meant to be an anchorman and I know you're going to hate it.'

'Whoa, Holly, where did all of that come from?' interrupted Tom. He sounded shocked, but Holly noted that he hadn't disagreed.

'I know we dismissed the idea of you being a freelancer. You felt obliged to take the anchorman job, but things change. Thanks to Sam at the gallery, I'm struggling to produce enough work to meet the demand—there's our security. I know being away from home is tough on both of us, but what if you did six months on assignments and six

241

months writing and researching? Doesn't that sound better than sticking you in a suit and painting a smile on your face in front of the camera every day?'

When Holly finally paused for breath, Tom was silent on the other end of the phone. 'I'm sorry,' she added. 'It's just I've been thinking about it and I wasn't going to say anything until you were home, but there you go, I can't keep my big mouth shut.'

'Or stop making plans,' Tom said quietly.

'Am I interfering?' moaned Holly. 'I'm sorry.'

'No, don't be sorry, don't ever be sorry. I love you because you know me inside and out.'

'Like you wouldn't believe,' whispered Holly.

'I know you're right. The new job does feel like it would be trying to fit a square peg in a round hole, but what about our other plans? What about a family?'

Holly had known this question would be coming. 'I want you to be happy, Tom,' she said. 'If we're destined to have children, we will have children.' Holly was quite proud of the answer she gave. It was as truthful as she could make it.

*   *   *

'It's no big deal,' argued Holly.

'No big deal? No big deal?' whispered Jocelyn with a suppressed screech that was just loud enough for one of the teashop regulars to raise his head from his steaming bowl of soup and give them a curious look.

'The nurse said they're waiting for more supplies. She's going to ring me next week when they get more in.' Holly was trying to sound casual about the

242

whole thing but even she had been a bit spooked when the nurse had told her that she couldn't have her contraceptive injection. Jocelyn's fears had been well placed. Holly's path was still leading her to an early grave, the battle with the moondial wasn't over yet.

'I can't believe you're not taking this seriously. Isn't there somewhere else you can go?' demanded Jocelyn.

'If it comes to it, I can go to a health centre I used to go to in London. I'll even go private if needs be. And worse-case scenario, I simply won't have sex with Tom,' Holly said chirpily.

Someone coughed and Holly and Jocelyn turned to face the old gent who had been slurping his soup. Holly blushed. So did the gent. 'Sorry to disturb,' he said. 'Could I have another bread roll?'

'Here,' Jocelyn told him gruffly, thumping down a bread roll onto the counter. She was in no mood to be pestered by customers.

The old gent returned happily to his seat and Jocelyn returned her attention to Holly. 'I told you it wouldn't be easy. Holly, you need to be so careful.'

'I know, honestly, Jocelyn, I do. I know that it's one thing living with the guilt of choosing not to have Libby but if I did accidentally conceive her I don't know what I would do. I couldn't have a termination, not when I've held her in my arms. So where would that leave me? I know how important this is,' Holly assured her.

Jocelyn nodded.

'There is one other problem this mess with my injection has created,' admitted Holly, biting her lip nervously.

Jocelyn looked at Holly and the puzzled look on her face deepened but then the penny dropped as did her mouth. 'It's the full moon tomorrow and you could still see Libby.'

Holly nodded and she bit down hard on her lip, the pain just enough to ward off the tears. 'I don't know what I'll do,' she said, pre-empting the question that she knew was on the tip of Jocelyn's tongue. 'I think I need you to persuade me not to visit Libby again. If I see her one more time, I swear I might not be able to go through with any of this.'

'Then you have two choices. Either you give the glass orb to me or you let me stay over with you. Or both.'

Holly suddenly realized that she couldn't hand over the moondial box. She was so overwhelmed by a sense of possessiveness that it surprised her. 'Technically that was three choices,' Holly argued.

Jocelyn raised an eyebrow in response but said nothing.

'I haven't got a guest bed.'

'We can share your bed,' Jocelyn told her. Her steely resolve wasn't going to be broken.

From behind them, the old gent coughed again. Holly blushed again.

'What do you want this time?' Jocelyn barked.

'I just wanted to pay the bill,' he replied meekly, handing Jocelyn the right money.

Jocelyn looked down at the coins. 'What, no tip?'

Jocelyn was in no mood to be argued with. She got her tip and she got her invitation to stay over with Holly on the night of the full moon.

* * *

244

It was late November and the night of the full moon was bitterly cold, the sky crystal clear. There wasn't a single cloud to offer any relief from the moon's gaze and Holly felt its brooding eye bearing down on her even though she had every curtain and every blind in the house closed tightly and the lights blazing in every room to push away the moonbeams. Nevertheless, Holly sensed the moon reaching out towards her, its light seeping through every crack and crevice in her self-made fortress.

Jocelyn had come prepared for their moondial vigil with shopping bags brimming with girlie night essentials. They spent a pleasant enough evening munching through popcorn, chocolates and watching a DVD. Jocelyn had picked a comedy rather than a tear-jerker. Laughter was the best medicine, she told Holly.

It was past midnight by the time they decided to call it a night and head upstairs to bed. It felt strange having Jocelyn stay over and Holly was a little self-conscious as she got into bed next to her. She had been alone for most of her life and with Tom away she had adapted easily to sleeping on her own again. She couldn't help feeling like Jocelyn was her prison guard even though she had been the one to request that she be kept under house arrest.

'Do you mind if I keep the light on?' Holly asked. She was looking towards the picture window and imagined the tendrils of moonlight reaching through the glass, through the folds of the curtain, stretching out towards her.

'Of course not. Do you think you're ready for sleep?' Jocelyn asked.

Holly shrugged her shoulders. 'I'll give it a try, but I can already feel the moondial pulling me,' confessed Holly. 'My legs are all jittery so I apologize now if I kick you in the night.'

'I've told you before, I've got the skin of a rhino. I doubt I'd feel a thing with one of your scrawny legs,' Jocelyn told her. She leaned over and tucked the duvet around Holly's shoulders. 'It'll be morning before you know it.'

'I hope you're right. I so want all of this to be over, but I'm scared it never will,' sighed Holly. The two women were now lying side by side, both staring up at the ceiling. 'How am I going to live with the guilt?'

'You just do,' replied Jocelyn. She turned to look at Holly. 'But don't compare what you're doing to what I did. Yes, I feel guilty, because I deserve to. I may not have held the gun to Harry's head and pulled the trigger but I did load the bullets. I set out to make him suffer to the point that he couldn't take any more.'

'But you were only turning the tables on him. If it had been the other way around, would Harry have felt guilty?'

'He was what he was, but he never consciously set out to end my life. I, on the other hand, knew what I was doing and where it was leading. But it's different for you. You can't torture yourself by believing you're taking Libby's life. You're taking the potential of life, yes, but not life. It's not the same,' insisted Jocelyn.

'It feels the same. Having seen Libby, having held her. It feels the same.'

The two women were quiet for a while and Holly began to think Jocelyn was drifting off to sleep but the old lady seemed determined to keep Holly's mind occupied.

246

'Paul's invited me over for Christmas,' Jocelyn chirped. 'I'll leave a few days before Christmas day and stay for about a week. It's still early days, but I think we've turned a corner.'

'You're staying over at his house? That's a big step.'

Jocelyn smiled sadly. 'I'll be staying in a nearby hotel. Like I said, early days.'

Holly felt anger welling up inside her but she held her tongue. She knew very little about Paul and, in some ways, he had been a victim of the moondial too, but then she looked at Jocelyn. If only he knew what he had been missing all these years by shutting her out of his life.

'So tell me about this Mrs Bronson,' Jocelyn continued when the silence that fell between them cried out to be filled. 'Are you ready to hand over your sculpture yet?'

'I've practically finished. I don't have a kiln here so I've had to send the top section off to be fired. It'll be back in a couple of days and then I've just got to put the two pieces back together and with a few finishing touches it'll be ready.'

'I can't wait to see it. I know it's going to be beautiful.'

'I'm quite pleased with it, if I do say so myself. There's a part of me in that sculpture that I never thought could have existed.'

'So do you think Mrs Bronson will like it even though it's not what she's expecting?'

Holly shrugged beneath the bedclothes, 'I couldn't care less. I like it and I'm proud of it.'

'You don't want to give it up, do you?'

Holly smiled ruefully. How did this woman get to know her so well? she thought. 'No, I don't,

247

especially not to Mrs Bronson. Now if it was someone like you, then I would.'

Jocelyn laughed to hide her embarrassment. 'I couldn't fit the scaled version in my little flat, let alone the proper one.'

'You know what I mean,' Holly said softly.

Jocelyn blushed. 'Yes, I do. Now get some sleep, it's getting late.'

'Yes, Jocelyn,' replied Holly like a dutiful child.

*   *   *

Holly did manage to fall asleep but the moondial wasn't ready to release its grip on her mind so easily. As she slept, Holly had one of the most vivid dreams she had ever had. She dreamt she was running through a field and the colours around her were dazzling. The blue azure of the sky and the vivid green of the grass beneath her feet were so bright that it made her eyes sting. She felt light and joyful as she ran because she was running towards a little girl with beautiful green eyes and soft blonde curls framing her face. It was Libby, but Libby as a young girl of perhaps four or five. Holly swept her up in her arms and then twirled her around in sweeping circles. She could hear Libby's squeals of delight as the sun shone brightly in the sky above. But the yellow orb grew paler and colder and the blue sky fell away to blackness. In heart-numbing seconds, the sun transformed into the moon and it glared down at Holly as the reassuring weight of Libby disappeared into the ether. Holly lost her balance and her arms flailed in front of her. She fell to the ground with a thump. She woke up with a gasp as the shock of the fall echoed through her body.

It was just after six in the morning and as Holly slipped out of bed, careful not to wake the softly snoring Jocelyn, she knew that sunrise was still over an hour away. Her need to see Libby consumed her and she could think of nothing else as she crept downstairs in her pyjamas. She picked up the wooden box and stumbled through the pitch blackness towards the moondial, ignoring the overgrowth that scratched and tore at her bare feet.

The orb clattered in the box as Holly grabbed hold of it in a trembling panic and slipped it into the brass claws. She could barely see the orb as it rattled into place but she waited impatiently for the first spark of life from its core. As she waited, her breath rasped against the cold and she felt like she was drowning in the darkness that surrounded her.

As the blackness of night closed in around her, she looked up desperately into the sky and it was only then that she realized why it was so dark. The full moon hadn't waited for her, it had floated away and taken Libby along with it.

Every muscle in Holly's body shuddered with tormented agony and she lashed out at the moondial, hitting her fists against its uncompromising surface. As she sobbed, she barely acknowledged the light from the kitchen window that reached out towards her or the blanket that was wrapped around her shoulders along with a firm pair of arms.

'It's all right,' soothed Jocelyn. 'Come in the house. It's going to be all right.'

'It's won,' sobbed Holly. 'The moondial has won.'

'I wish that was true, but it isn't over yet, Holly. You've got the hardest battles yet to face,' replied

Jocelyn. 'Now come away.'

As Holly let Jocelyn lead her back into the house, she thought about what Jocelyn had said. For the first time Holly realized that the battle she was facing wasn't with the moondial at all, it was a battle with herself. There were still choices to be made.

*   *   *

Two weeks before Christmas, Holly invited Mrs Bronson to the gatehouse to officially accept the piece before she set about organizing the tricky process of arranging for its installation at her client's country pile. She had known it would be a difficult meeting so she had also asked Sam Peterson to be there. She had a feeling that she would need someone to help fight her corner.

She had been right to worry about the visit, not least because she hadn't been in the best of moods to deal with the spoilt excuse for a mother anyway. Holly had other things on her mind. Her dream of Libby had plagued her since the night of the full moon and she deeply regretted giving up her last chance to see her daughter.

Holly's determination to save her own life had been seriously dented ever since and the thought of taking that last step to erase Libby from the future forever made her feel sick to the stomach. So much so that she hadn't made another appointment for her contraceptive injection. She needed to believe she was still there in the future somewhere, at least for a little while longer. She knew she was taking a huge risk, but she couldn't help herself. She wanted to keep that connection open, especially now she

250

was about to give up the only physical connection to her, the sculpture she had made in her image. Time was running out and by the end of the month Libby would be gone and so would the sculpture. Her only comfort lay in the thought of Tom coming home and of course the secret hope that Mrs Bronson would refuse to take the sculpture.

*　　*　　*

'She said what?' Tom gasped. Holly might not be able to see his face but she knew he was staring open-mouthed at the telephone.

'Mrs Bronson said she's going to sue me for every penny I've got,' Holly replied glumly. She was sitting at the kitchen table with a large glass of red wine which had already been refilled once. It was late afternoon but the weak December sunshine had already been beaten away by the descending winter's night.

'Can she do that? What does the contract say?'

'Oh, she could sue me,' Holly assured him. 'Sam's taken her back to the train station and I'm hoping he's going to use his best negotiating skills to get me out of this mess.'

'So what exactly could she do?'

'Well, worst case is that I'd have to return all the money she's paid me so far and then there would be some compensation too. How much, I don't know.'

'So if that's worst case, what other options are there?' Tom asked hopefully.

'I suppose she might demand that I remake the sculpture the way I was supposed to,' mumbled Holly like a naughty schoolchild. That was one option she really didn't want to contemplate. She

251

would refuse point-blank to create something that she didn't believe in. And she certainly wasn't going to dismantle the work she'd already completed, not when it included an image of Libby.

Tom laughed. 'I can't believe she didn't fall in love with it. Fair enough, it wasn't what she was expecting. You did change the concept, but it was only for the better. What was there not to like?'

Holly had sent Tom a photograph of the finished article and although she knew he was biased, there really was no reason why any normal person wouldn't love it. 'I don't think she liked the focus being on the child and not the mother. Besides, she said the mother looked like she had a man's body.'

Tom laughed even harder, despite the bad news. 'So she wasn't impressed with my muscles then?'

'Your muscles?' demanded Holly. 'I think you'll find those muscles belonged to Billy.' Holly was trying to see the funny side of it but it was going to be a hard blow to their finances. 'What am I going to do, Tom?'

'I promise, I'll work night and day to pay off the horrible woman. I don't want you to compromise your art, not for the likes of Mrs Bronson.'

'Sam's going to have to work wonders to get me out of this one. But anyway, we are where we are.'

'Well, that kind of makes my news a little easier,' stumbled Tom.

'What do you mean?' Holly heard a distant alarm bell ringing in her ears, although she was finding it hard to concentrate with the fuzziness that had been poured out of the wine bottle straight into her head.

'You know how you told me to start thinking about the direction of my career and look at other

252

options. Well, I'm not quite ready to throw away the chance of a secure job just yet, not when there's so much uncertainty and a lot of competition for the work out there, but . . .'

'But?' asked Holly. It was clear that the doubts Holly had planted about his career had not merely taken root but had sprouted up and taken on a life of their own.

'I've been putting some pressure on the studio. I'm not due to start my new job until mid January and these special assignments have gone down really well, it would be mad to give up now.'

'When and where?' demanded Holly, knowing he was talking about one more assignment.

Holly listened in silence as Tom explained that the new assignment was a documentary on the after-effects of landslides that had devastated China. The Chinese government had given the studio a small window of opportunity to enter the country. The problem was, that particular window was slap bang over Christmas for three weeks. Tom would be going directly from one location to the other with a few days stopover in Singapore.

'So Christmas is cancelled,' Holly said sulkily.

'No, not exactly. You could fly out to Singapore and we could still spend Christmas together, but I'd have to leave for China on Boxing Day. I know it sucks. But this really is a massive opportunity and great money, which helps you out of your little problem.'

'I suppose,' Holly said, not sure how this change of plan would affect not only Christmas but the rest of their lives and the deal she had to complete with the moondial.

'It might even be nice spending Christmas away.

253

I can get you a flight first thing on the twenty-first of December,' Tom told her.

Holly put down her glass of wine and wished she had stayed clear headed. The twenty-first was already a symbolic date in Holly's mind because it was the date of the next full moon. The full moon had opened the door to a world that held her daughter captive and it felt to Holly like the next time the moon crept out of the shadows that door to Libby would be firmly closed and her daughter would be lost forever.

The date, it seemed, was now going to be symbolic in other ways too. Holly had thought it was her doctor's appointment that would mark the point where her path into the future would change. Tom had changed all that by unwittingly giving her a choice. To join him in Singapore and risk becoming pregnant or staying at home and securing her place in the future at the expense of her daughter.

'Holly?' Tom asked, when the silence stretched between them.

'Sorry, I was just thinking,' she explained. 'It might be difficult getting away.'

'What? Why would it be?' stammered Tom with a mixture of surprise and disappointment.

'I have commitments too. Jocelyn is going away and I'll be working in the teashop.' Holly hated herself as the words came out of her mouth. She didn't want to take this decision. She wasn't ready.

'You're right, it's a stupid, selfish idea,' began Tom.

'Don't say that. It's not a stupid idea. I love that you've got another chance to do the job you love and you're not being selfish, I am.'

254

'But it's so far to travel and we'll only be together for a few days.'

'No, it's not too far to travel. Tom, I'd travel across the world to see you, I'd even travel across time.'

'So you'll come?'

Before Holly had a chance to reply, there was a knock at the door.

'That'll be Sam, I'd better go,' Holly told him.

'Tell me you'll come,' begged Tom.

'I'll come,' replied Holly nervously.

Jocelyn's warnings had been well founded. Holly sensed the path that secured her future was becoming irrevocably tangled with Libby's.

* * *

Sam looked weary and ready for a drink when he sat down at the kitchen table. 'Is there one of them for me?' he asked pointing to Holly's half-empty wine glass.

Holly put a glass in front of him and filled it up before asking him how it had gone with Mrs Bronson.

'Well, she's not a happy bunny,' he said.

Holly winced apologetically. 'Was she very angry?'

Sam raised an eyebrow. 'I won't even repeat the things she said about you.'

'And?' Holly asked impatiently. She didn't care about Mrs Bronson or even the money she would undoubtedly lose on the deal. She did care about her sculpture and was desperate to know what was going to happen to it.

'I think I've just about persuaded her to take the

255

artwork,' offered Sam, although he was obviously holding something back.

Holly's heart sank. 'Really?' she said miserably.

Sam almost choked on the mouthful of wine he'd just swigged. 'Holly! I don't believe you sometimes. I know you didn't want to take on the commission in the first place, but you've practically gone out of your way to make sure Mrs Bronson wouldn't get the sculpture. So, let me put your mind at rest, she doesn't want the grotesque piece of rubbish you've created. Her words, not mine. And in truth she didn't use the word rubbish, I was being polite.'

'Well, I'm not making another one for her,' insisted Holly. She was swirling her own glass of wine but wouldn't take a sip. There was too much to think about, although Mrs Bronson barely made the list.

'Don't worry, I wouldn't do that to you. She will accept the scaled-down version, if you finish off the finer detail on it and have it ready before Christmas.'

'Well done, you!' beamed Holly.

'Don't go celebrating just yet. You didn't deliver the commission so you have to repay her the advance and there'd be no charge for the delivered sculpture. Essentially, she'd be getting your work for free. You get to keep your full-size sculpture, but you will need to sign an agreement that you won't sell it on. You can either keep it or donate it. It might go down well with the pagans around here—they can perform all their weird fertility dances around it.'

'Country life really does scare you, doesn't it?' Holly observed.

'Not at all,' lied Sam. 'In fact, your local taxi

driver has just told me that there's a big freeze on its way and if I get snowed in here, he'll be happy to brave the blizzards and show me the sights. I'd bet he could name every sheep.'

'You're a bad man, Sam Peterson,' scolded Holly, but she couldn't help laughing at him.

'Yes, I am a bad man,' confirmed Sam and this time he looked a little guilty. He picked up his briefcase and took out a beautifully wrapped gift. 'A peace offering,' he explained.

Holly looked at him quizzically. 'What on earth do you need to make amends for? I'm the one who's caused all the trouble.' As she spoke, she carefully unwrapped the present. At first glance, it looked like a very soft, cream-coloured piece of cloth but as it unravelled itself, Holly's heart jumped into her throat. It was a comforter doll. It was the exact same comforter doll that Libby had been clinging to in her last vision and Holly held it to her cheek just as she'd seen her daughter doing.

Sam coughed nervously, taken aback by Holly's reaction. 'Apparently, the mother carries it around with her for a while to transfer her smell onto the cloth and then the baby feels safe sleeping with it when you're not there,' explained Sam. He smiled gently at Holly. 'Last time you were at the gallery, I thought I was a little harsh with you, mocking your brave attempt at motherhood. Of course you'll make a good mother, I can see it in the sculpture. You're going to surprise everyone, especially yourself.'

Holly tried to smile but she only managed to make her lower lip tremble. 'We'll see,' Holly told him.

12

'I know you don't want to hear this right now, but this might just be a blessing in disguise,' Jocelyn told Holly.

Holly had felt shell-shocked after Tom's phone call and although she still managed to function on a daily basis, she had stopped working at the teashop. She had told Jocelyn that she needed to spend more time finishing off the scaled-down sculpture for Mrs Bronson, but that was only partially true. She knew that Jocelyn would make her face the future head on and Holly wasn't ready to do that yet. It was only when Jocelyn came over for Sunday brunch and with less than a week to go before Holly was due to fly out to meet Tom that she had to stop living in denial.

She had always known that the day would come when she would have to turn from the path that held Libby in the future. Holly recognized what a dangerous game she had been playing by not going back to the doctors for her contraceptive injection and she accepted that she was being stubborn. She wouldn't be rushed into making the decision that essentially put an end to her daughter's life before it had even begun. But now it would seem that Tom's new travel arrangements were doing just that. There were two clear options: to go to Singapore and risk becoming pregnant, or to stay at home and ensure that Libby's life was erased once and for always. Holly knew which option Jocelyn was suggesting she should take. The old woman had once told her that the choices she had to make would be hers and hers alone, but it was becoming clear that she wouldn't rest until Holly chose correctly.

'You're right,' agreed Holly. 'I don't want to hear that right now.' She was sitting at the kitchen table with her fleece wrapped tightly around her. As she glanced out of the window, the snow was falling and the garden looked as if it had been covered in a white, sterile blanket. The moondial was unrecognizable, hidden beneath a thick layer of snow that had neutralized any power it might have held over Holly.

'You're supposed to be flying out on Tuesday,' Jocelyn continued, undeterred by Holly's reluctance to talk about the future. 'You still haven't been to the doctors, so you and I both know that if you go to Singapore you can bet your life that you'll get pregnant. And yes, the pun was intended.'

Holly carried on staring out of the window, almost as if she hadn't heard. 'Three times. I got to see Libby three times and I only got to hold her once.' Tears were brimming over her eyes. 'I can't believe I spent my entire life never even contemplating having children and now I'd give anything to hold Libby again, just once.'

'Even if you can't have other children, maybe there'll be other opportunities,' soothed Jocelyn. 'Tom's witnessed a lot of poverty and misery in his travels. There are so many children out there who need help, maybe you could adopt?'

Holly shook her head. 'I don't think that's really an option. Tom wouldn't be happy with saving only one child, he'd want to save an entire village.'

Holly had already tentatively gauged Tom's views on adopting and he'd told her as much.

259

Although his view was influenced by the immovable conviction that they would have a child of their own one day, Holly was fairly certain he wouldn't change his position on that issue.

'Besides,' continued Holly, 'that's not the point. I'm not even thinking about other children. I'm only thinking about Libby. It's Libby I see every time I close my eyes. It's Libby my arms are aching to hold. It's Libby's smell I try to recollect. I've lost her forever and what makes it worse is that Tom didn't even get to meet her. I know what we've sacrificed but he never will, not really. I'm not just betraying Libby, in some ways I'm betraying Tom too. How will our relationship survive that?'

'You love each other and you'll survive this,' Jocelyn insisted.

Holly gave Jocelyn a smile that broke her heart and her will. 'Yes, I will. For my sins, I will survive this.'

'You're not going to Singapore? Please, Holly, say it out loud. Tell me you're not going to Singapore,' pleaded Jocelyn.

'I'm not going to Singapore,' repeated Holly as a pitiful sob escaped. 'Oh, Jocelyn, I've lost her forever and I don't think I'll ever be able to forgive myself.' Her chest heaved as she felt the crushing weight of her decision bearing down on her, but she wouldn't let herself cry, she didn't think she deserved the relief it might bring.

Jocelyn squeezed back her own tears. 'Then I'm staying in the village for Christmas. You're not doing this on your own.'

'But what about Paul? He's expecting you,' Holly asked.

'He's invited me over on Christmas morning—

so far that's all. I would be spending the rest of my time stuck in a hotel room, waiting and hoping that he'll invite me over again. I didn't want to tell anyone because I was too ashamed. It's my punishment, I suppose.'

'Punishment? Paul should be proud to have you as his mum and if I ever meet him I swear to God I'm going to punch him!'

Jocelyn laughed despite herself, but the sadness never left her eyes. 'I don't deserve to be his mum and not just because of what I did to Harry. I was ready to take my own life and leave him to the whim of a wicked and violent father. The moondial gave me my life but not my son. I wasn't completely forgiven.'

'You're a good person, Jocelyn, and I won't hear another word said about you needing forgiveness. But if he can't recognize that then his loss is my gain.'

'Well, I'm staying here and that's final. I'll phone Paul and cancel. I think he'll probably be relieved.'

'I suppose I have a phone call to make myself,' sighed Holly. 'But I'm not going to tell Tom until the last minute. I couldn't face days of arguments and intensive persuasion. Christmas has been ruined enough as it is.'

'But at least there will be other Christmases,' Jocelyn reminded her.

Holly smiled bravely at Jocelyn but her face was a mask, a mask she was going to have to learn to live with for a very long time. Libby had sown seeds of maternal love in Holly's heart and Holly had amazed herself at how quickly she had nurtured and protected that love. With practised expertise, Holly closed her mind to all her hopes and dreams

261

of motherhood, and in time the seeds planted by her daughter would wither and die.

* * *

Holly worked on Mrs Bronson's sculpture with a sense of urgency. However, the urgency had nothing to do with the deadline or the imminent relief of finally getting Mrs Bronson out of her hair. It was Holly's guilt at failing her daughter that made her eager to finish the project. When the artwork was dispatched the day before Holly was supposed to fly out to Singapore, she closed up the studio. The full-size sculpture was still in there, draped in a dust sheet to hide the faces of the generations of mothers that Holly sensed were watching and judging her.

The emotional wall that Holly had built was enough to get her through the day, but the night before her flight Holly couldn't sleep. She wandered the empty house wrapped in a blanket trying to find a corner where she could curl up in a ball and hope that time would never find her. Every time she thought about the phone call she would have to make to Tom, her stomach lurched. First thing in the morning she would tell him that she wasn't setting off as planned.

With dawn still a long way off, Holly wandered into the spare room which was never to become Libby's room. It was cold and bare and empty, just like her heart, thought Holly. She squeezed herself into a gap between a pile of boxes and a suitcase, the suitcase that she should have packed ready for her travels. She brought her knees up to her chest and gripped them tightly, giving herself something to cling onto and stop her arms feeling so painfully empty.

The suitcase she was leaning against felt cold as she rested her head on it. It was made of dark brown leather but it triggered a memory of a bright tartan suitcase from Holly's childhood, the one her mum had hidden behind the sofa on the day she left. She had watched in horror as her mum stood waiting at the front door for her husband to come home. She had barred his entry at first, telling him she wanted a divorce, yelling at him that she would take him for everything, screaming at him to say goodbye to their daughter and to get out of their lives. Holly had been terrified at the thought of being left alone with her mum so she had a spark of hope when her dad started to argue back. He pushed his way into the house and told his wife that he was going nowhere, if she wanted a divorce, she would be the one to leave. Holly hadn't thought for a minute that they were fighting over her, it was the house he was refusing to give up. Holly had held her breath as the two stood facing each other in seething silence, neither parent moving, not until a smile started to creep across her mum's face. With a beaming smile, her mum had shrugged her shoulders and left her husband standing open-mouthed as she retrieved the suitcase from the living room and then headed for the door. She didn't look at Holly as she walked past her. There was no apology, no guilt to be wrestled with as she left the house, she didn't even say goodbye. Her parting words were to Holly's dad. 'At last I get my life back,' she had snarled at him.

Pushing away the memory, another one immediately took its place. Holly pictured herself standing in the room she was in now, holding Libby. She had told her daughter that she loved her, she had told her that she was sorry, but did that really make her a better mother? Holly wondered. Rather than answer the question, she tightened her grip on her knees until she could barely breathe. She looked beyond the space where she had stood and towards the window where the blind was open wide and the darkness that seeped through the glass seeped into her heart. She recalled Tom's gaunt reflection looking back at her, she remembered how he'd said he couldn't cope any more. It was this thought that Holly held onto, the only thought that stopped her picking up the suitcase and packing it up for a trip to Singapore and Tom. It was Tom's face that Holly held in her mind as she found something she had thought was beyond her grasp. Sleep.

* * *

It was only the insistent chirping of the phone that raised Holly from her slumber. She unravelled herself from her blanket and her body screamed out in pain as she forced her tensed limbs to straighten up so that she could reach the phone in her bedroom.

'Hello?' she asked. Her voice was raspy and her throat felt constricted.

'Holly? Is that you?' It was Tom.

Holly's stomach churned and a wave of nausea washed over her as she thought of the decision she was about to take.

'Yes, it's me,' she croaked. She glanced at the clock. It was half past six and Holly was expected to

264

leave for the airport in less than an hour.

'Are you OK? You sound awful. Are you ill? Are you going to be able to make the flight?' There was a growing panic in Tom's voice.

This was it, thought Holly. This was the moment she had to say goodbye to Libby. 'Tom!' Her voice was a sob now. 'I can't do this.'

'Christ, Holly, what's wrong? You're scaring me.'

Holly struggled to pull herself up straight. She took a deep breath. She had to remind herself that she was doing this for Tom.

'I can't come,' she told him. Her voice was still raspy but it was emotionless.

Holly had intended to tell Tom that it was the weather keeping her home. The country had been brought to a virtual standstill by the latest big freeze and Tom wouldn't take too much convincing that it made travelling for Holly impossible even if a thaw was already under way. But as soon as she answered the phone, Tom had assumed she was ill, so Holly just went along with the idea. The guilt of the lie barely registered with Holly; there were far greater burdens on her conscience. She was sacrificing her child's life for the sake of her own and she could almost hear the scratching of a distant pen on paper as the future was being rewritten.

Tom knew nothing of her betrayal and was only concerned about Holly's health. He hid his disappointment well and made her promise to stay in bed and to get help from Jocelyn if she needed anything. There would be other Christmases together, he told her, and Holly couldn't help but wonder about those future Christmases she had secured for herself. Would they still be together?

She had expected some sense of relief when

she put down the phone. The decision that had plagued her for months had at last been taken. But she felt no relief. She wouldn't allow herself to feel anything except the emptiness that engulfed her.

*　　　*　　　*

Jocelyn had been a little more difficult to convince that Holly was all right. They both knew it was the full moon that night and Jocelyn took a lot of persuading that she didn't need to keep vigil over her. Holly insisted the deed was done, her life was taking a new route and Jocelyn could breathe a sigh of relief. Jocelyn's sigh was more of resignation than relief, but she did eventually agree to leave Holly alone to find her feet on her new path.

And Holly knew exactly where her new path was leading her, at least where it would lead her that night. With the full moon rising above her, she headed straight for the moondial. She needed to put some final ghosts to rest and if she witnessed a future which realized her worst fears then that was surely her punishment for the decision she had just taken.

*　　　*　　　*

The night was cold and blustery. The scattering of bulbous clouds that glowed in the moon's backlighting scurried across the sky to reveal stars that twinkled with a sense of inferiority; it was the bold brightness of the moon which would dominate the night. Holly's heart was hammering in her chest as she stood in front of the moondial. She asked herself what she was doing, playing with her future

266

again, and it was her heartbeat that reminded her that she owed her life to the moondial. Now she needed to know what kind of life it was granting her. Was the sacrifice ever going to be worth it?

The thaw had exposed a ragged mess of long grass and weeds which poked through the icy carpet of snow. The temperature might have nudged above freezing but it was still bitterly cold and Holly zipped her winter coat right up to her chin. She held the glass orb in her hand but she still hadn't built up the courage to place it in the dial's expectant claws. She let it roll around her gloved hand and it glinted playfully in the moonlight. Holly felt entranced as it turned this way and that in her palm, but then the orb veered off course and dropped, falling where destiny dictated that it belonged, in the centre of the dial.

It happened so quickly that Holly was unprepared for the shower of moonbeams that followed. Her eyes were wide with fear as the claws snapped greedily around the glowing orb and she was temporarily blinded. She had to rely on her other senses to reveal her new surroundings and the first thing she noticed was the temperature. The night had suddenly become warm and the smell of summer filled the air. Holly didn't move other than to take off her gloves and unzip her coat. She reached out and touched the surface of the moondial. It felt warm and familiar.

As Holly blinked, her eyes slowly opening, she took in more of the garden. It was lit by a mixture of light from the full moon which had accompanied her on her journey into the unknown and the artificial light streaming from the kitchen. Holly's heart was still beating wildly and now it skipped a

267

beat at the thought of what lay ahead. For a brief moment, Holly considered staying where she was. She had been to hell and back in the last few months and she could be walking into another nightmare. She hadn't really wanted to see her future again, especially her rewritten future, but she had just given up her daughter and she needed to know what she had made that fateful sacrifice for. She realized that she needed to know more than ever if she was destined to become a mother beyond the realms of the moondial visions.

Holly stepped slowly across the lawn towards the back door. Her neck was tingling with sweat so she let her coat slip off onto the ground and carried on walking. She concentrated on her breathing to try to calm herself as she opened the back door and stepped into her future. Her breath caught in her throat as she looked around her. The kitchen was brimming with hope in the form of baby bottles and a highchair standing erect at the kitchen table.

With trembling hands, Holly scanned the kitchen for a newspaper but had to make do with a gas bill. The date on the bill was June 2012. The moondial was still pulling Holly eighteen months into the future. Holly stood paralysed by her thoughts, staring at the date and then she looked across to the highchair. A thousand butterflies took flight in her stomach, each carrying with it a question. There was only one question that Holly grasped and demanded an answer to. She didn't want to know if there were other babies, she didn't need to know if she had survived childbirth even. She only needed to know if the child that used the highchair that she was staring at intently was Libby. Holly took a step towards the door to the hallway, ready to spring into a run but then the lights flickered and went out. The kitchen plunged into darkness and the hairs prickled on the back of her neck. Before her eyes had a chance to adjust, before she could pick out anything other than the soft moon glow seeping through the kitchen window, the lights came back on again. Holly shivered but she pushed away the sense of foreboding that had crawled out of the darkness. She concentrated instead on the spark of hope that was growing inside her.

As she entered the hall, she heard Tom's voice coming from the study. Holly hovered at the door, listening to him chatting away. It was a one-sided conversation and Tom was obviously on the phone. He sounded like her Tom, not the broken man she had seen in her other visions. He laughed and the sound lifted Holly's heart. Tom was talking about work, planning an interview with someone and he sounded happy and animated and alive. What Holly heard next made her heart swell with joy.

'Sorry, Pete, but I really have to go. I was just putting Libby to bed. She's ready for her bottle and she's not a lady to be kept waiting.'

The words barely registered as Holly turned on her heels and leapt up the stairs, two at a time. She intended to stop at the nursery door and peep cautiously into the room but she was moving so fast that she couldn't stop and was in the middle of the nursery before she knew it. The room was lit up by a single nightlight but it practically glowed.

'Hello, sweetheart,' Holly gasped between ragged breaths of excitement.

Libby was standing up in her cot, holding on tightly to the rails and to her comforter doll which was even grubbier than it had been the last time

Holly had seen it. Libby smiled and jiggled up and down, sharing Holly's excitement. She jiggled so much that she lost her balance and fell onto her bottom with a thump. Her lip trembled and she reached up her arms to Holly. 'Mama!' she said.

The tears were stinging Holly's eyes as she rushed to the window to lift the blind, letting just enough moonlight into the room to allow her to do what she had thought had been stolen from her forever. She reached over the side of the cot and picked up her daughter.

Holding Libby in her arms, Holly closed her eyes and let her other senses take over. She took a deep breath to calm herself, at the same time taking in Libby's smell, which was a heady mixture of soap, sweat and something else that was just Libby. She felt the solid weight of Libby in her arms, heavier, sturdier than she had been the last time Holly had held her. She was now nine months old and there were other changes too. Her blonde, unruly curls tickled Holly's nose. 'I've missed you,' she told Libby. 'You don't know how much I've longed to do this. I can't believe I'm here. I can't believe you're here.'

Holly hadn't even tried to think about what was happening or why. Perhaps the actions she had put in place hadn't changed the future yet, perhaps it was only at that moment in time when Libby was supposed to be conceived that everything would change. Holly shivered and pushed the thoughts to the back of her mind. She didn't want to think about that now. After the longest time, Holly opened her eyes and smiled at Libby. 'I love you and I don't ever want to let you go.'

Libby smiled back at her. 'Dada,' she said,

reaching towards the open door.

Holly turned and could hear Tom on his way upstairs. 'I have to put you down now,' Holly whispered, not sure if she could let go but knowing that she had to. If Holly was still holding Libby when Tom came into the room then it would be like two worlds colliding and Holly couldn't face that. She wanted everything to be perfect and calm and right.

As Tom came into the nursery, he was rolling a baby bottle in his hands. 'Bedtime, young lady,' he told Libby, who was standing up in her cot again, jiggling with excitement. He looked over at the open blind in puzzlement and refused outright to see Holly standing staring at him in front of the window. Holly's presence was nothing more than a handprint on water, wasn't that what the poem had said? Tom closed the blind and gave his full attention to Libby.

Holly watched the two of them intently. Tom looked well, in fact he looked his normal dishevelled self. Dishevelled in a good way and not just because he looked in good health, physically and mentally, but because he didn't look polished. He hadn't become an anchorman, Holly was sure of it.

Tom picked up Libby and gave her the feeding bottle and a big bear hug. He smiled as she dropped her ragdoll and took the bottle in both hands. As she started to drink, she never took her eyes off Tom.

Tom smiled at her. 'Hello gorgeous,' he said, covering the top of her head in kisses. Libby blinked excitedly as his hair tickled her face. 'Oh, Libby, I love you so much. More than I thought I could ever love anyone ever again, that's how much.'

Tom rocked Libby from side to side and Holly couldn't resist the urge to reach out to both of them. She stroked the top of Libby's head and then ran her fingers gently through Tom's hair, which was as long and unruly as it ever had been, comfortingly familiar. She felt him shiver.

'Your mum once told me that I should look to what I have now, not always search for more,' Tom whispered. 'I know I can't wish for the impossible. I have you, Lib, and right now that's enough.'

Libby stopped drinking and, taking her cue from her mother, grabbed hold of Tom's hair. As Libby pulled his head down, he rested his forehead on hers and frowned, closing his eyes tightly. 'Oh, but I still miss your mummy,' he whispered. 'I always will.'

In response, Libby wriggled in his arms and then burped.

'Whoa,' cried Tom. 'You've got smelly breath just like your mum!'

Tom laughed and Libby giggled too as he lay her down in her cot to finish her milk. They were still staring intently at each other. 'So what story would you like tonight?' he asked.

Libby tore her eyes from Tom and looked towards Holly. 'Mama,' she said.

'Oh, so you want a story about your mummy do you?' Tom asked. He sat down on a beanbag next to the cot and rested his head on the bars, watching his daughter with pure adoration. 'Well, where shall we begin? Once upon a time there was a beautiful young princess and her name was Holly. The wicked king and queen kept her locked up in a tower and told her she would never be loved.'

As Tom told the story of how his princess was saved by a dashing young prince, Holly crept closer to the cot and sat down opposite Tom. She too rested her head on the bars of the cot and became just as mesmerized by the story as Libby. Tom had tears in his eyes but he was smiling as he told Libby how the prince and princess captured a star to make their very own baby but they left a hole in the sky that needed to be filled and how the princess had to go to heaven to fill the gap in the sky where the star had been. Holly felt the tears sting her eyes but the tears froze like icicles on her cheeks as the light flickered again. The image of Tom and Libby flickered too and darkness skittered across her vision as if Holly were watching the scene on a broken television.

Tom and Libby seemed to notice the flickering too. Libby dropped her bottle and sat up. As she began to cry, her daughter lifted her arms to Holly and her fingers grasped desperately at the air. Holly's heart pounded in her chest at the sound of Libby's cries which became more fearful. Tom and Holly both stood up as the flickering became more darkness than light.

'Libby?' Tom gasped, leaning over to pick up and protect their baby but Holly never saw him reach her. Somewhere in the distance, above the sound of Libby's mournful screams and the hammering of Holly's heart, a clock ticked.

The soft warm glow of the night light transformed into a cold blue as the moon peered through the window and cast shadows towards Holly. As the sound of the ticking clock retreated it was replaced by a hollow silence that was only interrupted by her ragged breathing. This time

273

Holly did have time for her eyes to adjust. She was still in the same room but it was now empty, devoid of life. It was the spare room that Holly knew only too well. There was no trace of Libby at all, not even her sweet baby smell, nothing other than the sound of her cries that still echoed in Holly's mind.

Holly looked around in disbelief. If her time in the future was up then she should have returned as usual to a spot in front of the moondial. She trembled with a growing fear that she was still in the future. Looking through the window, she found no comfort. The trees weren't covered in snow but were swelling with summer leaf. The lifeless room contained the familiar mixture of bric-a-brac and boxes but there were more boxes, more mess and squashed next to the suitcase that she had slept against the night before was another suitcase. Tom's. There was no remaining doubt. This was a new vision of the future being revealed to her.

'No, no, no,' gasped Holly. 'This can't be happening. I'm not ready. Libby needs me. I didn't get a chance to say goodbye. I have to say goodbye.'

The tears that welled up in her eyes mercifully blurred her vision and softened the tortuous sight of time unravelling and of Libby's life being erased.

'I'm sorry, Libby, I'm so sorry!' she gasped, stepping backwards out of the room. When she was on the landing, she turned and fled through the darkness. As she stumbled down the stairs, the lights flickered again and she stumbled as she took the last step and fell onto her knees. The house switched from one version of the future and then back again, from a dark lifeless place to one full of light. In the room upstairs, Holly could hear Libby sobbing and Tom's voice trying to soothe her, but he sounded frightened himself. She heard Libby cry out, 'Mama,' and then silence fell as the darkness descended with such force that it knocked Holly's breath from her body.

She scrambled to her feet and the need to run away consumed her. She reached the kitchen but then forced herself to stop and take stock, forced herself to take a look at the life she had been given at the expense of Libby. The kitchen, like the rest of the house was in darkness and devoid of life. In the dimness, Holly could see that the room was clean and clutter free. It even smelt sterile. 'Sterile and empty, just like your life will be,' she told herself.

Pushing herself onwards, Holly ran across the garden and didn't stop until she stood staring down at the moondial. 'I've seen enough, take me home,' she demanded.

The moondial glinted menacingly in the moonlight but it had rules to follow and it took its time, counting down the minutes that marked the end of Holly's nightmare and the beginning of the rest of her life.

*   *   *

Holly's vision of the future had left her feeling empty and devoid of hope but as the moonbeams whipped around her, sending her crashing back to the present she was consumed with an anger of such force that it shook her to the core, anger directed at the moondial. 'No!' she screamed. 'Why are you doing this to me?'

Her words sounded like the howl of a trapped wild animal, only to be whisked away dismissively by the cruel wintery gusts that gathered a storm around her. Only her painful sobs were left to echo hopelessly into the night. Holly couldn't move from the dial because she was gripping onto it with such force and staring at it with such an intensity that should have turned the stone into dust. She wanted to inflict the kind of cruel devastation that the dial had wrought on her life.

'I know what I am. I know I'm my mother's daughter. I always knew I was going to fail Libby.' Holly was gasping between sentences, her voice now a hiss rather than a howl. 'I should have trusted my gut instincts and told Tom I wasn't going to have children right from the start. I don't deserve to have children.'

Another sob escaped but Holly held back the tears, she hadn't finished venting her anger at the moondial. 'I knew how selfish I was being. I knew I was ready to take Libby's life for my own. Why did you let me see her? Why did you let me hold her and love her? Why did you let me do all of that and then let me watch her life being erased in front of my eyes. Did you think you were proving something to me?'

Holly took a deep breath, ignoring the icy chill running through her body. She loosened her grip on the dial just long enough to hit its surface with her fists. 'You didn't have to show me how I'd fail so miserably, how I'd put myself before my daughter, just like my own mother did. You didn't have to show me. You didn't have to let me listen to Libby calling out to me. What you've given me was never a gift. You haven't saved my life at all. You've given me a way to keep my body alive but you've taken away my soul.'

The tremors that were coursing through her

body were fuelled by her anger but as the minutes slipped by, the heat of her anger couldn't compete with the bitter winter's night. Holly could feel the cold seeping into her bones but she didn't know what to do next. It was pointless ranting at the moondial. What Holly desperately needed was something to anchor her.

She felt herself drowning in the grief of losing Libby and with that grief, there was also the immense burden of guilt. Sacrificing Libby was Holly's choice and now she had lost her forever. But still Holly couldn't let go of the moondial. She was about to take her first step onto the path that had been laid before her, a path that had come at an unimaginably cruel price and the thought terrified her because she didn't think her sanity could stand it.

Closing her eyes tightly, Holly tried desperately to recall every detail of Libby's face, her smell, the sound of her voice, the feeling of her breath as she snuggled against Holly's neck. Amidst the blackness of the night that surrounded her, Holly clung to the warmth of Libby's memories and they sent shivers coursing up her spine. Focusing on just a handful of sacred moments she had shared with her daughter, Holly fought against the despair. She took a deep breath of ice cold air which gave her the shock to her system she needed to let go of the dial.

It was the early hours of the morning and sunrise was still a long way off. The garden was consumed by shadows cast from the warm light coming from the kitchen but it wasn't towards the kitchen that Holly headed. She stumbled and then ran towards her studio.

The studio lights hurt Holly's eyes as they blazed

into life. The photographs of the smiling faces that dangled from the studio ceiling danced like menacing clowns in a funhouse with the breeze from the open door spurring them on. Holly felt them mocking her, showing her a glimpse of happiness that had been lost to her forever. Frantically flicking switches, Holly turned down the lights until she had pushed the photographs back into the shadows.

Ignoring the smiling faces that watched her, Holly was drawn to the centre of the room, towards a shadowy figure. It was the mother and child sculpture draped in the dust sheet. Holly stepped guiltily towards it and pulled off the cover. The countless faces in the spiralling form looked skywards, towards the baby held aloft by its mother and Holly followed their gaze. She sank to her knees as the last remnant of strength that had brought her to the sculpture was ripped from her heart.

Holly knelt next to the statue, not able to take her eyes off the baby figure while she held onto the base like a lost child. She didn't know if her body could stand the physical pain of her grief. She couldn't imagine how she would be able to bear such pain for the rest of her life, and she knew it would be for the rest of her life. She only now realized that she would be carrying her burdens alone. Tom would face his own rollercoaster of emotions when she eventually explained it all to him, but he would never feel how she felt now. The burden of guilt rested with her and her alone. Holly wasn't sure that their relationship would survive the gulf that would inevitably come between them. Perhaps that was what had terrified her so much when she had stumbled through the empty house. Was it just children that would be missing from their lives or would it be each other?

These thoughts and so many more tumbled through Holly's mind and she longed for Tom to take her in his arms and tell her it was going to be all right. Holly was overwhelmed by a sense of loneliness that she hadn't felt since she was a child. There was a huge wrenching deep inside her chest and she could almost believe it was her heart physically breaking, smashing once and for all the dam she had built against her emotions. Her first sob came out as a wretched howl and the tears that followed came in an endless torrent. As the weak wintry light of dawn trickled through the studio skylights, and with her tears still flowing, Holly slipped into a fitful sleep. Much as she longed to see Libby again, her daughter was lost to her even in her dreams. Instead, Holly dreamt about time ticking away. A hundred clocks stared down at her, their spidery hands twisting and turning, clunking and clicking, spinning around and around.

*　　　*　　　*

Holly woke up to the pounding of rain on the studio roof, which matched the pounding of her own heart. She had an overwhelming sense of panic and she didn't know why. Searching for an answer, she looked up at the sculpture. The mother figure held the baby aloft, lifting it upwards towards its future life. Holly had been that mother for the briefest while and that moment had been frozen in time by her own artwork. But then Holly had chosen a different path and she had sacrificed the beautiful

279

baby girl who had smiled up at her and called her Mama.

Holly got to her feet and let her fingers follow the spiral of the sculpture upwards, expecting to see a crack appear where she had broken the chain that had linked one generation to the next. With sickening clarity, Holly realized she had made the wrong choice, and the wave of nausea was quickly followed by a tidal wave of guilt and regret. Right now she should be stepping off a plane in Singapore and meeting Tom and then, at some point in the near future, make a baby out of their love, a love that would last for generations to come. That was the decision she should have taken, that was the right path. She desperately wished she had her time again, wished she had the chance to make a different decision, but time had run out. Her pulse quickened as she realized just how much she loved Libby and how much she was willing to sacrifice. She was a good mother, but she had realized it too late.

Holly's body froze as her last thoughts rattled around in her head. She would only be getting off the plane now, the point in time where Libby would or wouldn't be conceived still lay in the future. She hadn't reached the point where the two paths diverged. Her vision had shown two flickering realities, but the future hadn't been rewritten yet, it couldn't have been. Holly's heart skipped a beat as she realized that there could still be time to put things right.

*   *   *

'You're going to do what?' It was Jocelyn's turn to

be shocked.

No sooner had Holly rushed into the house and started making desperate phone calls than Jocelyn arrived. She had come under the pretext that she had some supplies to drop off in preparation for their Christmas lunch, which was to be hosted by Holly but prepared by Jocelyn. In reality, she had been looking for an excuse to check on Holly and it was immediately clear to Jocelyn that her worries had been justified.

'I'm going to Singapore,' Holly replied firmly. She knew it was going to be tough explaining her decision to Jocelyn and she had hoped to put off telling her until all the arrangements were in place. Unfortunately, getting a last-minute flight out to Singapore just before Christmas or even tracking down Tom had proven fruitless so far, but Holly wasn't about to give up yet.

'I don't understand,' stumbled Jocelyn. The colour had completely drained from her face. 'You can't go. You can't take the risk of getting pregnant.'

'No, Joss, that's exactly why I have to go. I have to do it for Libby. I'm her mum and it's my job to protect her. Above all else, above the need to save my own life or to protect Tom, my job is to keep Libby safe. My daughter comes first, I know that now. It just took a long time for me to realize it.' Holly felt warmth flooding into her heart as she heard herself say the words out loud. 'I'm going to get pregnant and I'm going to give birth to Libby.'

Jocelyn had sunk into a chair and was looking at Holly open-mouthed. 'Do you really understand what you're saying, Holly? You're talking about dying. The moondial was meant to save you. The moondial was a gift which was meant to save your life, Holly. You can't give that up. You can't!' Jocelyn's voice was breaking.

'Yes, it's a gift, I see that now. It's not only given me the chance to experience being a mother, it's given me the opportunity to be the best mum I possibly could be and to prove that history isn't going to repeat itself. I can be a better mother than my mum was to me. She sacrificed nothing, absolutely nothing. I'm ready to sacrifice everything. It's what I want, more than anything. You have to help me.'

Jocelyn grabbed Holly's hand and started pleading with her. 'But you still don't know what the future holds. You saw an empty house, that means nothing.'

Holly smiled as if that would be enough to prove to Jocelyn that she hadn't completely lost her mind. 'You don't understand. It has nothing to do with what the future holds. I don't know what the future would hold for me and I don't care any more, I really don't. Libby is my daughter, my living, breathing daughter. Maybe not now, but I've seen her and I've held her. I know her sweet baby smell and I know every golden curl on her head. And I know I'd do anything to protect her. Anything, Jocelyn.'

Jocelyn shook her head. 'But it's too late. You'll never get there now, will you?'

'I honestly don't know, but I'm not giving up, not yet. You've said yourself how difficult it is to change paths. I was destined to have Libby and I have to believe it can still happen, that there's still time.'

The grief and despair had been lifted from

Holly the moment she had realized time hadn't completely run out. It was only now, as she saw the look of horror in Jocelyn's face, that she was reminded of the price that would be paid if she was to carry out her plan. It might be her own life she was sacrificing, but it wasn't only her life that would be affected. Tom, Jocelyn, Tom's parents, they would all be affected too. They would still have to suffer the devastation that Holly's death would bring to their lives, the sense of loss that Holly had glimpsed during her journeys into the future. Then she remembered the way she had felt a few hours earlier. There was no argument in Holly's mind. The pain her own death would cause was nothing compared to the pain of losing Libby, and she would do anything and everything she could to stop that from happening.

'Holly, listen to me,' Jocelyn leaned over, gripping Holly's hands painfully tight. 'Think about what you're doing, what you're doing to the people who love you. What about me? I don't want to lose you.' Tears were starting to trickle down her face.

Icy tentacles of fear crept into Holly's heart. 'If I can't save Libby then I'm lost anyway. If I survive and Libby doesn't, then my life is over too.'

*   *   *

The hours ticked by mercilessly and the hope that Holly had grasped earlier that morning was trickling through her fingers. She had optimistically packed her bags and got dressed and changed as Jocelyn kept vigil on the two phones they were using to track down a plane ticket. Holly had called in every favour, every connection she could think of and there were countless travel agents doing their best to find her a seat on the next flight. So far, all their efforts were fruitless.

She had still been unable to get through to Tom. She had left messages at the hotel where he was staying but he hadn't returned her calls. His colleagues at the studio in London were next to useless; although everyone made vague promises, they were all too busy in the run up to Christmas to help Holly get to Singapore.

Holly's ears were red and sore from having a phone glued to the side of her head for hours on end without reprieve. 'I won't give up, I have to put things right,' she kept telling Jocelyn. She even recovered the dust-covered broken pieces of the China cat from under the sofa and glued it back together again.

'Do you think I should call Billy and ask him to come around and look at moving the conservatory doors back to their intended position?' she asked Jocelyn desperately.

'You can't put everything right. Perhaps now is the time to start accepting that there are things you can't change.'

Holly shook her head, but as she looked out of the window, the light was already starting to fade along with her hope. They were sitting at the kitchen table, hugging steaming hot cups of tea. As Holly's mood dipped lower and lower, Jocelyn did her best to hide her relief.

'You tried your damnedest, Holly. I know it's going to be hard and you won't want to forgive yourself, but at least now you know you were prepared to give up everything for Libby.'

'I was so sure I had time,' Holly whispered. She

284

put down her cup and stood up, peering into the darkness outside, looking towards the moondial. 'I spent so much time fighting it, and now that I'm ready to give in, the damned thing has let me go.'

'You'll get through this. You'll find a new path.'

Holly stepped over to the kitchen door. She fought the urge to go out into the rain and shake the moondial into life again. Instead, she looked at the window pane in the door and watched the raindrops hit the glass and then trickle downwards. 'I was so sure I could get back to the old path, the one that led to Libby.' Holly's finger traced a single droplet as it slipped down the window, sliding neatly into the path of a raindrop that had fallen before. 'I'm sorry, Libby,' she whispered. A shiver ran up her spine and tingled down to her finger which was still touching the glass. Out of the darkness, another finger on the other side of the glass reached out and met her fingertip. Holly gasped but she didn't withdraw her finger. Instead she looked beyond the finger, to a hand, a strong hand that could hold onto Holly's and never let go. Beyond the hand was an arm, one of two that could wrap themselves around Holly and make her feel like she was safe from anything. Beyond the arms, Holly looked on in wonderment at the chest, the neck, and the face of the man she loved and it took Holly's breath away.

'Are you going to let me in?' cried Tom, shivering in the rain.

Holly opened the door and flung herself into his arms. She fought back the tears only long enough to cover Tom's face in kisses.

'Hey, you're leaking,' he said.

'No, I'm not leaking, I'm crying,' Holly replied

285

with a triumphant smile before leaning in and giving Tom a very long and deliciously sweet kiss.

'You've still got stinky breath,' he said with a wicked smile.

'Me? You're the one who smells like he hasn't been washed in a fortnight.'

'Well, what do you expect from someone who's spent the last two days trying to get home to his poor sick wife?' Tom demanded.

Holly held onto Tom and let the rain beat down on them. Tom was a little more eager to get into the house so he lifted her up in his arms and carried her inside. Holly looked over his shoulder at the moondial and for the first time she smiled at it.

'Well, it looks like I've got my early Christmas present,' Holly said, turning towards Jocelyn, but Jocelyn had gone.

'Do you think I should give her a lift home?' Tom asked.

Holly took a sad, sharp intake of breath. 'She'll be all right.'

Tom looked tired as he stood dripping and shivering in the middle of the kitchen, still holding Holly in his arms. 'So is there anything I can do for you?' he asked with a mischievous grin.

'Oh, I've got plans, don't you worry,' she said.

13

Christmas was perfect and Holly couldn't have asked for more. She spent the festive season surrounded by family—family being Tom, his parents, Jocelyn, and Jocelyn's extended family, including Lisa and her daughter Patti, who was home from university and relished the opportunity to pick Tom's brain.

Jocelyn put on a brave face, but Holly knew her heart was breaking. She made sure they had plenty of time together and insisted on walking Jocelyn home after Christmas dinner and accepted her invitation to come in for a quick cup of tea.

Holly had never actually been in Jocelyn's flat before and it surprised her how small and crowded it was. There were two armchairs pinched around a portable television, but Jocelyn and Holly chose to sit at the small bistro table which was obviously a cast-off from the teashop. The table was in front of the one and only window, and a host of winter pansies trembled outside in the breeze. Beyond the window box, there was a view of the church and Jocelyn's face matched the greyness of its stone facade. It was the first opportunity they had to speak about the future and for Holly to give Jocelyn an extra Christmas present. It was the journal and the wooden box containing the glass orb and deconstructed brass mechanism.

'I can't use it again,' explained Holly. 'I can't take any risks, not while I'm pregnant. Besides, I don't need to visit Libby, I have her with me every day.' Holly patted her perfectly flat stomach. 'I need you to look after these now because I don't want the moondial to fall into the wrong hands. Tom must never know about the dial and what it can do. It's cast its shadow for long enough.'

'If I'd known what you would end up doing, I'd have taken the box off you sooner.'

'I know this is hard for you, but I need you now more than ever,' Holly insisted. 'For the last eight months, my emotions have been in utter chaos and it wasn't just affecting me, it was affecting my relationship with Tom too. Everything was becoming so fraught, there was so much distance growing between us and I don't mean just the miles. Right now I feel so at peace with myself, with Tom, and it feels wonderful. The only pain I feel now is my heart bursting with all this love for my husband and my baby.' Holly's voice was cracking with emotion and she was desperate for Jocelyn to find her own peace.

Jocelyn's cup was trembling in her hand and she took a sip of tea before she could bring herself to speak. 'What's done is done. I'll look after these and I'll do whatever I can to help you and Tom and when the time comes, Libby too. I let you down, but I promise I won't let her down.'

'You didn't let me down, don't ever think that. You let me take my own decisions and choose my own path. That's a decision for my conscience, not yours, and it was the right decision, you won't ever convince me otherwise.' It was Holly's turn to start trembling and her voice shook.

Jocelyn would only nod politely and Holly sensed she would never agree, at least not until she saw Libby.

'I'm going to have everything planned out and ready for Libby's arrival and for Tom's future without me, but I'll need you to keep reminding Tom of my plans when I'm gone.' Holly was surprised at how easy the words fell off her tongue. She wasn't ready to die yet, but nine months was time enough to get everything prepared. 'Tom's job is the only fly in the ointment so far. He's still determined to take up the anchorman post and when he finds out I'm pregnant, it's going to make it even more difficult to persuade him to rethink his options. The studio is livid with him for bailing out at Singapore and they'll make his life a misery, as if it wasn't going to be bad enough already. I'm determined to convince him to go freelance. He's made some good contacts in the last year and he can use that to his advantage. I think his globetrotting days are over, but then he is about to be a dad so that's not necessarily a bad thing. There's a better career for him out there, all I have to do is point him in the right direction.'

Jocelyn reached out and cupped Holly's face in her hands. 'Take a breath, Holly. Like you said, there's enough time to plan.'

Holly smiled and a tear rolled down her cheek. 'I know. And I know I'm going to hurt people. I just want to soften the blow.'

'You can't, but I'll do what I can,' Jocelyn said, smiling weakly.

Holly frowned, unsure where her next thoughts were leading. 'Patti is a lovely girl and very sensible for her age. Do you think she could help? She would have finished her degree by the time Libby's born. Maybe she could help Tom, be his researcher or even look after Libby?'

Jocelyn raised an eyebrow. 'You're not looking for a replacement for you, are you?'

Holly laughed nervously. 'Good grief, no. I want Tom to be happy, but right now he's mine and I don't want to even contemplate him having another woman in his life, but . . .' Holly couldn't finish her sentence, she let the word hover in the air.

'But?' pushed Jocelyn.

Holly looked out of the window and her frown

289

deepened. 'When the time's right, tell him I want him to be happy. Tell him to let go.' She turned to face Jocelyn with a wicked smile. 'Just make sure that whoever she is, she's good but not better than me.'

'I don't think that's possible. You're pretty unique, Holly Corrigan.'

*   *   *

New Year's Eve was a bitter-sweet moment for Holly, but there was no time to brood on how unfair life was. Holly had enough and she was happy; happy because she had finally accepted the gift the moondial had given her. It had given her the chance to be a mother and to meet her daughter before she died. Without the moondial she would never have been given the chance to hold her daughter.

'Would now be a good time to tell you I think I'm pregnant?' Holly said, almost in a whisper.

They had chosen to stay at home and were in the kitchen as the countdown to the New Year approached. Tom was in the middle of opening a bottle of champagne but his fingers froze as the news sank in.

'Really? Would you know so soon?' he asked cautiously.

Holly nodded. 'Believe me, I'm sure,' she beamed.

Tom still didn't move, he just stood in the middle of the kitchen and blinked. A huge grin began to appear on his face and he barely registered the loud celebrations blaring from the TV in the living room as one year moved seamlessly into the next. He dropped the bottle of champagne onto the kitchen table as he rushed towards Holly. The cork popped and champagne started gushing out but Tom was oblivious.

'Really?' he repeated.

'Happy New Year,' Holly told him, her smile a mirror image of his.

'Happy, yes, very happy,' he agreed. 'How could I ever have doubted it, it's in the plan after all.'

Holly's smile didn't exactly falter but it took a little extra effort as she pushed back more unpleasant thoughts about the future. 'Yes, this plan of ours, I think we need to work on it.'

A frown of suspicion creased Tom's brow but only for a moment. His smile reappeared, twice as wide as it had been and Holly knew he would happily agree to almost anything. He obediently cleared up the spilled champagne while she took out her notepad from the kitchen drawer and placed it purposefully on the table, leafing through until she found their current five-year plan set out in black and white. Holly sat down and Tom joined her, both of them staring at the open page.

'Do you mind if we have a supplementary plan?' she asked.

'One especially for me by any chance?'

Holly turned to him and it was her turn to look suspicious.

'One that sets out my career in a little more detail?' he continued. 'Don't look so surprised. Do you think I haven't noticed your less than subtle hints about me not taking the anchorman job?'

'I know I'm interfering. It's just that . . .' Holly began.

'Enough already,' laughed Tom. 'I know what

291

you think, I think the exact same thing. It's not the job for me, but you're about to have our baby and I want to do the best for you both.'

'But there's nothing to say you can't still provide for your family without taking on a job you're going to hate—and you will hate it, Tom, you . . .'

Tom placed his finger gently on Holly's lips.

'I'll take the job for six months, meanwhile I'll set the ball rolling to go freelance. By the time the baby's born, I'll have a new career all carved out. I might even have started writing my first book. Now, would you like to write all of that down, or shall I?'

Holly pulled his finger away from her mouth and kissed it innocently. 'It's your plan,' she told him sweetly.

'I'm glad you think so. I was starting to have my doubts.' The accusing look he gave Holly transformed to one of awe. 'A baby. We're going to have a baby,' he whispered.

*   *   *

When Holly wasn't meddling with Tom's plans, there were plenty of other things to keep her busy, Sam Peterson made sure of that. Fortunately Mrs Bronson hadn't caused too much of a fuss over the sculpture debacle. She had a piece of genuine Holly Corrigan artwork and she didn't want to devalue it by undermining the artist, especially when she'd acquired the work for free. But despite her reputation remaining intact, Holly refused point-blank to take on any more commissions. She still worked on small pieces for the gallery but not with the intensity she had previously put into her work. She wanted to spend as much time as she could enjoying life with Tom.

When she did venture into her studio, Holly found herself spending more time staring at her mother-and-child sculpture than she did working on her other pieces. A pregnancy test had given Tom the confirmation he thought they both needed and there were small changes to Holly's body that gave teasing hints of the life growing inside her, but it was still the baby she had moulded from clay that made Libby real. Holly felt comforted by its presence but she knew the sculpture deserved a more prominent and permanent home. She decided to take on board Sam's suggestion and donated it to the village. She chose May Day, the festival of fertility, as the perfect day to unveil the sculpture in the village hall, and Sam received an invitation he couldn't refuse. It was going to be a very emotional evening and Holly knew it was just one of the legacies she would be leaving behind.

*   *   *

Tom and Holly were getting ready for the great unveiling of her sculpture and as usual Tom had taken all of ten minutes to shower and change and then spent the rest of the time sitting on the bed watching Holly. She was running around like a lunatic. She tried on countless combinations of outfits but she was now four months pregnant and blooming, right out of her clothes.

'Nothing fits,' she complained, trying to pull one of her favourite dresses over her bump. It was a vintage sixties mini-dress in a loud orange and black print but it stretched so much over her stomach that it was indecently short, even for sixties fashion.

'Complaining?' asked Tom. He had worn a permanent grin from the moment he knew she was pregnant.

Holly pulled off her dress and slipped onto the bed next to him. 'No I most certainly am not.' She kissed him softly and started unbuttoning his shirt.

The gentleness of her kiss hit him like a steam train and he groaned in delight. 'Let's not go. Let's stay here,' he pleaded.

'Not a chance,' she told him with a reluctant smile. 'Our guests will be waiting and besides, your mum and dad are downstairs, they might complain about the noise.'

Holly whisked Tom's shirt off and then scuttled off the bed. She slipped it on and matched it with a pair of black leggings and a belt while Tom scrambled around for another shirt.

Eventually, with the help of his parents, she dragged a reluctant Tom out of the house, although she was the one who was feeling apprehensive about the evening. Unlike Tom, she wasn't used to being in the limelight and so she had used her pregnancy to persuade Tom to do the ceremonial speech. Even so, she knew she wouldn't be able to avoid being centre of attention.

The village hall was comfortably full with villagers and a few select outsiders. Jocelyn had helped Tom with the arrangements for raffles and auctions to raise money for the village community fund, and if that wasn't enough she and Lisa had also prepared enough food to feed the five thousand.

'You really shouldn't have gone to all this trouble,' exclaimed Tom when he spotted the buffet spread out along one side of the hall.

'It was no trouble, no trouble at all,' lied Jocelyn. Lisa pulled a face behind her to let everyone know she was lying. 'OK, I will admit I'll be glad to put my feet up tonight. My legs are aching like you wouldn't believe.'

'Well, you sit yourself down right now,' commanded Tom, taking Jocelyn by the arm and finding her a seat. 'I don't want to see you lift another finger all night. If you want something, you just ask me.'

Jocelyn's eyes twinkled with delight. It was obvious that she enjoyed being cosseted by a handsome young man. 'I could do with a drink, if it's not too much trouble,' she cooed.

'Excuse me, don't go escaping your duties,' interrupted Holly with a smirk. 'Let's get the unveiling out of the way first and then we can party all night. Jocelyn will just have to fend for herself a little longer.'

'Can I be of service?' Sam had slipped into the hall without Holly noticing.

'Perfect timing,' Holly replied slyly. 'Everybody, this is Sam Peterson, gallery owner and expert negotiator. Sam, meet the family,' Holly chirped, quickly going through the introductions, leaving Jocelyn until last. 'She's a very special lady,' Holly explained. 'And I want you to look after her. I think she could do with some liquid refreshment, if you'd be so kind.'

'Who died and made you queen?' retorted Sam.

'Nobody yet,' answered Holly and everyone laughed except Jocelyn.

'Come on, your majesty, let's get to work.' It was Tom's turn to try to pull Holly away. 'And don't you go anywhere, I won't be long,' he added, winking at

Jocelyn.

Up on stage, in front of the sculpture which took pride of place in the hall, Tom entertained the crowd with plenty of jokes at Holly's expense. It was only when it came to the dedication of the sculpture that Tom's tone became serious. 'I know Holly won't like me saying this, but twelve months ago, she didn't believe in motherhood, not for her anyway. She didn't think she could ever be a mother and if I'm honest I started to doubt it myself.'

Tom looked cautiously at Holly, unsure if she would be comfortable with his public confessions. Holly smiled tentatively at him. She would be the first to agree that it had indeed been a difficult journey.

'I thought I was the one who had been on an amazing voyage of discovery, off travelling the globe, but I look at the sculpture behind me and I can see the incredible journey that she's travelled. She thought she could never experience a mother's love, but the love is there, carved into stone for the whole world to see. I can't begin to tell you how proud I am of her and I can't wait for the day that the image she created in stone becomes real flesh and blood.'

Tom glanced at Holly. The last twelve months had also taught her how to cry and she was now crying like a baby. She was dragged towards the microphone and sniffed her way through all the thank yous. She thanked everyone for their love, support and patience, especially Tom, especially his parents, especially Jocelyn and even Billy too. The list just continued until she had to also thank the crowd too, mostly for their patience. Despite her reservations at giving a speech, Holly was starting to feel comfortable in front of the microphone, which Tom was now regretting handing over to her.

'I never could have imagined what a life-changing experience moving to the country would be. In a very short period of time, I've come to see Fincross as my home, the place where I've been able to put down roots that I hope will continue to thrive for generations to come. I'm just sorry I never had a chance to see Hardmonton Hall in all its glory. Now, I hope you won't think of me as an interfering busybody, but I was hoping that, perhaps, the money raised tonight could go towards the restoration of the gardens at the Hall. It's such an amazing site, it would be a shame to lose it to the past forever.'

Holly's gaze settled on Jocelyn, who was looking at her quizzically. This was yet another of Holly's intended legacies, one that would pay tribute to Edward and Isabella Hardmonton in particular. The world may never know what sacrifices they had made, but Holly knew only too well. There was also another reason for suggesting the plan. The project would help Jocelyn look to the future instead of dwelling in the past and it would satisfy her love for gardening far better than a single window box in her tiny flat.

Having kept her audience captive long enough, to relieved sighs all around, Holly declared the buffet open but warned people not to disappear. There were still plenty of fundraising activities on offer. She not only expected everyone to dig deep but then to dance the night away into the wee small hours of the morning.

Before they joined the throng, Holly turned to

Tom one last time. 'Thank you.'

'I think you've already said that,' laughed Tom. 'And in case I haven't said it enough, thank you, Holly. Thank you for making me the happiest, luckiest man alive.'

Holly wrapped her arm around Tom's waist and laid her head on his shoulder so he wouldn't see the look of sadness in her eyes.

'Hey, there's Billy,' Tom said excitedly.

'The second love of your life. It's a wonder I can trust you two alone with each other.'

'You? Trust me?' gasped Tom loudly as they stopped in front of Billy. 'You're the one who kept the poor man hostage in your studio for hours.'

'Hello, Mrs C, Mr C,' Billy said with an excitement that rivalled only Tom's as the two men shook hands. 'I'd like to introduce you to my wife, Edna. Edna this is Holly and Tom,' he stumbled.

The woman standing next to Billy was very matronly, with grey hair tied back tightly in a bun and a round face that was matched equally by her round body. She looked like she could easily keep Billy in check with a single withering look, but her smile to Tom and Holly was open and welcoming.

'Oh, how lovely to meet you both at last! I've heard so much about you from Billy, and of course, I've seen you on TV,' she said to Tom.

'I won't be on TV for much longer, not on the news anyway. I'm working my notice,' explained Tom with a palpable sense of relief.

'Does this mean you'll be putting the landscaping plans on hold?' Billy asked.

'Not a chance,' smiled Tom. 'I'll be working for myself and I've already got a couple of projects lined up.'

Billy raised an eyebrow in suspicion. 'I hope you won't be leaving your wife all on her own again,' he warned.

'No, of course I won't. I'll be staying put, don't you worry, and I'll still have time to help sort out the plans for the garden. Speaking of which, can I have a quick word about next week?' Tom asked.

'Do you mind, love?' Billy asked sheepishly, looking to Edna for approval.

'Just be quick about it,' she warned.

Once they were out of earshot, Holly couldn't help but laugh. 'I can see who wears the trousers in your house, and there was Billy giving the impression that he was master of all he surveyed.'

Edna joined in the laughter. 'You have to take a firm hand with him or goodness knows what he'd try to get away with. Actually, I'm glad I've caught you on your own,' Edna confessed. 'Billy is going to insist on decorating the nursery for you. He wants to do it as a thank you for all the work you've put his way.'

'Really? How sweet of him,' gasped Holly, genuinely touched by Billy's generosity.

'Is it all right with you, though?' asked Edna. 'It's just that he has a real soft spot for the gatehouse and its inhabitants and he'd be there all the time if you let him. Please let me know if you think he's becoming a pest and I'll put him off.'

'Billy? A pest?' Holly asked. She may have thought he was a nuisance at one time, but she knew Billy better now. 'He's kept a watchful eye over me while Tom was away and I really appreciate it.'

'We never had kids of our own and, I swear, he'd adopt you and Tom if he could.'

'Ah, but is he ready to be a granddad?' asked Holly, patting her stomach. The two women collapsed into a fit of giggles and they were still laughing when the men rejoined them. Holly insisted that Billy and Edna join the rest of their group so she could spend the remainder of the evening with her growing family.

The night was a huge success and Holly had never felt so alive. She was only sorry that Jocelyn had left not long after the buffet had been devoured and cleared away. She would be the last one to admit it, but the preparations for the evening had totally wiped her out so Holly didn't try to persuade her to stay.

Tom and Holly were the last to leave and although Jack and Diane had offered them a lift they were determined to make the night last as long as possible and said they would walk home. The full moon looked over their shoulders and pointed the way home as they passed the village green. Hundreds of daffodils bobbed their heads approvingly in the soft breeze and Holly allowed herself one of her rare moments when she felt sad and just a little scared about what she was leaving behind.

'I can't go on any more,' complained Tom and he sat down on the grass. 'I've danced myself out and my feet are killing me.'

'Excuse me, I'm the pregnant one. I'm supposed to be the one with sore feet.'

Tom pulled her down onto the grass with him. 'It must be sympathy pains,' he concluded.

'The only sympathy pains you have are with Sam,' laughed Holly.

'Well, someone had to dance with him. He was

mortified when he realized all the villagers weren't raving line dancers.'

'Hmm, you did have some good moves on the dance floor.'

Despite Sam's strange view of what village life was like, he was a hit with the locals and Holly suspected that he would be returning soon. He was staying over at one of the pubs and had been deep in conversation with the landlord when she had last seen him.

Tom and Holly both lay back on the grass and looked up into the night's sky.

'Just look at that moon. You never see a moon that bright in London.'

'It's not everything it appears to be,' answered Holly. 'It's a reflection of light from the sun, that's all. It doesn't hold any power of its own.'

'Tell that to the werewolves and lunatics,' slurred Tom lazily.

'I think it made me crazy for a while, but then I realized my fate lay in my own hands.'

Tom frowned at her. 'You been drinking too?'

'No,' Holly said with a rueful smile. 'But you certainly have.'

'I love you, Mrs Corrigan,' he whispered.

Holly was reminded of a grief-stricken Tom who believed he hadn't told her often enough that he loved her. 'I know you love me. Even when you don't say it, I know you love me. Don't ever think you don't tell me enough, because you do, every time you look at me, or speak to me, or think of me, I know you love me. Remember that.'

Tom grinned at her. She hoped he would remember through his drunken haze but she couldn't take away all of the pain or all of the guilt

301

that lay ahead for Tom. He would have to face the grief of her loss one day soon and she couldn't prevent that. All she could do was make sure that he had enough good memories to fill the void she knew she would be leaving in his life.

Holly bit her lip as she tried to stifle a sob. She didn't want to leave Tom. She wanted to stay with him for ever and she wanted to see Libby grow up. Holding back the tears, she took a deep breath and felt a faint fluttering in her stomach. She held her breath and her body tensed. It was like the gentle fluttering of a butterfly's wings.

Tom sensed something wrong and leaned over to her. 'Are you all right?' he asked, sounding more sober than he had done all night.

'I think I just felt the baby move,' she gasped.

Tom put his hand to Holly's stomach and she guided his fingers to where she had felt Libby move inside her for the very first time.

'I can't feel anything,' Tom said glumly.

'You've got the rest of your life to get to know her, be patient.' Tom was already getting used to Holly referring to the baby as a girl but he was still holding out for a boy.

Tom leaned over and gently put his head on Holly's stomach. 'This is it,' he said.

'This is what?'

'This is the moment you said to look out for. The moment when I can look at my life and think, this is enough. I know exactly what I have and I'm happy. I'm complete and I'm happy.'

Holly's heart skipped a beat and a tear trickled down her face. 'Yes, this is it,' she agreed. She looked up at the moon and realized she didn't have to wish for anything else. She had her husband and she had Libby growing inside her and she would have both of them with her until the day she died.

EPILOGUE

The twenty-ninth of September 2010 was a good day to die. The morning sky was crystal clear, if not a little on the watery side of blue. A small congregation had gathered at the front of the gatehouse, ready to wish the prospective parents well. Billy and his men had been working on the garden in stages and had reappeared that week to complete their work.

'With a little luck, we'll have the job finished before you come out of hospital,' Billy told Holly.

'Don't go wishing a long labour on her,' joked Tom. He was beaming with excitement, a stark contrast to Holly, who was carrying a heavier burden than just her unborn child.

'You'll be all right,' soothed Jocelyn, giving Holly a motherly hug.

'I'm scared,' Holly told her in a whisper so that no one else could hear. 'I'm not ready to leave them.'

'It'll be all right,' Jocelyn insisted and Holly didn't argue, although her eyes told Jocelyn she knew this to be a lie.

Jocelyn hadn't needed the urgent call from Tom to tell her Holly was in labour. She already knew the date Libby would arrive and had been preparing for it with as much detailed planning as Holly herself.

Holly froze in gasping pain as another contraction rippled across her stomach.

'Enough chatting, we need to get you to hospital,' Tom insisted, pulling Holly away from the well-wishers towards the car.

'I love you like the mum I never had,' Holly told Jocelyn, panic rising in her voice. 'I can't even begin to thank you for everything you've done and everything you're going to do. I don't know how I would have got through this without you.'

'Oh, Holly, I love you too. And I'm just glad you gave me the chance to be a proper mum again.' Both women were on the verge of tears, neither wanting to be the first one to break down.

'Hey, you two, you'd think you were never going to see each other again. Will you get moving,' urged Tom.

Holly kept looking back as she waddled down the driveway before easing herself into the car. Jocelyn watched on and it wasn't until the car pulled out of the drive and out of sight that she allowed the tears to fall, but even then, only for the briefest of moments. There was too much to be done.

'Will you do me a favour?' Jocelyn asked Billy, pulling herself up as tall as her aching bones would allow. 'I've a few things to do here but then would you be a dear and give me a lift home. I don't think I could manage the walk back today.'

'You wanting a lift? That's a first, but I'm glad to be of service,' smiled Billy before letting a frown of concern cloud his features. 'Are you all right, Joss?'

'I'll be fine,' Jocelyn assured him with a wink.

'Good, I can't have my favourite girl getting worry lines.'

'I think it's a bit late for that,' she told him before turning her attention back to the gatehouse. 'It's seen a lot of history, hasn't it?'

They were both looking up at the imposing facade, which hid its years and its secrets well

305

beneath newly painted woodwork and a sprinkling of honeysuckle around its edges.

Billy raised an eyebrow. 'Some things are best left in the past.'

'And some people,' added Jocelyn solemnly.

'Which is why today is so special. It's time to draw a line under the past and look to the future,' he said with a twinkle of excitement in his eyes.

'I couldn't have put it better myself. Now enough of this chit-chat, I've got work to do and so have you,' Jocelyn told him and sent him scurrying back to his landscaping.

Holly had given Jocelyn a set of keys and she was under instructions to make sure everything was ready and prepared for Tom's return home alone with his new baby daughter. Holly had stocked up on enough supplies to feed an army.

Jocelyn crept through the empty house for fear of waking up the ghosts from her past. She couldn't resist taking a peak upstairs at the newly decorated nursery, but her joints creaked almost as much as the stairs. By the time she reached the top, the dull ache in her back had upgraded itself to a searing pain despite the painkillers and she had to catch her breath before entering the nursery. The empty bassinet was in the centre of the room, awaiting Libby's arrival. Moving closer, Jocelyn realized that the bassinet wasn't completely empty. Inside there was the comforter doll Holly had told her about. Holly had been sleeping with the doll for the last week so that it would pick up her smell, a final gift that would create a tangible connection between mother and daughter.

Creeping back down the stairs, Jocelyn tried hard not to think back to the times when she had called this house her home. She could shake off the ghosts but the guilt that had followed her out of the door the day she left Harry had proven a little more difficult to leave behind. Despite the mournful time that lay ahead, Jocelyn felt that guilt, which had plagued her for decades, finally beginning to lift.

It was in the kitchen where she felt most at ease, here where she had made some good memories in the last eighteen months. She was supposed to start making a hearty stew for Tom's return, but she didn't have time to cook today, time was of the essence. She quickly unpacked the selection of pies and cakes she'd picked up from the teashop's larder on her way over, allowing herself a brief glance out of the window towards the moondial. The only items she left in her shopping bag were a white envelope, the journal and the wooden box.

Jocelyn took the shopping bag and headed for Holly's studio, which had a few ghosts of its own. It had been a long time since it had been her husband's workshop and despite the makeover Jocelyn felt Harry's presence here more than anywhere.

Jocelyn placed the box and the journal on Holly's workbench where they would be easily found. Looking thoughtfully at the box, she tapped its lid with her finger, a finger that was already starting to show the gnarled signs of arthritis. 'I'm ready to complete the bargain,' she told it.

Carefully, she placed the envelope on top of the box. The letter was tantamount to making a deal with the devil but, thanks to the wonders of the moondial, it was a deal that Jocelyn knew had already been sealed along with her fate.

Jocelyn locked up the studio and the house

before dragging Billy away from his work to take her home. The sense of relief she felt was almost euphoric as she was driven away from the house, leaving behind the last remnants of guilt. Not long now, she thought to herself as she pictured the scene that awaited her at home. The little bistro table had everything set out, ready for her return. The pills, the bottle of vodka and the photographs of the people she loved. Those would be the last faces she would ever see. The score was about to be settled.

My dearest Holly,
I expect you're wondering what on earth is going on, or perhaps more likely, wondering why the village is mourning the passing of a foolish old woman rather than a young mother.
Childbirth is a big enough shock for any woman, but for you, I suspect it's going to take a little longer to settle into your new life. You'll be feeling a mixture of anger and guilt. You'll be thinking that you've stolen someone else's right to life. I wish I had the words to stop you feeling like that, but all I can really say is, don't! I've wasted too much of my life feeling guilty and I don't want that for you. We both know that the moondial demands a life for a life but it shouldn't be yours, or Libby's or Tom's. So why not mine? Do I really want to spend my golden years bedridden as these joints of mine seize up? It sounds like a fate worse than death to me.
I look up at the full moon sometimes and it reminds me of my own life. It steals its light from yesterday's sun and that's how I've felt for a very long time. I stole someone else's life and my

penance has been to be left with a life that didn't quite shine bright enough, not until I met you, that is.

Your fate is going to be different because this is my gift to you and it's gladly given, and it should come as no surprise to you to know that the moondial has played its part in my bargaining. I'm actually sitting at your kitchen table writing this letter. It's the evening of the unveiling of your sculpture and you and Tom are no doubt still partying the night away. The full moon is shining through the window, winking at me now and again.

I wish you could see me, but rest assured I've got the biggest smile on my face you could ever imagine. Tonight I used the moondial one last time and I too saw the future as you had seen it, with Tom grieving for his lost wife, but only for a moment. I had already known I was prepared to sacrifice my life for yours but we both know the moondial has its rules. The life sacrificed has to be part of the family circle to settle the score. Take another look at your sculpture, Holly. It's you holding Libby but the foundation etched into the black marble, the maternal support that you never had as a child, I want that to be me. I've told you often enough that you're just like a daughter to me and thankfully tonight the moondial has seen that too.

As soon as I set eyes on Libby, that sweet child who had lost her mother, it firmed my resolve and the moondial accepted my offer. My life for your life. A mother sacrificing her life for the life of her daughter. Sound familiar? As soon as I knew I could and would make the

309

*deal, time unravelled before my very eyes and
I was able to see what we both thought was an
impossible dream. Oh, Holly, to see the three of
you together, it was such an amazing sight and
you were all so happy. Of course you tried to
dissuade me from putting my plan into action
but I'm a stubborn, old fool. Your words, not
mine.*

*The one thing we could agree on is that there
are a few insights that might help you take those
first steps on your new path a little more easily.
I know you're going to be worried about the
coming years—you've told me as much yourself.
In some ways, you're right to worry about
this balancing act the moondial demands.
I wish I could soften the blow, but time and
circumstance just won't allow. There will be
no other children for you and Tom. The Holly
I met wanted you to know that, if only to stop
you holding onto a false hope. You will come
to accept this but you need to share the burden
of this knowledge, and more besides, with Tom.
Don't waste years worrying that he'll be tempted
to use the dial himself and that the moondial
will continue to blight your life. He won't. He'll
be there to support you and help you, especially
with the next part of what is quite clearly a plan
that your future self has set for you.*

*You're still to go ahead with the renovation
of the gardens at Hardmonton Hall and this
is where Tom can help you track down Lucas
Hardmonton. Lucas deserves to know exactly
what happened to his family and the sacrifices
they made. You aren't to prevaricate over giving
him the journal and returning the moondial to*

310

its original site and you shouldn't waste time debating whether or not to simply destroy it. You won't destroy it, none of us ever could, could we? You will return it to the Hardmontons and that will be the right thing to do, for you and for Lucas. Just remember to keep Billy on his toes, even though, from the photos I've seen tonight, he'll do a good job on the restoration anyway. And when the time is right, tell him that I would have been pleased with the results but don't let it go to his head.

There, I've said enough. I refuse to give you any more information about your future. A life is for living and you should start each day with a blank page, although once in a while you might just notice the occasional glow from Yesterday's Sun. All I ask in return is that you go easy on Paul. He was meant to mourn his mother, it's come a little later than expected, that's all.

I could sit here writing for ever but I really must stop my ramblings. Don't worry, on the eve of Libby's fifth birthday, with the full moon gazing down upon us, we will have our last goodbye.

Until then,
My eternal love and gratitude,
Jocelyn

ACKNOWLEDGEMENTS

It was because of Nathan Valentine that I began to write. He is my inspiration and this book is only a small part of his legacy. I was blessed to have had him in my life but three years and ten months was not nearly long enough. My little boy taught me more than I was ever going to teach him and there were some tough lessons to learn. First and foremost, he taught me how to grab happiness where I can and to hold on to it, to appreciate what I have when I have it, which is why I hope he won't mind if my first acknowledgement is to my daughter Jessica Valentine, without whom I would be lost. She is growing into an amazing, beautiful, young woman and she has made her mum very, very proud.

I have so many other people to thank, so many friends and family that have helped me and supported me over the years. I can't name you all but please know that I'm still standing because of you. Special thanks to my mum Mary Hayes for being a mother to my children as well as to me, to Chris Valentine and Jonathan Hayes for the encouragement to pursue my dreams and to Lynn and Mick Jones, some people are blessed to have someone they call their rock, I have two.

Immense thanks to my agent, Luigi Bonomi for the insight, encouragement and most of all the courage to pull apart my manuscript and then put it back together again. A huge thank you too to everyone at HarperCollins for taking my dream and giving it wings, especially to Sarah Ritherdon

312

and Hana Osman for guiding me so gently and supportively through this new world of publishing that I've found myself in.

And finally, thank you to the Rainbow Mums (you know who you are), who learnt how to be brave from their sons and how to be strong from each other. In memory of our little heroes, Conor, Connor, Jordan, James and Nathan.